W9-CAN-170

THE
ILLUSIONIST

A NOVEL

Dinitia Smith

SCRIBNER

SCRIBNER
1230 Avenue of the Americas
New York, NY 10020

This book is a work of fiction. Names, characters, places, and incidents either are products of the author's imagination or are used fictitiously. Any resemblance to actual events or locales or persons, living or dead, is entirely coincidental.

Copyright © 1997 by Dinitia Smith

All rights reserved, including the right of reproduction in whole or in part in any form.

SCRIBNER and design are trademarks of Simon & Schuster Inc.

DESIGNED BY ERICH HOBBING

Set in Simoncini Garamond

Manufactured in the United States of America

1   3   5   7   9   10   8   6   4   2

Library of Congress Cataloging-in-Publication Data

Smith, Dinitia
The illusionist: a novel/Dinitia Smith
p.   cm.
I. Title.
PS3569.M526I43   1997
813'.54—dc21   97–22657
CIP

ISBN 0-684-84329-3

For David, always.

ACKNOWLEDGMENTS

Thanks for research help, support, and friendship to: State Supreme Court Justice Emily Goodman, Drs. Raymond Matta and Joel Solomon. Gioia Diliberto, Kathlyn Conway, Leslie Bennetts. Susan Moldow, my editor, and my agent, Amanda Urban.

Olivia: Are you a comedian?
Viola: No, my profound heart; And yet (by the very fangs of malice I swear) I am not that I play.

—*Twelfth Night*

PART I

THE MAGICIAN

CHAPTER 1

CHRISSIE

I first saw him one wild October night at the Wooden Nickel bar high up on the headland overlooking the river on Old Route 27. In Sparta in late October the wind sweeps in off the river, it can make your eyes tear, it can make you weep. Across the river, the sky over the palisades was dense with cumulus clouds, thick and silvery and shot through with light, and the leaves in the trees sang and rustled and shook in the wind. Down below, the great river glided by, like a sheet of gleaming metal two miles wide.

When I walked out of the cold into the Wooden Nickel that night, I spotted a young man I'd never seen before, sitting at a table in the big room adjoining the bar. A cone of golden light shone down on him from the ceiling, tiny specks of dust whirling about in it. He was surrounded by a small crowd and he was doing magic tricks—pulling quarters from behind people's ears, making his playing cards seem to leap from deck to deck and then magically rearrange themselves into groups of blacks and reds and aces and hearts. And as he worked, his hands moved as quick as water.

There was something about him that just struck you right away, that made your eyes rest upon him and made you puzzle. I know now that I wondered what he was, the question passed through my mind without being formed into words. I guess you always remember your first sight of someone who will become important in your life, even though you can't know it at the time. It stays a picture in your mind forever.

He was small and thin. He wore a black cowboy hat perched on the back of his head, and an old deerskin jacket with a fringe on it, even though it was hot inside and the wood stove was going full blast. Yes, he was beautiful. He had high cheekbones, reddened with wind, big green eyes, slightly prominent, shining like globes in his head, as if he had just been running. His mouth was full, with well-shaped lips drawing to two points under his nose. He had a little bit of an overbite, and long white healthy teeth.

His brown hair was short, but shaggy. And I noticed that he was wearing two flannel shirts, one on top of the other.

Brian Perez was his victim. Brian was sitting opposite him, watching him intently through his long, curly, light blond hair the color of burnt ashes that hung over his face, his mouth set in a thin smirk.

The atmosphere in the bar was thick with smoke, and you could smell the salty smell of wood burned over the generations, embedded in the walls of the place. Behind the dark wood-paneled bar, a mottled deer head hung, strands of tinsel dangling from its nose. Carl, the owner, liked to decorate. He made the place a home for us, and for himself. The old paneled walls of the bar were covered with calendars and clocks and neon signs for Genny and Michelob and give-aways from liquor companies, calendars with their pages stuck at 1954, and 1976, and black-and-white photographs of bowling teams, brittle and cracked and curled with age.

Aerosmith was playing on the jukebox. The Bills and the Giants were on the TV above the bar, but for a few minutes at least, no one was watching it. Even Carl had come out from behind the bar to watch the magician. Carl, white-haired, bright blue eyes, old boxer's body, stood holding his towel, and slowly wiping a glass. "Hey Chrissie," Carl said when he saw me. And then his eyes went back to the new person.

"Who's that?" I asked Carl.

"Dunno. Never seen him before. He just came here tonight for the first time."

Now the young man slapped his cards into three piles on the table. "Okay, pick a card from the top," he told Brian. "Look at it, but don't show it to me."

Brian took a card, glanced at it, said nothing. Then put it back facedown on one of the piles, keeping his eyes steady on him. Brian had hair like an angel, and pale blue, slanty eyes, Chinesey eyes. Brian would've been handsome if he weren't so empty, so dangerous and unpredictable. He was on parole, had just served three months in Sparta Correctional for arson. There was some kind of dispute with his landlord on Washington Street—he shared an apartment there with Jimmy Vladeck. One night Brian got drunk and just trashed the place and then he set fire to it. I saw it, the flames shooting up in the sky in the night, the families out on the street, the volunteer firemen and the fire trucks converging on the place, it was a spectacle.

Behind Brian stood his sidekick, Jimmy, big, pot-bellied, stupid, long brown stringy hair tied back in a ponytail, the odor of mildew somehow always around him. I'd known both of them all my life. I'd gone to grade school, then high school, with them, though both of them had ended up in Special Ed and neither one of them had made it to graduation. Brian's family was trouble, his mother's boyfriend beat him as a kid. Jimmy's dad was a deputy sheriff, but I think Jimmy was slow or something. I suppose Brian and Jimmy were a part of me in some way, like the air you breathe; the way anyone is whom you've known all your life.

Jimmy had a charge on him too. For car theft or something. There were always charges floating around Brian and Jimmy, all the time.

The new young man took a sip from the can of Mountain Dew next to him, and fluttered his long, thin fingers across the three piles of cards on the table. "Okay," he said to Brian. "You could've taken the card from here"— he touched one of his piles—"and put it here." He touched the other with his fingertips. "But instead, you put the card here. Now, cut the cards as many times as you want."

Brian cut the cards, all the time examining him, with his thin smile, his skinny leg jiggling restlessly beneath the table.

"So, what's your name?" Brian asked.

"Dean," he said, not looking up.

"I will now cause your unknown card to rise to the top of the deck." He spoke into his chest, his voice was vaguely hoarse.

Now, Dean closed his eyes, and passed his hand over the deck. "Okay, which card did you choose?" he asked Brian.

"Four of spades," Brian said. Every word from Brian was reluctant.

Dean nodded at the deck. "Okay. Take it."

Brian turned the top card. I peered over Brian's shoulder at it. Four of spades. On the top!

"Hold it up," I said to Brian. "So they can see." I was already taking Dean's side, though I hadn't even spoken a word to him yet. Dean had that effect on you, on women especially, drew you in, made you want to protect him.

Brian held the card up, reluctantly, so that people could see.

Dean raised his eyes to the crowd and smiled, a mischievous smile. I saw Brian's eyes flash in his anger. Then his face seemed to flatten out, became expressionless, as if he were trying to hide his humiliation. There was a ripple of applause.

I'd never seen anything like this in the Wooden Nickel, someone doing magic tricks. There was something old-fashioned about magic tricks. In fact, nobody did much with their hands in our town any more. They mostly just hung out, drank beer, played Nintendo, watched TV. For someone to do something creative—artistic—like magic was unusual, weird. But it wasn't unusual enough to hold people for long.

Soon the crowd grew restless, drawn back, as if they couldn't help themselves, to the football game above the bar, to the familiar things that had a greater hold on them.

He did a few more tricks. He made a rubber band jump magically from one of his fingers to another. He asked Brian for a quarter—he seemed to focus on Brian, as if early on, even then, he was drawn to trouble—and then made the quarter disappear and reappear.

Brian stood up. When Dean saw that he was leaving, he hurriedly started another trick, as if to hold Brian's interest. But Brian was deliberately walking away, Jimmy following him.

I sat down at the table, watching Dean. He took a shot glass from the inside pocket of his leather jacket and splashed some water in it. "I'm Chrissie," I said.

"Dean," he said, eyes on the glass, slowing the movement of his hands down, as if he were practicing the trick now. "Dean Lily," he said, not looking at me.

"Where you from?" I asked.

"St. Pierre."

"Where's that?"

"Up near the border."

He balanced the shot glass filled with water on the palm of his left hand. He had thin wrists, I noticed, bowed like bird's wings. Then he sealed both hands tightly over the shot glass, opened them. And the shot glass was gone.

"How'd you do that?" I asked.

"I'll never tell!" He smiled.

I looked up. Brian had drifted back, followed by big, lumbering Jimmy, drawn back again to Dean in spite of himself. Dean spotted Brian, smiled. It was almost like he was flirting with Brian or something.

"Wanna go outside?" Dean said, and swept me and Jimmy with his eyes to include us too.

Brian stood squarely above him.

"I got something good," said Dean.

"Yeah," Brian said. "What?"

"Come with me. You'll find out."

"I don't go anywhere unless I know where," Brian said.

Dean leaned back in his chair, hands on the table in front of him, looked meaningfully around the room. Then, "I got the best Humboldt you ever had. None of that Jersey swamp weed. Beautiful, big bud. Nice purple hairs on it. Guaranteed best you ever had."

"Better be," Brian said. I saw him hesitate, look at Jimmy, who never said anything. Jimmy nodded.

"Not here," Dean said.

"Down by the river?" I suggested.

"You coming?" he said to Brian. Brian nodded.

So we left, the three of us, me and Brian and Jimmy, following Dean.

CHAPTER 2

CHRISSIE

Outside in the parking lot, the wind swirled around us, sweeping the dead leaves across the asphalt. A big wooden sign stood at the edge of the road, lit by a spotlight, with a picture of an Indian in a headdress painted on it, one of the Taponacs who used to live here hundreds of years go.

There was the sound of cars pulling in and out of the lot, doors slamming, and of voices among the pine and spruce trees. The sounds still had the flighty, echoey lilt of summer.

"Let's take my truck," Dean said. "You can guide me, Chrissie."

Brian said, "We'll follow." He was challenging Dean to offer something good. He climbed into his blue Camaro with Jimmy.

Dean had an old red customized Dodge Ram with a cap on the back. There were white swirly decals running along the rusting sides, and a bumper sticker on the rear fender: In Order to Get to Hell You Have to Step Over Jesus.

Inside, the truck was filled with garbage, empty cans of Mountain Dew and Skittles bags. An old rug remnant was laid out in the back, with a sleeping bag on it, as if he slept there.

"Which way?" Dean asked.

"Make a left." We pulled out of the lot, onto Old 27, then made a left down the river road, Brian and Jimmy following behind us in the blue Camaro.

The river road was narrow, and led down through a steep

ravine. On either side of us were tall pines, hanging over the road, pines left over from when the settlers grew them for their whaling ships.

Through the dark trees as you drove, you could glimpse, now and then, an old mansion, where the lords of the manor who owned Palatine County and the land around it had once lived. The big houses belonged mostly to weekenders now.

As we rode, there was a tension in the air between us, like a charge, an unasked question hanging there. "So, where're you living?" I asked Dean.

He shot a grin at me, then nodded over his shoulder. "In back of the truck. . . . You from around here?"

"Yeah. All my life. You working?" I asked Dean.

"At the Laundercenter. Making change and selling soap," he said.

"I'm an aide up at the Nightingale Home."

We had come to the end of the road, and we were at the river. We stopped the cars. There was an inlet, with a little gray-shingled hut covered in scraggly vines, the roof caving in. It was an old ice house, it belonged to one of the estates hidden up in the trees.

Beyond the inlet, a steep embankment rose, and then sloped down again to the railroad tracks, which ran along the edge of the river. On the heights on the other side of the river, you could make out the winking lights of Manorville.

It was completely deserted here. There was the sound of the river lapping at the shore, and out on the water, the waves were shivery and silvery, tipped with moonlight. From somewhere came a faint wind, rustling through the dry leaves.

You couldn't swim in the river here because the bed was all mud, and as soon as you stepped into the water, you sank right down. Anyway, the river was poisoned, full of PCB's.

Out in the middle was what appeared to be a small island covered in scrub. In summer, there were water lilies there, but if you rowed over in a boat, you discovered the island was not solid ground at all, just mud and marsh, and there was nowhere really to land.

We got out of our cars, and Brian led the way through the long, dry grass to the ice house.

Inside, there were gaps in the floor slats, the black river water moving beneath, and a big round hole where they must have cut the ice in winter.

The floor of the hut was littered with beer cans, and tiny, brightly colored crack vials. An empty Dewar's bottle lay on the ground and an old hairbrush, and a sweatshirt sodden with mud. The ice house was where we always came when we were doing anything other than drinking.

Dean reached into the inside pocket of his deerskin jacket, and took out a little tin and a little wooden pipe, coffin-shaped, with a hinged lid.

"Humboldt," he said.

They didn't say anything, but kept their eyes on it. He opened up his little tin. Inside lay a roundish bud. He picked it up, held it out for them to see. "Beautiful," he said.

He broke off a piece and packed it into the pipe.

Brian watched carefully, missing nothing. That little smile, that fake calm. And suddenly, I pictured Brian dancing fiendishly in the flames of his apartment, laughing and screaming. Brian was like a deer tick, I thought, the only way you could kill him was to burn him.

Dean handed the unlit pipe to Brian together with his Bic. "You first," he said, focusing all the attention on Brian.

Brian fired it up, drew a long breath on it. Then he passed the pipe on to me.

I drew in on the pipe, and it was a taste like none I'd ever experienced, deep and rich, like burning leaves, damp and thick in the autumn, and a faint sweetness in it, as if the leaves had sugar in them.

I'd heard of Humboldt, but if truth be told, I'd never had any.

And neither, probably, had Brian. Cost way too much. Out of our reach.

We passed the pipe around, and soon the little hut was filled with the smell. I felt the dope spread through my body like a kind of liquid solvent, melting away all the soreness and tension.

"Okay," Brian said. He had to give Dean that.

Jimmy took some and I could tell even lumbering Jimmy appreciated it. Here in the hut, close to Jimmy, I could smell the mildew on his big body. He had opaque, greenish eyes, and thick, porous skin. He hadn't spoken a word since we'd gotten out of the cars.

"Huh, Brian? Good?" I prompted, wanting Brian, for no reason I understood, to like what Dean had given him, to like Dean.

Brian closed his eyes a moment, savoring, then nodded.

"You don't need to roll this shit, too expensive," Dean said. Talking like an expert, like he knew the streets. But we *were* the streets in Sparta.

Brian looked at Dean and his eyes narrowed. "So what *are* you anyway?" Brian asked Dean, his voice suddenly thick.

"Whaddya mean?" Dean said.

"I mean—what are you? Queer or something?" The dope had loosened Brian's tongue.

Brian had asked the question I wanted to ask, but was afraid to. Dean was like this blurred image, an image I had pondered, but hadn't let come into focus yet. I saw Dean's high, red cheeks, his liquid green eyes, the full beautiful lips. The cowboy hat was parked rakishly on the back of his head. He wore loose jeans over his small frame.

"What're you talking about?" Dean asked Brian.

"I'm talking about what you are," Brian answered, not taking his eyes off Dean.

Outside the hut, the wind breathed; dry leaves scuttled across the grass, and underneath our feet, we could hear the sound of the river water lapping at the pilings of the ice house.

Brian watched Dean. "You look like a girl," Brian said.

"I'm a guy," Dean said, relaxed, as if he wasn't bothered by the question. "Of course."

Most guys would get excited now, puff up their chests, and raise their fists. But Dean's eyes were on his pipe as he took a deep breath in.

Yet I thought I could feel, in the air of the ice house, Dean's fear.

"Yep," Brian said. He cocked his head back in a gesture of fake disbelief, a goofy look, ridden with the dope. "Could've fooled me. Don't you think so?" Brian said to Jimmy. "Don't you think it's a fag?"

Jimmy gaped at Dean. "Looks that way to me," he said finally in his deep, phlegmy voice.

"That's your problem," Dean said, still avoiding looking at them.

"Yeah?" said Brian.

I interrupted. "I'm cold. Let's go."

But Brian wouldn't be stopped. "You're like a—pervert?" Brian asked Dean, his eyes wide with fake innocence.

"Shut up," said Dean. He emptied the ashes from the pipe. I could see Dean's lips trembling as he poked at it. Then he tucked the pipe in his jacket.

"Let's get out of here," I said.

Next to me, Brian giggled. A stupid dope kind of giggle, loose and freaky, something that could easily go out of control. I shivered.

"Fag is what I think," said Brian, with a little giggle. "What about you, Jimmy?"

"I think fag too," Jimmy said.

I grabbed Dean's sleeve, pulled him away through the long grass. "He's an asshole," I said.

We moved off, and I looked back and Brian and Jimmy were following us and in the darkness I could hear Brian's laughter, silly and pointless, with no real object, it seemed, anymore.

We hurried back through the long grass, and got in our cars. And Dean and I drove back to Wooden Nickel in his truck. As we drove, I watched him out of the corner of my eye, his large eyes shining, thin fingers on the steering wheel. I was too shy to ask him again what *they* had asked him. Because if I pressed him, he might run. And I knew I wanted him to stay.

As we pulled into the parking lot of the Wooden Nickel again, he said, without looking at me, "Getting cold out. You know someplace I could crash? Just for the night?"

"You can stay at my place, I guess, for the night," I answered. I knew he wasn't asking for sex or anything, really did need a place to go in the cold. I sensed I would be safe, even though he was the stranger. It was he who needed protecting. "Don't mind Brian," I said. "He's just an asshole."

CHAPTER 3

CHRISSIE

So he came back with me that night to Washington Street. He slept in his sleeping bag on the futon in the living room, while I slept in the bed in the bedroom.

I had lived in this apartment a year, after I'd had to move out of my mom's house because I couldn't take it with Mason, my stepfather, anymore. Mason was acting like he was my real father, and even after I got the job at the Nightingale Home, he wanted to know where I was all the time, when I was coming home at night, everything about me. I hated Mason's thin, beige-gray face, his blunt beige hair, the way his clothes smelled of cigarette smoke even after they were laundered. Mason was a manager at City Shop. And my mom just went along with whatever Mason did, she let him scream at me because Mason was younger than she was, and she was so afraid he'd leave her. And she couldn't bear Mason to leave her like my dad did for Liz.

My dad and Liz didn't have room for me because Liz had her own two boys, the brats Fletcher and Timmy. Liz and Dad never told me I couldn't live with them, but it was obvious, when I looked around, there was no room for me in Liz's house.

This realization, that I had nowhere that was my real home, gave me an inner sadness. Because, though I was grown up now, maybe I was still a kid and I wanted to know there was a place I could still call home if I really needed it, if I lost my job or something.

During the day I worked at the Home, and at night I took courses at Sparta Community toward my associate's degree. Most evenings after class, or after work, I drove to the Wooden Nickel, which was about five miles out of town. The Wooden Nickel was where we had all hung out ever since high school. I would sit at the end of the bar, reading my book, doing my homework. Carl left me alone. He didn't care. Carl was like a father to us. He didn't card kids too closely. He knew all the troopers and the sheriff. But if a kid was drunk, Carl would find someone to drive him home. He watched over us. Carl wasn't married, had no kids of his own. We were his family, except we had to pay for drinks.

Washington Street, where my apartment was, was the main street in Sparta. It was paved in cobblestone, lined with false-fronted buildings of red brick and frame. Like everything else in Sparta, the street sloped steeply down to the river. Indeed, sometimes it seemed as if the whole place was slowly sliding down into the river, and that one day the entire town would just disappear into the water.

Long ago, Sparta was a thriving place, a whaling port, one of the most prosperous cities in the state, they said. The square riggers would sail upriver from New Amsterdam, their decks loaded with barrels of whale oil and bone. And when the ships reached the docks of Sparta, all the inhabitants of the town would gather to greet them, and the air would be filled with the boom of cannon fire. My dad said that the Pecks were an old Sparta family. There was even a Peck Street in town, named after us, he said, though it was only a little side street. But long ago, he said, we were probably rich people, though my dad worked at Sparta Utility now.

Then, suddenly, all the whaling ceased, and Sparta went into a decline. And then, after the Civil War, the city came to life again for a generation or so, with manufacturing. But slowly, that industry died down too, until there were only the husks of old factory buildings down by the river, covered in ivy and bindweed.

Over the years, the town fathers had tried periodically to revive the fortunes of the city. These days, Washington Street was mostly antique stores, run by gay people who'd moved up from New York City. The city government had gotten federal loans, put up fake gas lamps to attract tourists, but it seemed that every day another store closed. A group of weekenders, including the famous poet who lived on Courthouse Square, were trying to raise funds to restore the old Sparta Opera House, with its gargoyles representing comedy and tragedy above the entrance, which had been boarded up for years now, and turn it into a cultural center.

But today as you walked through the streets of Sparta, you saw mostly the outline of the beautiful old buildings within the abandoned structures that stood there now, buildings with elaborate moldings and pilasters, and stained glass windows and fine, thick front doors.

These days, the thing that kept Sparta going was that it was the county seat. The main businesses were law offices, lawyers representing the indigent, the prison, doctors getting paid by Medicaid, title search firms, the unemployment office, and the Early Childhood Intervention Center, to keep the unemployed from beating up on their kids.

And drugs. It was as if drugs had replaced whaling and manufacturing in Sparta's economy. On Washington Street, there was a store called New York, New York, which was nothing but a front for drugs, just a few Knicks caps in the windows, a nod to making it look like a real store. Geography was destiny. It was somehow no accident that Dean turned up with his Humboldt. Sparta was a natural destination point for drugs. Because of its location, on the railroad line, and just off the Parkway, it was a convenient drop-off point. The drugs came up from the big city by train to the station down on Front Street, and the dealers met the carriers there, or the couriers brought up the drugs by car on the Parkway. But these days they said the train was better for bringing drugs up from the city, because the state troopers staked out the Parkway on the lookout for rental car plates—the dealers usually drove rentals.

My apartment was in a worn red brick building at the corner of Washington and Third. Third Street was kind of a dividing line in Sparta. Above Third, mainly white people lived. Below Third were black people, the descendants of freed slaves who had come after the Civil War to work in the manufacturing plants by the river. Around the boundary of Third Street, people's skins were more varied, mulatto, as if the races had met and mingled here.

I imagined that once, long ago, some nice little family had lived in my apartment. I imagined maybe the father was a foreman in the thread factory on Third Street, the mother dutifully taking care of the little children who went off to school each morning carrying their lunch pails. The apartment was still in good condition, smooth wainscoting on the walls, brass sconces. When I rented it, it was empty and clean, as if it were not really meant ever to be a permanent home but only a temporary shelter.

All I had was my mattress on the bare wooden floor of the bedroom, and in the main room, a futon and the Formica table and the vinyl-covered chairs my mom had given me. I'd taped up a big poster of Mariah Carey on the wall. Mariah Carey was my ideal then, tiny and delicate, little-boned with long hair and big eyes. I am big, with broad shoulders. I wore my hair short in those days, and I always felt clumsy. It wasn't even a question then that Dean might come onto me. Guys just never did. So I was one step ahead of them, made them my friends right away, and that way I could never get hurt.

In the morning, I woke up to the pearly light, the sound of voices outside on Washington muffled by the wavy glass in the windows. I went into the living room and I saw Dean there, curled up on his side in the sleeping bag, his head resting on his elbow, his mouth open, his long thin teeth gleaming on his lip, the lashes curling on his red cheeks. I saw that Dean was still wearing his two shirts, one on top of the other.

He was like a child, I thought. The object of your love, but completely unaware of how much you adored him. Innocent, I thought. For the moment.

And I wanted to lean down and touch his hair, all soft and shaggy and brown, put my lips to his cheek, inhale his skin. But I didn't dare. Dean wasn't the kind of person you touched without permission, I knew that instinctively, without his having told me.

As I moved close to where he lay, I could hear the even sound of his breathing. Suddenly, as I stood there, his eyelids fluttered, and he shifted onto his back. His body jerked, as if he were fighting something, as if I had startled him, and I stepped away.

I returned to my room and waited for him to wake up. Eventually, I heard the floorboards creaking in the other room, and then a burst of water from the shower. A few minutes later, Dean emerged from the bathroom, his hair damp, his skin clean, fully dressed, as usual.

He just stayed. He moved his stuff in, his magic books, *Modern Magic,* and *Magic Secrets of the World,* a duffel bag with some old clothes, his ditty bag. In the morning, he would go to work, chucking down Skittles for breakfast on his way out.

We lived like two bachelors. The place was a mess, we never cleaned. But then we didn't really have to clean, because there was almost no furniture.

Those first few days, I rarely saw Dean. At night, sometimes he wouldn't come home till late, till after I was in bed. Or else he'd sit at the table, practicing magic tricks, one eye on his book and the diagrams on the page, the other on his pile of cards, or his glass and quarter. I never saw Dean any other way but fully clothed, in his jeans and his two shirts, one on top of the other, though I saw his bare feet, the long, soft toes, the high, delicate arch.

After a couple of days, when Dean got paid, he gave me $120 cash for half the rent—he didn't have a checking account, he said. He was planning to get one, but he'd had some trouble upstate with an ATM and he had to wait.

I didn't ask more.

What did I know then? Only what I wanted to know. That he was a strange and beautiful creature, living in my house. I didn't pursue what Brian had said. Yes, he might have been a pervert—some in-between creature. But he was clean and intoxicating, and I was lonely. I was too young, or too stupid, to frame the question. I was only intrigued. And I was afraid that if I asked too many questions, he would flee, and I would be ordinary again, living alone, going at night to the Wooden Nickel, doing my homework at the end of the bar.

A few days after he moved in, I gave him an old denim shirt of mine that had shrunk in the wash. Dean was smaller than me, an inch or two shorter, and maybe ten pounds lighter. He was delicate next to me. "Try it on," I told him.

He went into the bathroom and shut the door tight. A couple minutes later, he reemerged, holding the shirt in his hand. "Too small," he said, looking at me, a question of sorts, a little smile on his face. I allowed my eyes to focus on what I didn't want to see, the two faint mounds on his chest, where his breasts would be.

The imponderability of it all was too weird.

"Dean," I said, "what's that?" I pointed to his chest. "Those breasts or something?"

He was suddenly straight-faced. "No. It's a deformity. I've always had them. Don't worry. I'm all guy."

"So—how come you got—those?" I asked, nodding at the bumps.

He was serious, his large eyes cool. "I got them on the top. Inside I'm a man."

I was confused. "So—you're like a—lesbian?"

"No," he said, calmly. "I'm *not* a lesbian."

"So, what are you then?" I asked.

"I'm not a lesbian. A lesbian is really a woman. I'm not. I'm a man," he said. "I'm a real man."

CHAPTER 4

CHRISSIE

I waited. From down on the street below came the sound of Saturday morning business, cars driving by, voices, the clatter of footsteps on the concrete sidewalk. Dean was not smiling now. "It's like another state of being," he said. "If they did an operation, they'd see men's things inside. They'd see I was a man."

"How do you know?"

"I know, because of the way I feel," he said.

"What's your real name then?"

"Dean."

"I mean your *real* name?"

"They baptized me Lily. Lily Dean." He looked up. "When I was born I had these—these little deformities. They were confused. I just changed it around. Cool, huh?" He grinned. "It worked for my ID and everything."

"What about your parents?"

"You couldn't tell about it when I was a kid. I just looked like a girl, so they just thought I was. It started happening later. Then the truth came out."

Dean told me he came from this little hamlet way upstate. His father was a purchasing agent for the county, his mother the town clerk. His father didn't want to know the truth about it, Dean said. But he thought his mother suspected from the start.

Dean also had a brother, Raymond, two years older, whom he

worshiped. Right from the beginning, Dean said, he wanted to do everything Raymond did, to tag along with all his friends. But his brother hated him. Raymond and his friends would tie Dean up and then beat him with sticks, anything to get rid of him. The mother would try to protect Dean. But no matter how much Raymond tormented him, Dean said, all he ever wanted was for Raymond to love him.

And when Dean got hurt, he'd try desperately not to cry, because only girls cry. He would wear only boys' clothes, refused to play with dolls. If his mother brought him a doll, he'd just leave it in the package to die. One time, when he went to his grandma's house in Syracuse, he came home and his mother had redecorated his room. She'd painted the walls pink, hung pink curtains, ordered a canopy bed from a catalog, and put down a pink rug—as if to make Dean more a girl. But when Dean saw what his mother had done, he threw a fit and refused to sleep in his room until she'd changed it all back again.

At first Dean didn't really understand what he was, but he just *knew* somehow, though he couldn't give it a name. He was a stranger in his own body. And as he got older, as he reached adolescence, he understood more clearly that he was a boy. His voice grew deeper, he started lifting weights. About that time, he became interested in magic, started ordering stuff from catalogs, magic tricks and books on the subject. Doing magic tricks was a way of getting other kids not to beat up on him, something to make them like him. He was good at the magic tricks, real fast, and soon the other kids began to tolerate him.

He started selling a little dope here and there. He had this connection up near the border. Pretty soon his mom lost all control over him, and he was hitchhiking all over the place anyway. He brought this stuff down and kids loved it. Strangely enough, he really didn't smoke that much himself. He used it kind of like bait, and to buy affection. And sometimes he used it as an aphrodisiac. The other kids still thought he was a weirdo, but they stopped beating up on him.

"So—I'm fifteen," he continued, "and this girl calls the house. It's a wrong number—but she thinks I'm a guy. We start talking, and we make a date to go RollerBlading, and the whole time she thinks I'm a boy.

"I start shaving to make my beard grow in, so it'll be all bristly, and my mom sees this, but my dad's pretending nothing's happening. I tell my parents I want them to call me Dean. But it's like my dad just doesn't hear it. My mom starts trying to obey me, but she can't make herself do it. I can feel my mom watching me now, her eyes all full of sorrow. And meanwhile, my brother Raymond is dropping out of school, and he's hanging out and getting drunk and doesn't come home at night.

"One day, I'm in the bathroom shaving myself, and I look at myself in the mirror, and I'm still seeing traces of girl there from the deformity. I see this face, and I'm afraid that nothing can get rid of that girl stuff that doesn't belong there. Maybe it'll never go away, and it'll always be like this, this shadow of a girl there.

"And so I just start crying. And my mom hears me, and knocks on the bathroom door. She sees me standing there with the razor in my hand. 'Honey, honey,' she says, and she just—holds me. 'Oh God,' she says, 'It's so hard.' And it's like she knows the truth now, and how I'm suffering, and she starts to cry too.

"She sits down next to me there on the hall floor, and she says, 'If it's gonna cause you so much suffering, then maybe you should live as a boy,' and from then on, she tolerates me, and doesn't try to change me, and my dad continues to pretend there's nothing weird going on."

He started dating a girl. He had had other girlfriends before, he said, but he and this girl were really in love. She was beautiful, he said, his ideal, a cheerleader. She loved him, but they didn't have sex like other people. One reason the girl loved him, Dean said, was that he didn't hit on her like every other guy.

But then one day this other girl he'd gone out with—before the cheerleader—she called his present girlfriend, and laid it on her, told her that Dean was really a female. And the cheerleader just went crazy! She turned on Dean, called him a freak. "She said I disgusted her, and she never wanted to lay eyes on me again as long as she lived."

Dean paused here in his story. I saw his eyes fill with tears. "You don't have to talk about it," I said. I couldn't bear to see him cry, because then all his efforts to be a boy would come to nothing, and he would be naked in front of me.

Dean took a swallow, and continued. "*Then* I cried," he said. "Like a fuckin' girl. I didn't even want to go on living anymore. Her name was Sharon. Fuckin' cheerleader—Princess Normal. Now she tells me I'm a sicko, a lesbo, and I tell her I'm not a lesbian!

"She breaks up with me, and I just want to die. I swallow a whole bottle of antibiotics and they put me in the state hospital for thirty days. I tell the doctor I'm not a girl!" Dean drew his head back, mimicked the doctor's pompous voice, " 'Miss Dean,' he says, 'I think this is what we call a crisis of sexual identity.' "

Here Dean spluttered with laughter. "Fuckin' A it is!" he cried. "It's a fuckin' crisis for him. But it ain't no crisis for *me!*"

CHAPTER 5

CHRISSIE

So, I let Dean live with me, he had wormed his way into my heart.

I would see him sometimes at the Laundercenter when I went to wash my clothes. There, in the warm, damp atmosphere, condensation running in rivulets down the windows, the machines churning and rumbling, he would hold court. He would stand at the center of a group of girls, and regale them with stories, and perform his magic tricks, making his cards disappear and reappear, drawing quarters out from behind their ears, making his rubber bands jump from finger to finger, his hands moving as fast and smooth as water.

There were always girls hanging round Dean, young girls, thirteen- and fourteen-year-olds. Like birds, chattering and flapping their wings in a ceaseless motion, their hair all puffed up because they'd just been to Trendsetters, which was next door to the Laundercenter, and there would be fresh blusher on their pale cheeks. And Dean would flirt with them and goof around, and smoke his cigarette so the smoke made his eyes squint in a manly way. Now and then, he'd interrupt himself to give change to customers, to sell little containers of Tide and fabric softener, all the time surrounded by his little girls.

But despite how strange Dean was, despite the crowd around him, the people at the Laundercenter didn't fire him, because he was so good at the job. He would help women customers carry their laundry baskets out to their cars, and if the dryer was finished and a woman was still at Food Mart next door, he'd unload the clothes for her, and put them safely aside till she returned. If a customer was there for the first time, he would show them patiently how to run the machines. And he always had change. Plus, he was offering free entertainment to the customers with his magic tricks.

What did they know, I wondered? What did they really think of him? Maybe the younger girls just weren't old enough, wise enough, to see the truth about him, or to admit it to themselves. And maybe to them Dean really was a guy, only without a guy's strength and threat.

I never heard people say anything out loud to define him, though the older women would stare and smile at one another. Maybe people said nothing to me about him because they knew I was Dean's friend, and that he lived with me, and they figured I was weird too, and that we must be lovers or something—which we weren't.

The guys, they would drift toward him, and stand there watching his antics. Occasionally, they bought dope from him. I could see them holding themselves back, and sometimes I thought I could see this little gleam of fear in their eyes, fear and doubt.

Most nights after work, Dean would go to the Wooden Nickel, where he would do his magic tricks for whoever would watch. Sometimes the crowd would break away from the TV set or the jukebox to watch. Whoever did magic around there? Whoever did *anything* in Sparta? There was nothing to do except drink and hang out and go to your lousy job and have sex. Maybe people in Sparta—at first at least—wanted to preserve the mystery of Dean because it was more fun that way, he was something to do—like watching TV. Dean was entertainment for people's idle hours.

CHAPTER 6

CHRISSIE

Girls would call for him on the phone. "Is Dean there?" they'd ask. Tiny little voices, voices like the tinkling of wind chimes.

"He's out," I'd say, stifling a laugh.

Sometimes when they'd phone and hear my voice on the other end instead of his, they'd hang up. Or, if I said he'd be back soon, they'd call ten times in an hour to see if he had returned.

I ran interference for him. If I knew he was on a date, I didn't tell his callers. I'd just say he was at a friend's house or something. There were a lot of girls. Mostly little girls, younger than him. Sometimes they'd call up in groups, and you could hear the others in the background trying to keep quiet, shushing each other, giggling. Oh the tension, the terrible nervousness in that little voice at the other end of the phone! How they'd had to work themselves up to make these calls. They'd have gotten together in one of their houses in a group, in order to screw up the courage to phone him—they needed that mutual support.

Now, automatically, whenever the phone rang, I'd yell out, "Dean—yeewh!" because people hardly ever called for me.

The whole thing just made me laugh. And if I couldn't be one of his little girls, then I could watch it happen, and be entertained.

Jennifer, Maureen, Latasha, Megan, and a host of others— calling him up on the phone, loving him. Dean was like this game. And if you were young enough, scared enough, if you hadn't lost

38

it yet—your virginity, that is—then Dean was a nonscary way to go. He was small and skinny and his skin was soft and he didn't have a beard that scratched your face when he kissed you. And somehow, he could understand your body—for reasons maybe *you* couldn't quite understand yet. You had the illusion, somehow, that Dean wouldn't hurt you.

Sometimes the little girls would come for him personally. One day the doorbell rang, and there was little Stacy. Stacy was maybe thirteen, with big dark curly hair, and makeup carefully applied.

"Dean here?" Stacy asked, in her tiny little voice.

"Sorry, he's out."

She sidled in, carrying her purple backpack, and as she passed close to me, I could smell the fresh shampoo on her hair. Her breasts underneath her pink cotton sweater were just little buds, and the bones in her face still had that undefined look of child-hood.

Stacy glanced around the room, searching for him. I could feel her focused only on finding him, I recognized her child's secretiveness, her intentions encased like a bud in its petals.

"You know where he's at?" Stacy asked.

"I don't know." But I knew exactly where he was. Out with Latasha, driving around in his truck somewhere.

"Can I wait here?" Her voice was so tiny it seemed to float across the air.

She sat down on the futon in front of the TV. *Ricki Lake* was on, with women who'd shaved their heads and become racists. The audience was in a rage, yelling and screaming at the women on the podium. "It's got to do with I'm proud of my race," one of the women said, "proud of who I am . . ."

Stacy watches the television screen. Hardly moves there on the futon. As if she's scared that if she moves she'll bother me and I'll make her leave. Every now and then her hand goes absently to her full, dark hair, pats at it, in case *he* should suddenly walk in.

She is still, like a deer frozen at the edge of the road. The teenage girl's capacity to stay still, to wait in one spot for love! In those Greek myths we used to have in school, the maidens pined so much for the object of their love, or for their own reflections, that they grew rooted to the spot and became trees and hyacinths or rocks. No other category of human being is like the teenager in love, has that ability to wait, to wait motionless on doorsteps, in hallways, outside the classroom where the love object sits, or his place of work, for simply a glimpse of him.

Now the light in the room is waning, and the TV casts a blue reflection on her face. We watch the television together for a while. And then I say, "Isn't Dean kind of old for you?"

"No," says Stacy.

"What *is* it about him?" I ask.

At first she doesn't react. And then, suddenly, she loses her cool. She sticks her lower lip out, the big round blue eyes fill with tears. "He's not like other guys," she says. "He's just so—nice," she whispers.

She bends her face down into her hands, her long dark fragrant hair like a veil around her head now. "I just *love* him," she says. And suddenly she's all pathetic, the black eye makeup smudged on her cheeks and her tears have washed away all the blusher, and there is the little girl underneath, with her full child's face.

He never does come home that night, and eventually, I make her leave. I tell her she has to, because her mother will be worried. I know she would stay all night if I let her.

I wondered if he made love to them. I wondered how he did it. If he used his hands. His tongue. For just a second in my mind, a picture formed. But then—I stopped the thought. Didn't want to picture it, wanted to keep those thoughts away.

I was overweight, but not fat. I had never had a man of my own. That need just hadn't woken up in me, yet, whatever it was. I was the big girl with the heavy walk, everybody's buddy. Nobody's lover. I was quiet and I did not intrude. I just hung back and listened. I read my books, my mysteries and my romances, and people left me alone, and I survived.

But, sometimes at night, as Dean lay in the other room on the futon, I did dream about him. Then, the movements in my body would wake me up, as if the bones in my pelvis had softened, and they were rippling outward and then pulling together again. And when I woke up, I could never remember the dreams, except for little flashes. Those flashes were of just a moment, his face close to mine, his green eyes, my arms around him. But that was all I could ever remember, and when I woke up and I let the morning in, the images would dissolve immediately. And as the day wore on, and I tried to remember the dream, I couldn't remember any of it. Which was probably a good thing.

One night, after Dean had been with me awhile, when he wasn't home, the phone rang, and there was a woman's voice on the other end of the line. "Dean Lily there?" the woman asked. She sounded older, her voice was husky, sweet.

"He's not here."

A pause. "When *will* he be home?"

"I don't know. Want to leave a message?"

Another silence. Then, "Where is this I'm calling?"

"Who is this?" I asked. I could hear her breathing at the other end. "Who are you?"

"I'm an old friend of Dean's. This is the five-one-eight area code," she said. "This is New York State?"

"Yeah."

"I've been looking for him. . . . Are you his friend?"

"Yes."

"His *girl*friend?" the woman asked.

"No. Are you?"

"I was. . . ." A hesitation. "So—is he just living there?"

"Kind of."

She was silent for a moment on the other end. "I gotta tell you," she said. "Watch out for him. Watch out for Dean."

"Why?"

"He stole from me. He stole a hundred fifty dollars. He was living with me and my little girl—and—" I heard her sniff at the other end. "On top of everything—I come home and I find he's stolen from me! He lives in my house for three months, and he's like a—parent to my little girl!"

"I'm sorry," I said.

"I trusted him. And my little girl loved him. I don't even care about the money—a hundred and fifty dollars, except for what it means. It means he just—he just didn't care about us. And I want my money back." She paused, her voice was muffled, like she was crying. "I guess he's got someone else now?" she said.

"I don't know," I lied.

"But he's living there with you, and you say you're not his girlfriend?" She was begging for information now. When people are in love, I realized, information is like food to a starving person. And the person who's got the information has the power, by withholding it, then doling it out, bit by bit.

I heard a child cry in the background. "Oops, I gotta go," the woman said.

"Want to leave a message?"

"No—I'll call back. I want my money. . . . Oh boy, she's at the cat again! I gotta go."

I hung up the phone.

What was his secret? What was *her* secret that had made this woman turn to him, boy that he was?

It was late afternoon, and very still. The light was failing, the radiator hissed. Outside, the street was busy with shoppers, and I could hear the clatter of footsteps on the sidewalk beneath my window.

I looked around the room. I had left my wallet and my keys thrown down heedlessly on the Formica table. Everything seemed exposed now in the still air of the apartment. And suddenly I felt vulnerable.

I kept everything valuable I had in a green fireproof box by my bed—my Social Security card, my birth certificate, the $100 savings bond my dad gave me for graduation. That savings bond was like my insurance, in case I ever lost my job, it was a symbol, something my dad had given me to show he cared.

The green box lay on the floor by my mattress, and I went into the bedroom now, and opened it. The envelope from the Bureau of the Public Debt lay there.

The savings bond was still tucked inside it. He wouldn't steal from *me*. It was the law of the jungle, you don't shit where you eat. You don't steal from the person you live with, who you depend on.

That night I lay in bed waiting for him to come home. Washington Street grew quiet, except for the occasional car driving past at high speed, a whoosh of sound, kids screaming out the windows, the sounds swelling and then receding.

Around 2 A.M., I heard the key turn in the lock. The floorboards creaked. The toilet flushed. Then, silence.

I lay there, listening in the dark. Who was he? A bird person. A brother and sister both. A creature who could change his shape at will, fill any form you wanted.

I sat up in bed, and went quietly into the other room. I could see the mound of his body on the futon. He lay on his stomach, his hand wedged up underneath the pillow. The street lamp outside the window shone in on him. He seemed fast asleep.

"Dean, you asleep?"

"Yeah." I could tell by his voice he nearly was. His levels had exhausted him, whatever they were.

"You got a phone call," I said.

He didn't open his eyes. "Yeah," he mumbled, his voice muffled in the pillow.

"A lady. A woman."

"Yeah." Still, he didn't open his eyes.

"She was upset."

"Ummm."

"She said she was looking for you. She said you'd been with her, and then you left, and you stole from her."

He rolled over on his back, flung his arm across his face.

"Do you know who it was?" I asked.

"No . . . But I gotta go to sleep now."

"She said she had a little daughter."

"Cindy," he said, his arm still flung over his eyes.

"Did you steal her money?"

"Of course not. She's just pissed, that's all, 'cause I left her."

"Why'd you leave her?"

"Too old."

"Too old?"

"Yeah—she was a wo-man!" he said, emphasizing the word.

I stood in my flannel nightie by the door, waiting for him to say something else. Then I said, "You wouldn't steal from me ever, would you?"

He rolled over on his side, and pulled the edges of the sleeping bag up under his chin. "Oh for heaven's sake," he said. "You know I wouldn't do that, Chrissie! . . . Please, Chrissie, I gotta go to sleep now."

CHAPTER 7

CHRISSIE

It was deepening November now, the sky was thinning, a watery gray. The trees were all stripped of their leaves, bent in the wind; weather to pull your collar up around your neck for.

It was as if Dean could read people's minds. It was as if now, since the woman's call, Dean could sense some doubt in the air, in me. He started trying to do me favors. He bought flowers for the apartment, which I had to stick in an empty milk carton because I didn't have a vase. He even bought me a book, a paperback, *Anthology of Contemporary American Poetry,* something he'd picked up at a tag sale or something. (He, of course, never read a book himself.) I didn't tell him I already had the book for Lit-Comp II.

During the week that November, I went to work as usual at the Nightingale Home. The Home was in a brick building high up on a rise overlooking the town and the river down below. I was a nurse's aide there. I liked the job, though the smells, of urine, of dentures, of disinfectant, hung over the place constantly. And sometimes the bodies of the old people, the crinkly lizard skin of their hands with the liver spots, frightened me. But when I read to them, they would put their faces up to me like children. They would clutch my hand with theirs, and the warmth of their skin would permeate mine and would comfort me. They called me "sweetheart" and "darling" and they would tell me stories of the old days in Sparta, when people had jobs, when all the mills and the cement plants along the river were running. When the place was a real town, with churches not abandoned, and Sunday worshipers strolling the streets on a spring morning full of hope because there was a future, with possibilities, for the young.

My supervisor at the Home was Terry Kluge. Terry was tall, a couple years ahead of me in school, gangly like a colt. Terry did nothing with herself, wore her slate brown hair straight, wore thick, froggy glasses with flesh-colored frames. Yet I found Terry beautiful, her hazel eyes, her clear skin devoid of makeup, even her big nose, which was always red from the cold. Terry had high full breasts, and she stooped a little to make herself seem less tall. She wore thick-soled shoes, and granny cardigans.

Terry fascinated me. I was in some way deeply curious about her. I found Terry beautiful because she was so pure and so straight and so honorable. But sometimes I hated her too, for being so responsible. I resented her because she could tell me what to do, give me orders, even though she was close to me in age. If I were just a couple of minutes late, Terry would reprimand me. She was always watching me, making me do my job, follow the rules. Once when I had my coworker B.J. punch in for me because I had a hangover and wanted to sleep late, Terry yelled at me and told me that next time she'd tell Mr. Hanley and we would both get fired. "That's stealing, Chrissie," she said. "That's theft. You took money from the Home."

"What do you mean 'stealing'?"

"You took money that wasn't yours." When she said the words I could feel it in the back of my head, my hair seemed to rise up. She made me so ashamed that day I felt the tears sting my eyes. I hated the rightness of her words, the truth.

One morning in November, Terry said, "Chrissie, I need to ask you a favor. My dad had to use my car today to take Bobby to the doctor, and I wonder if you could give me a ride home."

I knew Terry hated to ask me for a favor because she was my

boss—Terry was very proper. But I said yes, I could help her out. I explained that my roommate Dean was picking me up because my car was in for inspection, but I thought he'd drive her home.

At noon I called Dean, and since he was in the mood for doing favors, he said yes, he would.

At four-ten promptly, Terry was waiting for me outside on the white-columned porch. There was a raw, wet wind sweeping in from the river. She was all bundled up in her navy wool coat, the sleeves too short for her long arms, and her gray scarf tied around her head as if she didn't care whether she looked old-fashioned or not, or like somebody's grandmother.

Terry was raising her child by herself. The father was Eddie Lasko, Coach Lasko's son. Eddie was a big football star when we were in high school and Terry and Eddie'd been together since ninth grade. They never married.

Then, last summer, when the baby was only two years old, Eddie left her. Couldn't take the responsibility, he said. The boy had asthma, and Terry's dad took care of him during the day while she worked. They lived way out in the countryside, in West Taponac.

Now, in the shelter of the porch, Terry and I waited side by side for Dean, Terry sniffing in the cold, her prominent nose bright red, both of us stomping our feet to keep warm, not talking because it was too freezing. Because she was my boss, she was holding herself a little away from me.

The Nightingale Home looked out across the river, and you could see on the other shore the tall towers of the cement plant spewing thin columns of steam, which thickened into a permanent cloud in the sky. It was the last working cement plant in the region. And the sound of it was with you always, wherever you went in the town, a low rumble, a steady, clanking beat of machinery echoing through the river valley. If you grew up in Sparta, the sound of the cement plant was part of your consciousness, it was like your breathing, you ceased, after a while, to even notice it. And if the sound had stopped, it would have been like the cessation of a heartbeat. It would have been as if there was suddenly no more life left in the river valley.

Then I saw Dean's red Dodge truck pull in and curve around the elliptical driveway. He stopped in front of the porch, reached over, rolled his window down. Looked from me to Terry with a smile, a question in his eyes, and I made the introductions. "Terry," I said. "Dean."

Terry, serious at all times, in a hurry, stepped toward the car. And then she stopped and met Dean's eyes.

Funny, seeing Terry's coolness disappear. I saw her eyes lock on him, in spite of herself. The curiosity at first, I thought—yes, what *was* he? And then—something else . . . and I smiled inside myself.

Dean shot her that quick smile, that flirtatious look you couldn't resist. I saw Terry catch herself, then she looked away.

"Dean," he said, and he held out his hand.

It was curiosity, I thought, that always drew them to him.

As we climbed in the truck, he swept his hand across the floor, and moved aside all the junk, the empty cans of Mountain Dew, the Skittles bags.

I sat in the seat next to Dean, between him and Terry. Terry, by the window, folded herself practically in half, bending her long thin legs up close to her body so she could fit inside the front of the truck. Terry's awkwardness was sweet.

"My dad had to use my car to take my son to the doctor," Terry said, nervously, though no one had asked, and I had already explained this to Dean.

Seeing Terry nervous made me happy.

He drove the truck down the driveway that curved around the home. We passed the hospital, and the beige stucco house on Noland with the big willow tree and the plaque in front of it saying the Queen of Greece had visited there once in 1959 on her American tour. Actually, they said, the queen had really stopped at the house just to go to the bathroom.

We passed the Fireman's Home, and the park and the Kiwanis

Olympic Torch Memorial. In the park, the Christmas Village was set up permanently, the little wooden houses on the green that only a child could enter, a train that went 'round and 'round. My mom and dad both said the town had had the Christmas Village when they were little kids.

Terry was huddled against the door of the truck, gripping the dashboard so she wouldn't fall against us. Every now and then, I'd catch her glancing at Dean. Couldn't help herself, I thought— they never could. It was so funny, I thought, to see Terry unhinged because of Dean.

PART II

ARE YOU
A COMEDIAN?

CHAPTER 8

TERRY

*Aug. 23. Eddie has gone and we are all alone now in the
middle of nowhere xxxx there is this silence xxx nothing,
no way to eat my body shocked. When you have seen the
worst and you have survived and you realize that you are
still alive . . . I called Dad and he came right over and
he's going to help us. . . . I feel like I am getting flu or sick
after the crying.*

—Excerpt from the diary of Terry Kluge

As we drove along in Dean's truck, he sat at the wheel, staring out
at the road ahead, slender and slight. I noticed the soft flesh of his
neck above the rim of his collar, so vulnerable there, the tender
curve of his flesh, made me want to put my tongue on it. I noticed
he had high cheekbones, delicate bones. The little smile on his
face, like he knew he was cute, and was in charge of the situation.

I wondered about where Chrissie found him. Something so
clean and perfect about the curve of his full lips. His features so
fine, different from the other guys around here, like he was an
aristocrat or something.

I couldn't help myself, kept looking at him, hoping he wouldn't
catch me. I couldn't wait for Chrissie to leave. I knew he and
Chrissie couldn't be lovers. Chrissie just wasn't the type somehow. She held herself in, away from that. Chrissie always had guys

as friends. He was waiting for her to leave too, I could tell. I knew it from that sly little smile of his.

When we got to Chrissie's place she looked quickly from one to the other of us, and then couldn't get out of the truck fast enough, climbing over me to reach the door. Like she had set us up, and could sense it had taken. She ran across the sidewalk to the front door of her building, not even looking back at us. It's funny how people cooperate when it comes to love and sex, I thought.

As we pulled way from the curb, I sat as far away from Dean as I could, next to the passenger door of the truck, so that I was leaning against it, almost falling out. We bumped along saying nothing. The truck needed new shocks, and I gripped the door handle to stop myself from sliding toward him.

Dean said nothing. He reached forward and put a tape in the deck to fill the silence. *This wild heart, it beats for you, baby, my heart in a storm, beats for you, babe-e. . . .* And he bumped his body up and down to the music, tapping his fingertips on the steering wheel.

It was cold in the truck. Heater must be broken too. I dug my nails into the palms of my hands, like knives, until my flesh hurt. Always did that when I was nervous—a secret way of being terrified so no one could see you.

We passed through the outskirts of Sparta. Up on the hill was the prison warden's white mansion. Below the big house were the outlying buildings of the prison, board and batten with gingerbread trim, a black wrought iron fence running along the perimeter of the prison farm. The little gray clapboard houses for the guards and their families. The prison itself was hidden down below in the valley, at the end of a long drive.

Behind a chain link fence were the abandoned cement factory, the lifeless silos, big asphalt yard filled with weeds poking up through the cracks. Next, the old stone tollhouse with the windows bricked up. Some local artist had painted scenes in the windows, to make it look as if there were life there—an old woman knitting in a rocking chair in front of a glowing fire.

Across from the tollhouse, the Sparta Utility plant, fuel tanks and giant transformers enclosed by a high wire fence. Right under the fuel tanks, that strange blue house, too vivid a blue for the usual color of a house, and peeling all over, the white showing underneath. The occupants must have bought the paint cheap somewhere, then painted it themselves.

Down below, to our right, was the river, a ribbon of water running through the valley between high cliffs.

We were on Old 27 now. There were wooden farmhouses, red barns. The abandoned Carvel's, Minter's vegetable stand, closed up for winter. Gradually, the town gave way to fields, dried stalks of harvested corn sticking up from the gray earth. This was when the county was ugliest, I thought, when the ground was waiting for the first snow. It was as if the ground were pregnant, like a woman is when she's first pregnant, when she is ugly and exhausted, and has morning sickness, before she becomes beautiful. I always thought in terms of pregnancy then, because of Bobby.

It had been a long time since I'd had sex. Months, since that night last summer when Eddie had lain on me, our bodies dripping wet from the heat, sticking together, Bobby asleep in the other room, his little body covered with sweat too, all of us too hot. It was so hot, the windows were all sealed up because Mr. Jukowsky painted them shut, there was no air. This was Eddie's last desperate, passionate encounter. Outside, in the fields, the cornstalks were stippled with moonlight. He was on top of me, plowing away at me, working working as if, with every movement, he's trying—trying—one last time to love me. I hope it will be over soon and it's like I'm outside us both, across the room watching. And I'm dry and no amount of his plowing can make me wet. I know I'm getting raw there and will probably get an infection or something. But still I love him, feel this tenderness toward him, and as he goes at it I stroke his silky hair like he's my child.

The next morning, the heat was blinding even before eight o'clock. I got out of bed, went into the kitchen, and found Eddie already awake. He was sitting very still at the oak table, as if he'd been up for hours, drinking coffee and smoking a cigarette. His thin dark hair fell over his square face, almost in bangs. I knew Eddie was supposed to be handsome, he was so tall and lithe, with tapering limbs and dark eyes, almost Arab eyes. His penis was big like the rest of him, but too big for me.

That part of life, desire, had always been silent in me. Maybe it was because Eddie was more a brother to me than a lover, and what I loved was having love around me, the state of it. We had been together since ninth grade, when my mother got sick with the breast cancer. I felt so undeserving of Eddie's love, so lucky, because he was so handsome and already a football star and I was tall and plain. Maybe he loved me because I was steady and did well in school and I kept him on the right path. We were a couple, waiting outside class for each other, so regular you could set your watch by us.

My dad was so stunned by my mother's illness that he could do nothing, and he just sat there helplessly, watching her, while I took care of her. I'd come home from school, make dinner, clean the house, and bathe her, fix her hair.

It was funny how, for a while when she was sick, my mother got even more beautiful. She was thinner, her eyes were bigger and shining and after they gave up on the chemo, her hair came in softer, like a baby's, and she let it grow to her shoulders. Her hair was a pinky blond color and it had a wave to it, and I'd brush it for her, and rub lotion on her body. She'd smile up at me, "Thank you, sweetheart. You are so sweet." Just having me bathe her and wash her hair would exhaust her, and she'd have to take more oxygen and she'd go right to sleep. . . . Please do not make me remember this. . . .

And it was killing my dad. He just could not handle it. That was when I began going with Eddie. Everyone envied us, because

Eddie was a football star already, and he was only with me. Even though Eddie was big and handsome, there was a secret part of him that was vulnerable. He had a little stutter sometimes, when he was nervous; not many people realized that. I loved him for it, it was an imperfection that made him human, that I could love, that made him seem not so big, not so imposing. And we were a solid couple, almost like parents to our friends, to be counted on to be a unit.

But I was never attracted to Eddie in the right way, and that was my secret. I figured it had something to do with that we made love for the first time right after my mother died, and maybe it was bad-luck love because it was the day after she died. I let him go inside. For two weeks I was too scared to do it again. Then I let him because he said he was so desperate, I felt it was his due, he was like a husband. And I couldn't bear to see him suffer, if he needed it so much.

When I got pregnant, the Laskos didn't want me to have the baby, they didn't want Eddie saddled with the responsibility. I stood my ground, I was not going to give up a life when my mother had been taken from me, faded into wind.

We found the little house in West Taponac in the classifieds, got it for almost no rent because Mr. Jukowsky couldn't get farmhands to live there. Bobby came three weeks early. He had hyaline membrane disease and on the second day, blew a hole in his lung. They kept him in the hospital three weeks. He was so skinny, and right from the beginning I thought he would never make it, that he would die too.

Of course, he didn't die, and we brought him home eventually. Eddie worked at Happy Clown after school and his parents gave us money. Eventually, I got the job as an aide at the Home. Even though Bobby was still a baby, there must have been something in me that sensed Eddie would leave us, and I had to be sure I could always take care of Bobby.

I wanted us to be a little family. I tried, tried, tried. I fixed up the little house with stuff from the Salvation Army in Sparta. Then Bobby had a croup attack and we had to rush him to the hospital, and I lay with him in the oxygen tent. Eddie was more scared than I. The croup turned to asthma and every time Bobby got it, gasping for breath, his little chest heaving, Eddie would pace frantically, his eyes flashing in terror.

I could feel Eddie growing quieter and quieter, sadder and sadder. He would look at Bobby and me as if from a great distance. He started spending more and more time at his parents' house. He was always sweet to us though, treated us well. But I could feel him slipping away, and there was nothing I could do. Nothing.

Then, on that hot morning last summer, standing in front of Eddie in my T-shirt, the heat trapped in the little house—it is not insulated—I hear a fly buzzing in the window, which is sealed shut with paint. And Eddie is watching me with those dark, Arab eyes. "I-I'm sorry," he says, with his little stutter. "I'm so sorry." And I can tell he wants *me* to comfort *him*. "Please, forgive me. . . ." he says.

"So, when are you leaving?" My voice is flat.

"I don't know. . . ."

"Do it now. If you're gonna do it, do it now."

That summer, all around me the fields filled with color—purple vetch, black-eyed Susan, goldenrod. Butterflies drifted across the tall grass. I heard nothing from Eddie, from the Laskos, since I had called them and they said they didn't know where he was. But I knew they were protecting him. They hadn't wanted us to have the baby, and now they just pretended I didn't exist anymore.

At night, sometimes, after we ate, I'd take Bobby out into the fields to look at the stars. Above us was the harvest moon, almost as big as the sky itself, the tips of the long grass lit up in the moonlight, and Bobby rendered into silence with his crazy mother carrying him out there way past his bedtime under the huge sky. As we walked, he'd stare up at the sky intensely, his eyes like black jewels, I could see the moonlight pooled in them. "Look, honey," I said. "See the stars." I wanted to be able to tell Bobby the names of all the stars, to point out the forms they took, the Big Dipper, the Twins, all the mythological figures. But I'd stare up at the sky and I couldn't find them. I wondered if you had to be a rich person to name the stars? In books, it seemed like only rich people knew.

Bobby, in my arms, weighed nothing. I would have given anything to have Bobby be heavier, stronger, not to have this feeling that any moment he could die on me, fade away.

And I was scared here in the long grass, but excited by the two of us being alone, the immensity of the sky, though my dad was ten minutes away. Only a mile away from here, a 300-pound black bear had been sighted by a farmer and the farmer took a picture of him, with the animal looking straight into the camera. The picture appeared on the front page of the *Ledger-Republican*.

Standing in the middle of the field that summer and holding Bobby, I looked back at my little house on the hill. A speck of white in the moonlight, the light in the window. Just him and me now. But my dad would help us.

I keep a diary, always have, ever since I was ten years old. My diaries have pink or blue leatherette covers, brass locks that tarnish and flake, and little keys. . . .

August 30. He has left me but all his life what he has done will live in him. Even when he has his own family he'll have to remember what he did and his other child he left behind and it will weaken him and poison him and that's my only revenge.

Now, four months after Eddie has left us, next to me here in the truck, there is this creature, this person I am afraid to look at.

"Which way?" Dean asks.

"Left here onto Church Road. I have to pick up my son at my dad's. Bergen Falls, just before West Taponac."

We turn onto Church Road and the truck glides along the curb through the little settlement. There is a scattering of houses, the

Lutheran Church, the graveyard with its soft, rainwashed headstones, wonderful names carved on them—Proper and Stockings and Hogeboom—tiny stones of buried children jutting up through the ground, their names and dates washed away.

There is only one tiny general store, in a white clapboard building, which sells newspapers, and a thin stock of milk and bread, canned goods and lottery tickets. I always wondered who lived here, what work they did. I knew there must be a history here—perhaps once this had been a mill town, or a horse stop with an inn.

You hardly ever saw anyone outside here, except for an occasional kid on a bicycle, or an old person walking a dog, or a woman pushing a stroller along the edge of the road, some young single mother who didn't own a car. And yet you knew people lived here, the houses weren't abandoned yet. The grass was cut, you could see curtains in the windows, satellite dishes in some of the yards.

Off to the left was my dad's apartment, above the video store, which was closed up now. My dad had gotten his own car back, and my black Toyota was parked next to his.

"You can drop me off here," I said. "I'm okay now if you've gotta get back." I said it praying he would say no, knowing somehow he would, though not sure till he said it, knowing that we had unfinished business between us.

He stopped the truck. "I'm making dinner," I said. "If you want some. . . ."

"Yeah, sure," he said.

He sat with the engine idling while I climbed up the outside stairs to my dad's door.

I could hear within the sound of Barney on the television set. "Oh ho hi, everybody! Oh ho . . ." My dad and Bobby were sitting on the couch, watching TV. "Two fellas together!" I cried.

Bobby looked up, saw me. "Mommy!" He jumped down from the couch, ran across the floor, flung his skinny frame into my arms—and bumped the top of his head on my chin. "Ouch!" I cried and I rubbed the top of his head to make the pain go away.

My father rose from the couch, a smile on his face. He was so thin and gray, and bent, the flesh seemed to hang loose and transparent from his bones. "Hello, sweetheart."

Bobby was overexcited from his asthma medicine. You could tell he was tight, his eyes were too bright, his cheeks flaming.

I bent my head down, inhaled the fragrance of his hair, the smell of shampoo, the smell of life itself. Bobby had dark, thin, silky hair like Eddie's. I hated cutting it and it was still like a girl's, and his cheeks were like the pulpiest fruit, made you want to bite them.

Bobby grabbed both my cheeks. "Where Mommy go?" he asked, looking into my eyes, his voice mock ferocious.

"You know I went to work, honey. . . . What did Dr. Vakil say?" I asked my dad.

"Just give him the mask tonight. He thinks it's under control. Said call him if you're worried."

My father stood there stooped, smiling, a tremble in his body, I noticed, as I gathered the Pulmo-Aide machine, and packed Bobby's things into his little backpack.

"He's a good guy, ain't you, buddy?" my father said. The two of them spent their days together struggling for breath, my father with his emphysema from the cement plant, Bobby with his asthma.

"I got a friend downstairs in his truck, waiting," I said to my father. "Hurry up, honey," I told Bobby. "Let's get your jacket on."

"Barney!" Bobby shouted. "Barney got a headache."

"Yeah, yeah," I said. "Barney got a headache."

I carried Bobby outside, down the steps. Too light, too light, I thought.

Down in the yard, in front of the building, I presented Bobby to Dean sitting in his truck, as if I were giving Dean a gift. "This is my son, Bobby."

From the truck window, Dean smiled at Bobby. "Hey there, little guy." I was happy that he had greeted him this way.

Bobby stared at him with those dark, steady eyes of his, his fist jammed into his mouth. I strapped Bobby into my Toyota, and we drove out, me leading the way, Dean following behind in his truck.

It was ten minutes from Bergen Falls to my house. And as you approached it, driving along the road, inevitably, your eye was drawn to it, my little house on the hill. Way up there, a good half mile from the road, just a tiny white speck. The only building in sight.

Behind the house the sky was darkening. For miles and miles around the fields were dipping and rising; and then on the horizon beyond, there was a harsh ridge of trees. Behind the ridge, the sun was setting, and the thin, spindly branches of the trees melted together like lace, the orange light like coins spinning between the threads.

From the road, looking up, you might think at first my house was abandoned. If you were an outsider in the county, you might think my house was just one of those odd buildings that were scattered all over, buildings that seemed to have no actual function—neither houses nor barns. Isn't it strange, you might think, a building so small no one lives there, so far up off the main road? But then at dusk, at night, you saw a speck of light in the window, a sign of life, and you realized someone did live there.

At the entrance to Schermerhorn Road, I stopped my car, and left the motor running while I opened the mailbox, number 105A, Dean waiting in his truck, at the edge of the road.

I reached in, got the mail, and stood for a second examining it. From the big oak beyond there came the sound of screeching, the pulsing of wings. The oak had thick, gnarly old branches, circling upwards, and its limbs were bare of all leaves now.

I peered at the black branches. The tree was infested with birds. The branches were alive with them, they seemed to move and undulate, swarming with birds, sparrows, flying in and out of the tree screeching and chattering. Beyond, in the field, a crow skimmed the surface of the ground, looking for something alive.

No good mail in the box today. Only the electric bill and a sale flyer from City Shop. I got back in my car, and we continued up the hill, me leading the way, my little car straining against gravity as I drove.

At the top of Schermerhorn, we pulled into the yard in front of my house. The house was just a little frame box, really, which had been painted white a hundred times over. Once, maybe, it had been a chicken coop or a storage shed. It was one story high, with a gray tin roof rusted at the joints. A wooden porch clung to the front of it, and there was a huge freezer left over from some previous tenant long ago that nearly filled the space, and the rest was cluttered with Bobby's toys, his wagon, his plastic trike.

The yard in front was rutted, frozen mud. We climbed out of our cars and we both paused a moment, instinctively listening to the wind dipping and sighing through the fields all round us.

I unlocked the front door and we went inside. The house was low-ceilinged, the floor covered with worn blue linoleum, patches of wood plank showing through. There was a big woodstove.

It was furnished with the stuff I got from the Salvation Army and leftovers from previous tenants over the years, a round oak table, chairs with broken braces, the windows had little white cottage curtains, the fabric worn and torn. To the side of the living room were two tiny bedrooms, one for me, the other Bobby's.

As soon as we got inside, Bobby cried, "I'm hungry!"

"Just a minute!" I said. "Gimme a minute."

I pulled off Bobby's jacket. "I'm going to make his dinner," I told Dean. "Fish sticks. Want some?"

"Sure," he said.

While I put the cookie tray with the fish sticks into the oven, Dean sat on the floor and played with Bobby. "Let me show you a magic trick," he said.

He reached behind Bobby's ear, pulled out a quarter. Bobby smiled up at him, but he didn't get the magic of it. Too young to understand the trick, and Dean didn't understand that Bobby was too young.

"How'd you do that?" I asked from the stove.

Dean smiled. "I'll never tell."

"You could be a professional."

"That's what I want to be. I'm not working at the Launder-center selling soap my whole life. . . . I want to have like a traveling show. Go from place to place. Maybe do it out of the back of the truck. People'll pay money. Once I really get it perfect, I'll be able to charge."

"I'll bet you will."

He started pushing Bobby's big yellow dump truck across the floor. Then he made a road with Bobby's blocks, giving Bobby his close attention, concentrating on the game, a cigarette dangling from the corner of his mouth, making his eye squint. I wished he wouldn't smoke, because of Bobby's asthma. But I was afraid to say anything. I already knew I wanted Dean to be happy here. I wanted him to stay.

And Bobby, sitting on the floor in his denim overalls, legs spread out, was gaping up at him, fascinated by this new person.

After dinner, I gave Bobby his bath. As I knelt beside the tub, I was so tired there was a buzzing inside my skull. It was if all the blood had drained from it. Only a half hour more, I thought, and then he'd be in bed. As I washed Bobby's thin, white body, I could hear Dean in the kitchen, clearing the table, stacking the dishes in the sink. I was grateful for his help.

Outside the bathroom window, a velvety wind rose over the fields, then, after a few moments, subsided like a breath. Not a summer wind with all its fullness and sweetness, but a damp, November wind, brushing the surface of the hills, promising worse.

Bobby was chattering up at me. "This the submarine . . . this the boat . . ."

"Yeah, honey."

I lifted him from the tub, and he ran naked into the living room, a tiny white body on skinny legs, and I ran after him. This chase was part of his bedtime ritual.

In the big room, Dean caught Bobby in his arms, and I swept him up and carried him back into the bathroom.

I dried Bobby off, and put my ear to his chest. "Sshh. Stand still. Let Mommy listen." Coming from deep within his chest was a sound like the whistle of a train, a sound far away in the distance. It was the asthma. But there was no retraction, no struggle for breath. Dr. Vakil had taught me how to detect the danger signs. "Trust yourself," Dr. Vakil said. "Always listen to the mother, that's the first thing they taught us in medical school. The mother knows."

When I'd pulled Bobby's blue feet pajamas on him, I sat him down in front of the TV to watch *Jeopardy!* and hooked up his Pulmo-Aide machine.

"What's that?" Dean asked.

"His medicine. Gets there quicker with this."

With the eyedropper, I mixed the medicine into a little container, fitted the transparent mask over Bobby's face, and switched on the console. Air hissed through the tube that led from the console to the mask and Bobby sat there breathing it in like a good boy. With the plastic mask over his face, he looked like a little spaceman.

After only a few minutes, the hissing stopped. It was all used up.

Dean asked, "Can I give him a kiss good night?" That pleased me, and I held him down to Dean so he could kiss him.

Then I put Bobby into bed in his own room, tucking the covers around his tiny frame. As I reached the door, his voice came to me. "Sing!" He sensed I was in a hurry to get to Dean. He wasn't going to let me get away without giving him his rightful due, without the ritual of my nighttime departure being complete. So I went back, and I sat on his bed. "Go to sleep—go to sleep," I sang. "Go to sleep, little bi-ird. . . ." Our own special words for the song.

He lay on his back, sucking on his thumb, listening intently to make sure I sang the words exactly the way I always did, exactly as I had a hundred times before.

* * *

After Bobby had fallen asleep, I went back in to Dean in the living room. I washed the dishes Dean had stacked for me in the sink, and Dean dried them. Above the kitchen sink, there was a small window that looked out across the fields behind the house. Beyond the house were fields, the grass brown and matted, waiting for the snow.

As Dean reached next to me into the drainer for the dishes to dry, I could smell him, the fresh, washed flannel of his shirts, the scent of wind and air on his skin. His green eyes shone, his cheeks were flushed red, there were soft golden hairs on them. He had this little smile, his teeth resting on his lower lip, as if he was aware of being watched, would burst out laughing at any moment.

A sudden energy seemed to knit my flesh. I was wide awake. Dean looked at me, a teasing smile on his face. He reached out his hand, touched my cheek, and under his fingertips, the pores of my skin rose. It was as if an electrical current were somehow magnetizing my skin, drawing it up, toward him.

He leaned over, touched his lips to mine. He was shorter than me by an inch or so, and I had to bend my knees slightly to receive the kiss. His lips were full, unexpectedly soft, his mouth fresh and moist, though not too moist. His breath was sweet, like spring or dawn.

I stepped closer to him and reached to put my arms around his neck. But he backed away, as if he didn't want me to touch him, danced a little shuffle step away from me, and smiled. Then he stepped forward again, leaned over, kissed me, but he held himself away so our bodies didn't touch.

At first his kisses were dry, subtle, feathery, his full lips barely touching mine. Then he'd pull away. Making me want more. Eddie's kisses were always too wet, his tongue too big, filling my mouth. When Eddie kissed me sometimes I felt I had no room to breathe.

Dean's tongue was making darting motions in and out of my mouth, entering, then withdrawing. Each little kiss made my body seem to swell more. And every time, he pulled back so that it almost hurt me physically. It was like he was torturing me, teasing me, making me want it more and more.

He wouldn't let me catch his tongue with mine—he'd pull it away just in time. It was like a dance he had designed, all the moves planned out.

Then, finally, he gave me his full mouth, all ripe and healthy, tasting sweet like fresh fruit.

"Take your glasses off," he ordered.

I said, "I can't see without them."

"You don't need to see."

I removed my glasses, and he peered into my eyes. "Your eyes are kind of hazel—greenish. Then, there's like these brown specks in them. . . ."

I knew I had permanent red marks on the bridge of my nose from my glasses. I rubbed at the marks now, knowing they were there. But the marks never went away, they were like scars on my face.

He led me by the hand into my bedroom. The wrought iron bed, with its chipped coat of white paint, took up nearly the whole space. There was a quilt, faded and torn, that had been left behind by some other tenant, and the old mattress sagged in the middle. In the corner, jammed up against the bed practically, was a little bureau.

Outside, the wind rose, the window rattled in its frame. For a moment, the house trembled. It was dark in the tiny room, except for a shaft of light coming through the door from the main room.

Dean lay down on the bed beside me, the springs squeaked. But he still held his body away from me so that we didn't touch. Then he curved his body toward me, but it wasn't touching mine, and kissed me so nothing touched but our lips.

All these months, I thought, all these months . . .

His hand moved to my breast, and when he cupped it in his hand it was as if all my body were centered there. He lifted my blouse, pushed up my bra, reached behind, and unhooked it like he was practiced at this. But again when I reached out to touch *him,* he shrank away.

Now his lips were on my breast, his cold wet tongue flicking the nipple and as he did that, he unzipped my skirt, loosened it, pulled down my panty hose, pushing up the skirt. I cooperated, lifted my hips for him. Didn't care anymore. Had been so long. In fact, it had *never* been. I felt the air on my naked skin and I was so wet there it was like a pool. It was all for me and not for him, if that was the way he wanted it. . . .

He whispered, "Take as long as you want."

And then he was down there, taking my swollen body into himself.

Every now and then he'd come up for air, kissing me, and I could taste myself on his wet lips, the lemony taste, detect the faint smell of myself on his mouth.

He didn't go inside me.

Afterward, I lay with my back to him, and he wrapped his arms around me, his body warm, warmer than any body I'd ever lain next to before, at least the one man I had ever known.

CHAPTER 9

TERRY

The next day Dean brought all his stuff over from Chrissie Peck's place. Chrissie was his "bud," he said, just his friend, a good person. Dean didn't have much to bring, just what he carried around in the truck with him, his backpack with some clothes, his magic books, his ditty bag. In the bathroom, I peeked inside the ditty bag—there was a razor, a roll of Ace bandages, Polo aftershave, a toothbrush, some pills, with the name of the drug on the label blacked out with Magic Marker. The label read L. Dean. Pharmacist's error, I thought.

That night, when we made love, Dean again insisted that it be dark. And when I touched him on the chest, I felt a thickness there, from the long underwear he wore, and then—maybe something underneath that. When I tried to touch him at his waist, or below, he pulled my hand away, and gripped my wrist tight. But I didn't mind, for now, at least, if he only wanted to give *me* pleasure. He arched his body over mine, pulling himself up on one arm, thrust his fingers inside me, then his hand, until it seemed like his whole fist was inside me. As he did it, he studied my face, like he was reading a book—though I was a book in motion, my head sweeping from side to side.

I felt him push one finger into my other hole, then another finger, prying me open, and I could feel my flesh part, a place exposed that no one had ever known before, and I could feel myself close around him tight enough to kill him.

After it was all over, I fit my body into the curve of his, my back close to his chest. I could feel two soft lumps there. As I turned, he stirred. "Hi," he said.

Now, as I turned to face him, he opened his eyes, caught me looking at him. Then he closed his eyes again, smiling and pulling my head down to rest in the crook of his neck, so I couldn't look at him.

"Dean," I said.

I pulled back away from him a little, and reached my hand out, almost afraid to touch him, but I did, on the chest, and his flesh gave way under my fingertips. I realized that before he must have been wearing a bandage around there. But now he was naked underneath his long underwear top.

I slid my hand under his top. He was wide awake now, watching me, and I felt his warm, smooth skin, the mounds of flesh so soft they gave away instantly under my fingertips, and his nipples had hardened into little stones.

I pulled his underwear top all the way up to his neck and I could just see, in the light from the fields, the smooth skin of his chest. Now a fragrance seemed to rise from his body toward me. It was familiar, a warm perfume that seemed to emanate from the very pores of his skin. It was the perfume of breasts, I realized.

"What?" I said. "What's this?"

"It's a deformity," he said. "I usually wear a bandage around it, but I took it off because it was itching." Indeed, the Ace bandage lay on the floor by the bed.

"A deformity?"

"Like nature made a mistake. It happened when I hit puberty. I usually hide it."

I slid my fingers around the breasts. The breasts were small and soft. "Does it feel good when I touch them?"

His eyes were closed now. "Yeah."

"Like a woman's?"

"Ummm . . ."

I saw the smooth skin, moist-looking, the aureole around the nipple wide and dark, the skin puckered, long soft hairs sticking out. I squeezed his nipple between my thumb and forefinger, and watched his face. He closed his eyes, and turned his head from side to side.

Slowly, I slid my hand down to the place between his legs, but he grabbed my wrist, as he always did when I tried to touch him there, and he brought my hand up again.

Now I inched my head down, took each of his nipples in my mouth, flicking them with my tongue, licking him there til his skin was wet. There was a low, moaning sound in the back of his throat.

Abruptly, he sat up in the bed and jerked his body away from me. Then he lay down on his back again. He arched his hips above the mattress, and he thrust his own hand down and dug it between his legs.

Later, as I was drifting off to sleep, I felt him get out of bed, the mattress tilting down to my side, the breath of cold air, and I heard him go into the main room. I roused myself, forced myself to climb out of the bed and I followed him.

He was sitting in the middle of the room at the round oak table. It was warm here, warm inside the house from the woodstove, which was still burning. But outside, the wind was blowing, I felt the house rattling. In the other room, Bobby slept through.

Dean took a pack of cigars and a bag of reefer from his backpack. He sliced open one of the cigars with his nail and unrolled the skin from around it, emptied out the tobacco, and repacked the cigar skin with weed. He sealed the skin down with his tongue, then lit up and offered the thing to me.

"No, I don't do that." Drugs always frightened me, losing control. And the evil it did to people in Sparta.

71

"As an experiment," he said. "See what happens."

He looked at me with those liquid eyes, the deep light shining within them. His cheeks were red, windburned from playing outside with Bobby. He had given Bobby a good run today. He smiled. "Good for fucking," he said. "We're not going anywhere."

Bobby in bed, safe, asleep. I took the blunt from him. I'd tried it once or twice, and as then, when I inhaled the smoke burned my throat, and I started choking and my chest hurt and my throat burned.

"Try again," he said. "One more time. Once your throat's a little burned, you don't feel it as much the next time. Makes it like scar tissue."

I inhaled again, and this time the smoke went right down into my lungs. I could feel the stuff begin to permeate my body, softening my limbs, and I let out a little laugh. I wasn't really high, but just the gesture of inhaling had giving me a new license.

"I want to see you naked," I told him.

The smile disappeared from his face. He took another puff on the blunt. "Can't," he said, avoiding my eyes.

"C'mon!"

"Sorry."

"But why? You see *me!* I'm not afraid. It's not fair."

I giggled, and I leaned over and pulled down at the top of his jeans, but he jerked his body away from me, as if he were irritated.

"I want to," I said.

"Please," he said. "Stop."

"Just tell me why. I love everything about you."

He hesitated, composing his words. He opened his mouth to speak, then seemed to think better of it.

"I want to understand," I said. Besides, there might be something even better, sexually, something we hadn't done that we could do now. And now, because of the dope, I could ask him.

"Please," I begged. "You can tell me."

He paused, studied me a moment as if planning how he would

put it. "See," he said, "I wasn't born like other people." He stopped. "I was born different."

"You told me that. It doesn't matter. It just doesn't matter to me."

He sighed, and suddenly he looked tired. "It's more complicated," he said.

"So. Tell me."

"Hard to explain."

"Try me." I stood up from the table, walked over to his side, knelt down on my knees in front of him, and took his hand in mine. "Nothing'll make me stop loving you," I whispered.

He hesitated. "I was born with both things," he said. "As a man *and* a woman. On the outside, I *did* look like a girl, but inside I've got male organs. I don't have a uterus or a cervix—or whatever . . ."

He looked away, as if embarrassed for the first time. But he had nothing to be embarrassed about around me.

"Don't be afraid," I said.

"My grandparents, they gave me money to have an operation."

"An operation?"

"Yeah." He wouldn't meet my eyes. "They take your thing and they make a—" He didn't finish describing it.

The thought of what they had done to him made me dig my knuckles into my eyesockets. "It hurts me to think about it!" I cried. I looked up at him again, seeing white, blind from the pressure on my eyeballs. "It's all done?" I asked him.

"Yeah, sort of." Still not looking at me.

"So, why can't you—I mean—why can't I see you now?"

"They don't do it all at once. It isn't finished yet. I gotta save up money for the second half. They still have to do one more operation. I got the hormones now. That helps."

"Hormones?"

"I take pills."

The ones with the name of the drug blacked out, the pharmacist's error, the name back to front. "I don't mind seeing you, whichever way it looks."

He shook his head.

"I told you," I said, "nothing about you can upset me."

His face was drawn, shadows etched under his eyes, around his mouth. "But you're happy?" he asked, as if for reassurance. "This is the happiest you've ever been—right?" He was eager for me to say yes.

"Yeah."

"So—why change things?" he asked.

"But *you* don't get any pleasure?"

"I do," he said. "I get off watching you."

CHAPTER 10

TERRY

*Dec. 1. Sometimes it is as if all the cells in my body are
singing, I am all cleaned out. . . . I worry that all our
lovemaking is just for me . . . but then I cannot think
about it when he does it to me. . . . I go to work and I
cannot concentrate I am a stranger just going through the
motions. People have no idea though I guess that maybe
Chrissie suspects. She keeps looking at me Dean if you are
reading this it is okay because what I cannot tell you
myself you will find here. . . . This is a message. . . .*

During the day Dean and I went to work and, as usual, I left
Bobby with my dad. All day long at the Nightingale Home, I
moved through my tasks as if I were sleepwalking, thinking only
of him, and I couldn't wait for four o'clock when I would return
to him.

At night, after we'd had dinner, I'd hurry to put Bobby in bed,
so we could be alone together, so we could make love.

I guess that during the day when I was at the Home, he wasn't
showing up for work at the Laundercenter or something, because
after he had been with me ten days or so, he got fired. They said
he was late for work too much, and that sometimes he wasn't
coming in at all.

So now Dean had no job, and I had to support him as well as

myself and Bobby, and that left almost nothing of my paycheck at the end of the week. But that was okay, I couldn't let him starve, I couldn't throw him out.

During the day, while I was working, he'd drive around in his truck looking for work. Sometimes he'd take Bobby with him, just to give my dad a break from baby-sitting.

And when I came home from work, he would be there waiting for me, and we could begin our secret life. As I made dinner, Dean would stare at me, wouldn't take his eyes off me, a faint smile on his lips, like he was sending me a message, teasing me.

But it was always for me, not him. He'd never let me touch him there. And after a while, I forgot to care because I was so lost in what he was doing to me.

He would prolong things, hold himself back, his hand, his tongue—stretch it out until I was in pain wanting it, until it was torture and I'd be begging him, please please and he'd laugh at me and my agony. Everything focused on this place, or that, my breasts, between my legs. Then he'd take pity on me, and it would all come together like a wild storm.

We were like a little family, he and I and Bobby. On Saturday, we'd go into town to Food Mart and do all our shopping, and then we'd go to Uncle Dom's Pizza for lunch—a little family of Saturday morning shoppers, walking along the street surrounded by the warmth from our love. And sometimes we were so heavy with love, from what we had done the night before, that we could hardly speak, could only smile.

On Sunday, Dean would study his magic books for hours, concentrating on them while Bobby played on the floor at his feet.

Dean held a piece of string in his hand, looking from his book to the string and back again. There was a knot in it. He cut a piece from the string, then wound it around his hand.

"Pull it," he said to me. I pulled, and suddenly the string was miraculously in one piece again and the knot had disappeared.

He made me choose four crayons from the box. "Don't let me see—hand one to me under the table. Don't let me see which one you picked."

I handed the crayon to him, under the table, and he felt it without looking down. "Green," he said.

When he took it out, of course, the crayon was green.

At night, he would rouse me from sleep to make love. And I was so tired, I didn't think I could do it, but I could, I could . . . and we'd go at it, the warm, damp smell of sleep filling the air around us in the tiny room. And I'd whisper, "What about you? This is all for me."

"Doesn't matter," he said, his breath fluttering on my cheek.

Dean was a jealous lover, too. One evening, Bobby was having his last few minutes of play before bed. I could see him through the door in his own room, kneeling on the floor in his blue feet pajamas, in front of his toy box, methodically removing his toys, one by one, and placing them on the floor.

I started washing the dishes. I was waiting, waiting for Bobby to be in bed . . . for Dean's and my time alone together. It was as if everything in my life was directed toward that time. Here I wanted my own son to go away.

I moved around the kitchen sink, conscious of my own body, of Dean's body across the room, of the special silence and stillness before we were drawn together.

Dean was studying my figure with his eyes, as if I were an object, and I was glad, because I knew he was imagining tonight, picturing himself making love to me.

After I finished the dishes, I began folding the laundry from the bag into little piles on the couch, smoothing each piece out with my hand. Dean's T-shirts, his jockeys. Bobby's little clothes, my panties and bra. All our clothes mixed together like a little family.

Dean had been watching me. Suddenly, he asked, "Was sex good with Eddie?"

"It was hardly even sex," I said. That was the truth. Didn't know it then, of course. I had thought there was something wrong with me, that I was just frozen that way, that what counted was the love I felt for Eddie, the spiritual feeling, and that maybe the other side, the physical feeling that I had read about in books, would come later. Or maybe that stuff I read in books was just an exaggeration.

"You think about Eddie much?" Dean asked.

"Never."

"Who else've you been with besides Eddie?"

"No one. He was the first."

"I think you're shitting me," Dean said suddenly.

"Don't be crazy." I laughed. This was funny. He knew he was the only one that mattered.

He sat forward, tense, over the round table, his eyes fixed on me. "Is there anyone else you're attracted to *now?*"

I laughed. "You're crazy!"

He didn't smile. "I'm serious."

"How can you worry? Can't you tell the truth about the way I feel about you from—the way I am with you?"

He stood up from the table, strode across the room to the sink, where the little window faced out to the fields and the ridge of trees beyond. He was angry—I didn't understand why.

I stood by the couch, my hands frozen in the gesture of folding his T-shirt. I put the garment down, walked over to him by the window. I touched his cheek. "How can you worry?" I asked.

He jerked his body away from me.

"What's the matter?"

"Thinking about you with somebody else just makes me crazy!"

"What started this? We were having a nice time. Who said anything about anybody else?"

I had no one else, wanted no one else. He knew that. Was he just pretending—acting the way he thought you were supposed to act when you were in love?

I stood next to him, smoothing his hair down with the palm of my hand. But it stuck up in the air like baby hair, the cold made static electricity in everything. So I carried Bobby's clean laundry into his room, opened the door to the bureau, and folded it away.

Bobby walked up to Dean. The ends of his thin dark hair were damp and curled from his bath, his skin was all shiny. He was wearing his blue feet pajamas, carrying his *Runaway Bunny* book, and he held the book up to Dean. "Read!" Bobby commanded. Bobby usually didn't even have to say hardly anything to Dean, Dean would just scoop him up and do what he wanted. But now Dean pushed the book aside.

Bobby stood there, staring up at him, his lip trembling. Dean had never pushed him away like that before.

"C'mon, Bobby," I said. "Mommy read it. Dean doesn't feel good. Let Dean alone now, honey."

A half hour later, after I had finally gotten Bobby to sleep, and Dean and I were in our own bed, I turned to Dean, but he rolled away from me to the other side of the mattress. "What's the matter?" I asked.

He mumbled into the pillow, "Jealous."

"But why? I don't get it. I love you. You *know* there's no one else."

"I can't help it. It's the thought of it. . . . Let me be. Let me try and work it out."

And that night, for the first time since I had known him, he didn't make love to me.

I couldn't sleep. I lay next to him, listening for his breathing. And he seemed to fall asleep without difficulty, as if he didn't need me. But it was hours and hours before sleep came to me.

Then, the next night, he made love to me again, as if nothing had happened, as if all his anger had disappeared. We had finished making love, and though I was satisfied, I felt only half complete, that there was this whole other realm of pleasure—*his* pleasure— to be explored. I whispered, "What about *you?*" These were things we talked about only in darkness.

"Doesn't matter," he whispered, smoothing the hair back from my forehead. Then he kissed it. "What counts is seeing you happy."

December 10. We are a little family! Bobby has a daddy now. We've got our little routine down. It is real winter now. The pipe in the bathroom froze in the night and we had to go to Dad's house. My dad likes Dean, maybe he doesn't see so well, Dean is just one of my friends to him. It's funny how the brain gets dull with age to protect people, and everything is concentrated on your own survival. There was not much damage to house from the water. Mr. Jukowsky put in a new pipe section I feel like we got the asthma under control because of the mask at home. Dean lost his job. Now I have to support three of us but that doesn't matter because we are all together now.

CHAPTER 11

CHRISSIE

Saturday mornings, I'd see Dean and Terry and the boy shopping at Food Mart. Or on Washington Street on one of those bright winter Saturday mornings when the sun is shining and there is a surge of happiness in town and everyone is released at last from their overheated homes where they've been fighting with each other and the kids have been driving them crazy with cabin fever and they come out joyously into the sunny winter morning.

Some stores on Washington Street were boarded up, but people still came downtown on Saturday mornings. As if they were trying to recover something that had been lost, the sense of a real town, a vital community.

Dean would glance up and spot me and give me that secret smile. He would help Terry with the boy. Reach inside the truck for the child, carry him like he was his own. Really loved that kid, it seemed.

I'd see them go in the balloon shop on Washington Street, then they'd stop in at Uncle Dom's Pizza.

Terry had a grave way of walking, she was taller than Dean by about an inch. Terry was so serious, and you could see the weariness on her face sometimes. Always focused on her boy, worried about her boy. She'd held herself together after her boyfriend, Eddie Lasko, the father of her kid, took off and left her stranded with the kid. She'd gotten herself a job and raised the boy basically by herself, with a little help from her dad, and her dad was sick too.

They were a weird trio—Dean and Terry and Bobby. But not any weirder than the deadbeats who hung out in downtown Sparta. The young women without teeth, the retarded people. The obese people with their pale bodies. People leaning out of their windows over the street, shouting at one another across the way, fighting. Women worked up on drugs, with their tottering, swaying gait and their arms flaying out, hookers stumbling on high heels. All those people left behind in Sparta because they couldn't get jobs elsewhere. People with something wrong with them. Mutationally speaking. Genetically speaking. The people who lived off the dirt roads in the countryside, in worn-out farmhouses and trailers under strange circumstances, trailers you weren't even sure were inhabited when you drove by them, because there wasn't even a car parked outside and the windows were shuttered. But then, if you looked closely, you could see a thin column of smoke rising from the metal vent on the roof, and you'd know that someone must be home.

So what did people know about Dean? Did they guess? One moment, you were looking at a boy. The next, you shifted the angle of your sight just a little and—and lo and behold—he was a girl! And you were left squinting and wondering. But maybe people just didn't want to know the actual truth. It was more fun that way anyhow. Dean was like going to the movies. He was entertainment. Watching him was something to do, he was someone to look at and smile about if you saw him on the street, or at night when you were drinking at the Wooden Nickel.

If you were an old person, and sitting there in the window of your house day after day looking out onto the street, you'd see Dean strutting down the sidewalk, handsome and cocky, in his cowboy hat and boots with their thick heels. He'd catch you staring at him and he'd grin and he wouldn't let go of your eyes, he'd force you to look at him, and you'd just keep staring and staring, in spite of yourself.

At work, Terry was private about Dean. Terry knew I was Dean's friend, but she tried never to mention him. If I brought him up, she'd respond as briefly as she could. Maybe it was the overwhelmingness of her love for him. Sometimes I'd talk about Dean deliberately, just to see Terry look uncomfortable. And because it gave me power over her. As if to say, "You better be nice to me, girl, because I'm his *original* friend, I introduced you." I liked having power over Terry. It would be harder, I thought, for Terry to discipline me now if I were late or something, because I was his original friend.

One night, Dean brought the boy to the Wooden Nickel. Terry was working nights that week to get the differential because she was supporting them both now that Dean had lost his job at the Laundercenter. Dean must've gotten bored being home alone with the child. It was eleven o'clock when he came in with Bobby. You weren't supposed to have kids in the bar really, but Carl didn't say anything. I saw Dean carrying Bobby along the bar, showing him all Carl's crazy clocks and objects, the deer head with the tinsel hanging from its nose.

Then Dean started dancing with him to the noise of the jukebox, holding both his little hands in his.

The boy was getting overexcited, his eyes were too bright and wet, his cheeks flushed. He looked up into Dean's eyes and Dean made faces back to him and stuck his tongue out and wiggled it at him. Then he sat the boy down on his lap at the bar, and they watched the TV news together, the boy leaning back against Dean like he trusted him completely, was comfortable with him, like Dean was his family. Dean was showing him off, like this was his real, biological son.

People walked over to them, touched Bobby's hand, as if they'd never seen a kid before. "Hey fella, how ya doing, little guy?" The kid was special because he was small for his age, and yet he was intelligent and alert like an older child. He had long fine dark wavy hair, dark eyes, long eyelashes. The discrepancy between his small size and his mental capacities intrigued people. Someone offered him a sip of beer, and he took it, then made a terrible face and spat it all out and it made everybody around him laugh. It was as if he were a pet monkey or something, a little performer, a conversation starter. He had replaced Dean's magic tricks as the attention-getter.

I was sitting at the end of the bar reading my book that night. "Terry know you got Bobby here?" I asked Dean. "It's late."

"She knows," Dean said. He jiggled the boy on his knee, looked at him. "He loves me, don'tcha, guy?" he said.

Bobby giggled, slid off Dean's lap, scampered into the other room in his little denim overalls and his red sneakers, his curls bouncing.

"Hey you!" Dean cried. "Come back here to Daddy!"

So, Bobby was calling Dean Daddy now.

In the middle of the room, the child stopped and turned. He spotted Dean watching him and his face lit up. Back he ran—too fast, he was going to trip. "Daddy!" he shrieked. "Daddy!" And then, right in the middle of the room, he did trip, and he fell right down on the floor.

Next thing, he was crying hard. His voice rose to a wail. The sound of a child weeping was incongruous in the bar, drowning out the noise from the TV and the jukebox. Everyone had stopped what they were doing and were staring at Dean and Bobby now.

Dean lurched off the bar stool, ran to Bobby, picked him up, and held him. The boy was sobbing like his heart was broken now, his little chest heaving, rubbing his eyes with his fists.

Dean pulled the boy's snowsuit on, trying to soothe him, and hustled him out the door of the bar. As the door slammed behind them, you could still hear Bobby wailing from out in the parking lot.

CHAPTER 12

CHRISSIE

The first snow came, falling silently and steadily on Washington Street, fresh and pure, announcing itself with a purpose. All day long, it kept on coming. Like a baptism. Below my apartment window, kids ran outside to play, shrieking, opening their mouths to the sky to swallow the flakes, sliding down the sidewalk on toboggans.

Throughout the day, the snow built up on the sidewalk. It swirled across the street, drifted up the steps of buildings, blocking front doors in windswept motions.

As evening came, the children came inside for dinner, and outside my window, the quiet deepened, the only sounds now were the scraping of metal shovels on the sidewalk. Nothing moved. There were no cars. The snowplow hadn't come through yet. There were lights in the windows of the building across the way, but the street itself was empty.

I put Mariah Carey on the tape deck.

There was a knock on my door. The buzzer downstairs was broken. "Who's there?"

"Me," he said through the door. He didn't even have to say his name. He expected that everyone would recognize his voice, that he was at the center of everyone's thoughts even when he was absent.

I opened my front door and he stood there, snow melting on

the brim of his cowboy hat and the shoulders of his jacket. His cheeks were bright red from the cold, his green eyes shining, his gleaming teeth resting on his full red lip. "Mind if I come in?"

But he already knew the answer, and he stepped right across my threshold.

"What're you doing here?" I asked.

"Nothing. Haven't seen you in a while." He threw his jacket and his hat on the floor, and the snow from them melted on the floorboards in little puddles.

He sat down on the futon and pulled off his cowboy boots, his big socks steaming in the air.

Then he stood up, walked over to the refrigerator, opened it as if this was his own house. He took out a can of Mountain Dew, and in one quick gesture popped the tab up with his thumb. I could never do that, but Dean had all those cool guy gestures down. Better than any guy.

"Got anything sweet?" he asked.

"Nope. Your teeth are gonna fall out from all that sugar."

"My teeth are fine," he said, baring them to show me. His teeth were big and white.

It was very warm in the apartment. The old boiler downstairs overheated us sometimes.

"What's up?" he asked. Sometimes he just made me laugh. Just looking at him, he was like a little juvenile delinquent, mischievous and seductive.

"Fine," I said. "I'm doing homework."

"What homework?"

"English. I'm reading this." I showed him *I Know Why the Caged Bird Sings.* Dean would never read a book. All that seemed to matter to Dean was sensation—drinking and sex and any other pleasure.

"How's Terry?" I asked.

"Fine."

"And the boy?"

86

"Cute."

"So where's Terry at?"

"Working double shift. B.J.'s out sick."

"Where's Bobby at?"

"I left him at her dad's. I needed a night off from baby-sitting."

He moved about the room, the can of Mountain Dew in his hand. His jeans were drawn tight at the waist with his belt, the pants legs loose over his skinny legs.

On the floor by the phone lay my address book. He bent down, picked it up, then sat down on the futon next to me and began paging through it.

"What're you looking at?"

"Names."

"Names of what?"

He reached into his jeans pocket, took out his weed. He rolled a blunt, lit up, and dragged on it, offering it to me. I took it from him and sucked.

He said, "Show me who's in here."

"What do you mean?"

"I want to meet someone."

"What about Terry?"

"Just looking," he said, and smiled.

Terry had power over me, she made me toe the line. Terry was my supervisor. I felt guilty.

I said, "I thought you were with Terry."

"I just want to see what else is around."

I snatched the address book from him, feeling a sudden guilt about Terry, slammed it shut. But then suddenly . . . I liked the idea of going around Terry.

I opened the address book again. "Let's see," I said, studying it. "Shannon Attwood."

"She pretty?"

"Yeah."

"Tell me."

87

"She's got black hair . . ."

"Don't like black hair." He laughed. "Tell me who's the prettiest of them all—all your girlfriends. Go through the book and tell me. Describe them—each one."

I came to the B's. "Cindy Betts." For a moment, I imagined him making love to Cindy Betts. Then I stopped the thought.

"What's she like?" he asked.

"Pretty. Blond hair—"

"How does she wear it?"

I tried to picture it. "Shortish, I think."

"I like it long." I realized that his remark cut *me* out—he didn't even realize what he was saying. I, Chrissie, wasn't even in the picture for him because I had short hair.

Dean had never come on to me. I guess I would've been surprised if he had. Always the friend, I thought. I was an insider, almost invisible. But I let it happen that way. Maybe even encouraged it.

I kept on going. "Long hair," I said. "Ummm . . ." I paged through the book. He must like the long hair because it was a challenge. Someone truly feminine he could deceive. "You're so bad!" I said. He laughed again. I came to the S's. "Here's one," I said.

"Who's she?"

"Melanie Saluggio."

"Tell me," he said.

"Well—Melanie's very beautiful, I guess."

"Describe her," he ordered.

I closed my eyes, tried to visualize Melanie. "Got beautiful hair. Fine, long, shiny, reddish-brown, little highlights. Small, everything about her kind of delicate. Melanie is—complex. She could be a model if she wanted. . . ." In some circles in Sparta, that was the highest compliment you could pay a person.

"Where's she at now?"

"I don't know what Melanie's doing. She's with Brian Perez

sometimes, but I don't know whether they're going out or what. She was County Schoolgirl Queen our year."

He looked up. "Brian? She goes out with Brian?"

"Melanie's weird. She takes pity on people. The weaker, the sicker they are . . . Anyway, Brian's good-looking. I think she kind of looks on him as her brother. They've been friends since they were little. Melanie's always defended him."

Dean said, "Fuck Brian."

"Yeah. Brian's an asshole."

"You got a picture of her or something?" he asked.

"In my yearbook."

"Let's see."

I stood up, took the yearbook down from the shelf. The yearbook was one of my few personal possessions, one of the few things I'd brought from my mother's house, that I carried with me. I opened it, leafed through it till I came to the pages that had the individual class photographs.

There I was. Too big. Not fat, but just big-boned. Big jaw, big nose. Nothing I could do would ever make me pretty.

"I hate my face," I said.

Dane studied my picture. "You look good," he said. "Don't put yourself down."

"Yuck."

He turned to me. "Why do you feel so bad about yourself?"

"I'm too—big," I said. "Clunky."

He scrunched up his eyes, studying me. "Y'know—when you smile—your face is just—sweet. You got the sweetest smile. You're not fat. Your eyes—they're beautiful. Real dark. Your skin's clear. There's nothing phony about you—and your smile's really special."

It was a strange moment. I knew he meant it. Though it didn't mean he was interested in me, and I still thought I was plain. But it was if a little bit of truth—on his part—of genuineness, had beamed through all his bullshit. He really did think that.

"You're strong and steady and good, Chrissie," he said. "Ten times smarter than all the assholes around here."

I was embarrassed by the scrutiny. I slapped my palm down over my photograph. I hated photographs of myself. I wasn't even going to let them photograph me for the yearbook. I just wanted one of those blank spaces on the page, with only my name and my clubs under it, but then my mom made me have my photograph taken.

I kept on turning the pages of the yearbook till I came to Melanie Saluggio. There was the photograph from when Melanie was Schoolgirl Queen. In the photo, Melanie wore a peaked gold crown on her head and carried a bouquet of flowers. She had long, fine, shining hair, high cheekbones, large eyes with big, dark pupils, almost like straight vertical lines in her eyes. Eyes like a cat. As if she could see in the dark.

The photo was black and white, with deep contrasts and shadows. Melanie's eyes were lit up weirdly from the flash. In real life Melanie's skin was olive-colored. Her smile in the picture was shy, beautiful. She had a little chin, delicate, perfectly formed lips. A curved smile like one of those Greek statues. Everything about Melanie was delicate—her small breasts under the white, strapless gown, her thin arms. Melanie was just born lucky. She was everybody's honey. Don't know why she hung out with Brian.

You could never quite reach her. She was vague, you couldn't put your finger on her. Except she was so sweet and kind and she hated injustice. When someone was mean, or called another kid "nerd," Melanie would always rush to the defense of the weaker person. She would use the strength of her popularity for justice.

"I gotta meet her," Dean said. "How can I get to her?"

"What about Terry?"

"She'll understand," he said, his eyes fixed on the photograph of Melanie.

"What do you mean—'She'll understand'?"

"It's different with us," he said, still studying the photograph.

"Like how?"

"Because of—what I am."

"What does *that* mean?"

He didn't move his eyes from the yearbook. "Just—how I am. That's all."

"Terry's going to freak," I said.

"No." His voice was distracted. "I know what!" He looked at me, smiled at his bright idea. "My birthday's coming up. You can give me a party!"

"A party?"

"Yeah. A twenty-first birthday party. I'm a Christmas baby. Invite her."

"Invite Melanie?"

"Call her up."

"Who's going to pay for this party?" I asked.

"I'll chip in. We'll have a party, man!" he said, taken up with it now.

"What about Terry?"

"Say you can only do it on Fridays. She's working Friday nights because of the differential." Terry had to make the money for both of them because he wasn't earning any.

"Terry'll take the night off for it, if it's a birthday party for you," I said.

"I'll tell her we'll have our own party—me and her together."

I sat there quietly, thinking. I owed nothing to Terry. Terry made my life tough. Terry was on their side. Terry . . . so good . . . so pure.

I felt mean tonight. I guess I was jealous a little, too, that they were a unit, that she had him in a way I never could. Even though I didn't ever expect him to be my lover.

While he was still there, I dialed Melanie's mother's house and asked for Melanie and told her about the party.

"Think you can make it?" I asked. Over on the futon, Dean listened carefully.

There was silence on the other end. "You know Dean?" I said. "Dean Lily? He was working at the Laundercenter?"

Still silence. Melanie often answered questions with silence, I remembered. This had the effect of making you concentrate on her answer.

After a pause, she said, "I'll try and get there." And then she gave that soft little laugh, that laugh that told you nothing.

I hung up. And now I was excited. It was the excitement you feel when you are going to cause a big change, alter the course of events, disrupt things, and you are sitting back to watch it all unfold in front of you.

CHAPTER 13

CHRISSIE

On the night of the party, Dean arrived early, at nine o'clock. And what do you know—who should walk in with him but Terry? "What happened?" I asked Terry. "I thought you were working."

"Couldn't miss this," Terry said.

She looked completely different tonight. I'd never seen Terry like this. She was wearing a black lace top and tight black jeans, spike heels, long silver earrings. And makeup. And it was like she wasn't used to wearing makeup—the lipstick was dark red, and painted in a harsh, jagged line over the lip line. Her eyeliner was too thick. I liked plain old Terry better. What was she doing to herself? Just for *him?*

Dean's face was pale from his shower, he had his hair all slicked down, he looked punk. He was wearing his usual two torn flannel shirts, and a black t-shirt underneath, and his cowboy boots. There was a tiny gold hoop earring in his ear—as if he were daring everyone—What am I, he was saying, take your pick—boy or girl?

I'd decorated the apartment for him, put up a Happy Birthday banner across the wall, and balloons, and I'd taped red gel over the windows, and screwed red lightbulbs into the fixtures. The room had a deep, red glow, and it was dark enough so people could misbehave without feeling observed.

Around nine thirty, the guests began arriving. B.J. came, from work. B.J. was black, a little older than us, maybe thirty-five or forty. He was a Vet. He had a soft, southern voice, and though his skin was black, he had blue eyes. B.J. was kind and private. I believed he had a past. I didn't even know if he had a family, if he were married, or had kids.

There were people from down the block. Latasha came from down the street, bright faced, caramel-skinned, eyes laughing; one of Dean's ex-girlfriends. And some kids from our high school class that never seemed to leave Sparta, that seemed to show up at every party, whether or not they were invited, even though we'd left school long ago.

The arriving guests stood around, drank paper cups of wine and beer, pretended not to be scrutinizing one another.

I found the Salt n' Pepa tape, slid it into the deck, turned up the volume, and it blasted through the room.

As the night wore on, the apartment door kept opening and closing, more people arriving. The room was filled near to capacity now. People were cramped together in the tiny kitchen area. Some had drifted into my bedroom. The more people in a small space at a party, the better.

The sound of Salt n' Pepa pumped through our bodies. The beat of the music was like a heartbeat, and you could feel the blood pump through your body like the tide sweeping in, out, in, out.

Dean stood near the door, eyes riveted on it, drawing on his roach in short little bursts. I sensed the tension in him. Everything about him was directed toward that door, all his senses were strained toward it, to where he knew Melanie would have to enter.

Someone put another tape on. I heard Terry ask Dean, "Want to dance?" But he shook his head. Terry looked at B.J. as if to extend an invitation, and together they moved into the center of the room. The icebreakers! Terry was so tall in high heels, like a tree. A different woman today, released . . . She jiggled her shoulders to the music, twisted her hips, knees together. *My guy makes me crazy . . . crazy . . . O crazy . . . does it to me . . . does it . . . does it . . .*

Terry and B.J. were really getting it on. B.J. was dancing like he was experienced, watching Terry's crotch as he moved his body in rhythm with hers. B.J.'s age made me shy, he could be our father.

I'd never seen Terry this loose before. I knew she was really dancing for Dean, she wanted him to pay attention to her. But Dean wasn't looking at Terry. He was watching the door.

He was sitting on the futon with his legs out in front of him and he seemed unhappy. He wouldn't look at Terry, though every now and then while she was dancing, Terry glanced over her shoulder at him to see if he was watching her.

Now Terry moved toward Dean, gate-legged, pelvis tilted, knees apart, in rhythm to the music. She stood right above him, moving her hips at him, looking down at him. Terry babee! It was an invitation. She wanted him to dance with her.

But Dean avoided looking at her, wouldn't look at her. Wouldn't meet her eyes. I knew—and maybe Terry knew too—one reason Dean wouldn't dance. If he got up and danced he might show those very few people in the world who didn't know, what he really was. If he moved his body around, somebody might notice the little swellings on his chest—his breasts—they might notice the roundness of his hips—which were almost like a real boy's, but not quite—it helped he always wore the baggy jeans.

Oh, Dean was so unhappy waiting there! Oh boy . . . *D-o-o-o me, do me . . . Go right throoough me . . . Inside . . . Upside . . .* And Terry had that bright look on her face, like glass that could shatter. Terry wasn't drunk enough. Dean was going to break her heart. He was! He was! Terry had lost him. I knew this was going to be like dying for Terry. Terry didn't quite realize it yet. But it would be like dying.

Melanie hadn't arrived. Wasn't coming. Just like Melanie. Made you want her by being scarce. Only, I didn't think this habit of Melanie's was deliberate. This tendency of hers toward scarcity just came naturally, out of some complexity, out of her guilt, from something difficult inside her.

By eleven, the apartment was packed. People dancing close together. The room had a hellish red glow. There was a nice pungent smell of dope now, hanging in the air. Groups of people locked in the bathroom doing lines. People dancing by themselves, stoned out of their minds, absorbed in themselves. The music so loud my throat was sore from shouting over it. A stack of empty beer cans was piled high in the garbage pail, empty boxes of Uncle Dom's. The room was all smoky, and the smell of reefer hung in the air, so warm, comforting, like food. Most delicious smell in the world, I thought.

Then suddenly a draft of cold air swept through the room. Cold, cold December air. The cigarette smoke in the air roiled. And I knew she had arrived. I knew it from Dean, from his face. He was transfixed.

Melanie stands in the doorway. Small and delicate, her thin, wispy brown-red hair gleaming. Gold eyes like a cat's, fragile smile, little pointed chin.

And I can't believe it. She's with Brian. There is Brian, standing right behind her.

Melanie is wearing a black leather jacket that hangs to her knees. The jacket is open. She wears a black leotard underneath it, which is tight over her small breasts. Melanie's skin has a rubbed look, as if she has just made love. There are soft brown shadows around her eyes, cat's eyes. So delicate.

Brian Perez is standing behind her, much taller, towering over her. Brian's long, blond hair is beautiful tonight—hair so pale it's almost white, like burned ashes, fluffy around his face as if he's shampooed and blow-dried it just for this occasion. But his slanty blue eyes give away nothing. His thin mouth is tight. His face is wide, flat, with high cheekbones. He is wearing only a denim jacket though it's cold—Brian never seems to feel the cold. And underneath the jacket, he wears a white Indian-cotton shirt across his broad chest.

Behind Brian stands Jimmy Vladeck. Big lump of stupidity Jimmy, slouch-shouldered, pot-bellied, brown hair tied back in a ponytail, bits of hair hanging in greasy strands around his puffy face. Wearing a huge dirty dark blue parka.

Abruptly, Dean clambers to his feet. Dean's movement catches my eye. And suddenly, Dean grabs Terry's arm, pulls her out into the middle of the room, and he starts to dance with her.

You can see the burst of joy shoot through Terry's whole body as he summons her. And as they dance Terry is like a young tree swaying in the wind, tossing her hair back, arching her body, kicking out her long legs as she dances.

I'd never seen Dean dance before. . . . His cigarette hangs from the corner of his mouth, his eyes squint from the smoke. So cool! He's got a special, unique way of doing it. . . .

The way he dances hides his body. He draws his elbows in close to his ribs, darts his head out from side to side like a bird pecking. Doesn't make any eye contact with Terry. Little flash of gold in his ear. Soft hair sticking up at the top, sideburns, little tail behind at the neck.

People at the party glance at him out of the corner of their eyes—they're not sure. And even if they are sure—they're fascinated. Who *is* he?

It's midnight. I bring in the birthday cake, candles blazing. I'd bought it at Food Mart, stuck in on a plate with a doily. We all sing "Happy Birthday—Happy Birthday—" "Hey, Dean," someone says. "Do some magic tricks!" Humoring him.

"Yeah, Dean. Do some magic!"

And they stand around him while he does his routine. He folds his handkerchief around a quarter, then shakes the handkerchief loose. Nothing falls out. The handkerchief is empty, the quarter has disappeared.

He curls a dime around his fingers and it changes into a penny. He covers a shot glass with his handkerchief, removes the handkerchief—the shot glass has evaporated into thin air! The partyers watch him, mocking smiles on their faces, skeptical. They only half believe what he's doing is magic. They've seen his tricks

97

before. They know he's an imposter and a con man. But at least for tonight, they *want* to believe. And they love him anyway! Dean is entertainment.

He finishes his act. People start dancing again, laughing and flirting in the shadows of the room. They go in and out of the bathroom, slamming the door behind them, busy in there.

Two figures drift together across my line of sight and block my vision. For a moment, I can't find either Dean or Melanie.

Then, there's a shriek of laughter from somewhere. The bodies in front of me part. And next thing I know, Dean is sitting on the futon, right up close to Melanie.

He's leaning in toward Melanie, saying something to her, and making her laugh. And Melanie's bending her head down, listening intently to him, the side of her face hidden by her fine hair. And I can see Brian standing against the wall across from them pretending not to look, but knowing everything, seeing everything they do.

PART III

My Profound
Heart

CHAPTER 14

MELANIE

At Chrissie Peck's place that night, the new boy didn't even say hello to me. He just looked deep into my eyes. Didn't even introduce himself. As if he'd been waiting for me all along. "You *are* beautiful," he said, as if confirming something, as if he already knew all about me. So direct. So frank. He had oval eyes, I could see the light shining through the moist green lens, long, dark blond lashes with the pale tips curling on the high cheekbone. White teeth, ridges on them gleaming like white coral. I saw a soft brown mole above his upper lip, like a tiny patch of velvet.

"You *are* beautiful," he said again, as if satisfying himself. That was all.

And then, just as suddenly as he'd sat down beside me, he stood up from the futon, and he walked away.

And now there was a gap of air, a sudden, cool space. I felt weird. I wasn't used to being left at parties. There was always someone trying to talk to me.

The music beat through the crowded room. *This wild heart . . . it beats for you . . . my wild heart . . . it weeps for you . . .*

I tried to follow him with my eyes through the fumy red air, through the crowd of partyers. I tried to keep my eye on his thin, small frame in the loose jeans, the little tail of hair in the tender groove of his neck, the clunky cowboy boots. I always thought that magic tricks were hokey; you know the magic isn't real. But he was so fast—the way his long, tapered fingers moved and you couldn't keep track of them. Everyone around here was such a bunch of dufuses, never did anything but drink and play computer games and watch TV and smoke dope. At least he could *do* something!

Chrissie Peck's place was packed. No room hardly to dance or sit down. The green canvas blinds were drawn over the windows so no one could see in. People were standing on the landing in the hallway. Someone had brushed up against Chrissie's Mariah Carey poster and torn it. Now it hung down from the wall at a weird angle, Mariah Carey's face cut in half, one of her big eyes lopsided and staring out.

The smoky air stung my eyes. I glanced up and suddenly, Brian was standing right above me, very close. I hadn't seen him approach. He was leaning back against the wall, his eyes focused across the room, pretending he didn't even know I was there. And Jimmy was lounging next to him. As always, waiting for Brian to tell him what to do, attuned to Brian's every need.

Brian pretended he just wanted to be my friend, just wanted to hang out. He'd discovered there was a party at Chrissie's place, and he'd offered to give me a ride. I didn't have my own car because I had no right to own a car as I didn't have a job. So I had said yes, you can drive me.

Now he was standing above me, silently waiting.

I searched through the crowd of partyers for the new boy, Dean, the boy with the lick of hair, and the two shirts, one on top of the other.

I glimpsed him standing by himself in the corner on the other side of the room, drinking a can of Mountain Dew and smoking a blunt. Had he forgotten about me so fast? After that big intro, he didn't want me anymore. Somehow, I hadn't measured up. Usually, people didn't walk away from me like that. I knew I was lucky that way, that everybody loved me. And realizing it didn't mean I was stuck up or anything, or conceited. It just meant that because people love you so much, you have an extra responsibility to them.

But now, this new person had aroused my curiosity and I wanted to know more about him.

Around midnight, I stood up to leave. Brian, who had been standing over me, came to attention. "I guess I'll go home," I said. "It's late."

And I knew Brian had waited all night for me just so he could take me home.

CHAPTER 15

MELANIE

Brian drove me home from Chrissie's party, big old silent Jimmy in the back. As we rode through Sparta, the snow-covered streets glittered in the headlights. This city was so lonely at night, so empty, all boarded-up buildings, all the people who remained living on Social Security and welfare. Its size was so limited. You knew everyone, and yet you were lonely, and the night, when the streets were deserted and all the antique shops on Washington Street closed, their hollow windows lit up, only emphasized the loneliness.

Brian beside me, hands on the wheel, silent. Jimmy sitting in the backseat. The earthy, mildewy smell of Jimmy filled the air of the car. I knew Brian was simply grateful to be with me, to be able to transport me home, because then he would know exactly where I was tonight.

Brian was like a shadow in my life, always present, attached to me by this thin, dark strand, expandable. Mostly, he tried not to be obtrusive, just hung in the background, but I could sense him there. Always.

When we were in kindergarten, Brian would sit at the back of the class. He'd sit there blinking blinking like he was flinching at a fist raised against him. No one would sit next to Brian, or play with him, because he smelled of dried pee. "You stink, Brian," they told him.

But I defended Brian. "Leave him alone. Go away. Stop it." Something in me made me always come to his defense. Brian looked like an angel with that blond curly hair. Maybe because I had been so lucky in life, God made me pretty, gave me my mommy—though God had taken my daddy away from me—anyway, I wasn't afraid to stand up to the other kids, because I was already popular.

One time, in the schoolyard, I found Brian sitting alone on a swing, sitting in a square of too-hot sunlight, blinking blinking all alone. I said, "Brian, why don't you *wait* to go to the bathroom? If you have an accident, you should change your clothes."

He said, "Don't have no other clothes."

"You do too, Brian. Why do you do it in your pants instead of waiting to go to the bathroom?"

"Cecil, he hit me on the butt til I pee. Then he makes me wear my dirty pants to teach me a lesson."

"Cecil? Who's Cecil?"

"He's my mom's boyfriend. He lives with us."

I wondered what kind of person would do that to a boy. I was so lucky, so loved, I couldn't understand it. I knew his secret, and it was a mystery to me.

Being loved made me strong. Now sometimes when the other kids excluded him, I'd sit down by him in the cafeteria, in defiance of his tormentors. And when we had to choose a group for a class project and nobody picked Brian, and he was sitting there all alone pretending he didn't care, I'd feel sorry for him and invite him into my group.

They took Brian out of his home, away from his family, put him in a foster home for a while, but then they gave him back to his mother and Cecil. All those Perez kids were trouble. They all looked like angels, with that curly blond hair and those pale blue eyes, seemed like they all had tans, but if you looked close, their skin was covered with a thin film of dust. They were all learning disabled and truant, always getting in trouble. Brian should've been a beautiful boy, but was not because of that blank, hard look on his little face.

The family lived in that strange, blue-colored house underneath the big fuel tanks by Sparta Utility. The front yard was always littered with toys and old engine parts.

One day when we were ten, Brian arrived at our house. He had on the blank-faced look, his flat, bony face was streaked with dirt. He had only his jeans on, his skinny little chest was heaving, his ribs sticking out through the skin, the muscles on his shoulders and arms tight and sinewy even then.

"What's the matter?" Mommy asked him.

"They locked me in a room, Cecil did. They won't give me nothin' to eat. I escaped. Climbed out the window."

Mommy took him in, gave him a bath, and called B.C.W. and they removed him again, and placed him in a group home. At school, he was put in Special Ed, and we didn't have any classes together after that.

When we were in junior high, Brian was always sitting on the bench outside the principal's office, white-blond curls framing his face, slitty blue eyes blinking blinking. "Now what've you gone and done, Brian?" I asked.

"Mohammed says I pulled a syringe on him."

"A syringe is a lethal weapon, Brian. Somebody could get AIDS. That's negative attention, Brian." I was a conflict mediator now and we'd studied "negative attention" in Conflict Resolution Workshop.

His eyes darted to me. "You're my only friend, Mellie," he said.

Around then was when he first started setting fires. The first one was in the basement at school, he and a group of boys set fire to a cardboard box and watched it burn. It set off the alarm and we were all evacuated for twenty minutes, and he got suspended. I don't know what it was in Brian that loved fire, the warmth of it, the light, the power it gave him, to create something beautiful, to destroy.

You must love the weak and the destitute, Mommy said. And I was a Christian, or trying to be.

"When you get mad, Brian, just count to ten," I told him. We'd learned that in workshop too. "Just sit there and meditate. I'll show you how." I touched him on the shoulder and suddenly his skinny body froze under my fingertips, all tense with love, I knew even then. "Breathe deep . . . one—two—three," I told him. "See . . . how relaxed you feel . . ."

Later on, after he started really getting in trouble, after he got arrested for setting the fire in that apartment building on Washington Street, where he and Jimmy were squatting, Mommy said to stay away from him, but he would come around or I'd run into him, because he was waiting for me and I'd give in out of pity.

In a way, Brian was saved because he became a stud. As he got older, he got handsome. He was tall and thin now, with a nice long line to his torso. A lot of girls liked Brian—but they were trash girls. He'd date them a few times, then abandon them. He was always hanging around me, but I only cared about him like a brother, or like my child.

He'd turn up at my house suddenly, just like that. Want to talk. Pour his whole heart out to me, his voice all breathless, as if he'd been storing up all those feelings for months. And I'd try to talk to him about Jesus. "Jesus accepts the most pitiful sinner," I said. " 'I am the light of the world; he who follows me will not walk in darkness, but will have the light of life.' John eight, twelve."

"Fuck," he said. "I'm too far gone for Jesus!" And he laughed.

Last August one night, he turned up at my house in his car and begged me to go for a ride with him. He'd just gotten fired from his job at Allbright's Auto Shop. They'd accused him of stealing parts. "Fuckin' bullshit man, they had it in for me right from the beginning!"

I let him drive me out to the Wooden Nickel. He parked the car in the lot overlooking the river, and we sat there, the summer air around us thick with heat and moisture, kids standing in the shadows, darting in and out of the trees. You could hear the sound of voices rising, falling, car doors slamming, the sound echoing off the palisades.

Suddenly, next to me in the shadows, Brian turned to me. "I *love* you, Melanie," he cried, as if his voice was tearing out of his throat.

"I love you too, Brian," I said. I didn't mean love-as-romance, or love-as-sex. I meant sympathy-love.

Then he reached out and gripped both my arms, and his fingertips dug into my flesh and it really hurt. "Ouch!" I cried. Next thing, his lips were on mine like metal bands tight across my mouth and I couldn't breathe.

Brian was strong and the muscles on his arms and hands were taut as wire. I could taste peppermint on his lips as if he'd been sucking on them, and *planning* to kiss me.

"Stop it, Brian!" I cried, cutting the edges of my palms down on his forearms.

He swung around, glowering at the windshield, breathing deeply.

"Don't be hurt," I said, my voice soft now, cooing at him as you would to a child. "I love you too, Brian. But I love you like a brother."

Ever since then, he hadn't asked again for love. He seemed content just to drive me around in his car. And he asked nothing of me. Brian was like my bodyguard. Sometimes when he was with me, he didn't even look at me. But he always seemed to know exactly where I was.

I let him drive me around. I was looking for a job, but I hadn't found anything yet.

Now, in the car after Chrissie's party, Brian circled around the town onto Route 7 in the direction of the mall. We were in the newest part of Sparta now, in an area built in the nineteen fifties. It used to be farmland here, and in between the car wash and the dry cleaner there was still an old wooden farmhouse, the wood gray and weathered, the windows crowded with objects as if some old hermit lived there. Beyond Route 7 were flat fields, and a muddy road leading to the skeletal form of an unfinished housing development. You could see a big wooden sign with the words *Palatine Manor.* But they never finished construction on the place because the developer had gone bankrupt, and now it just sat there, rows of empty townhouses in the distance, no sign of life.

My house was right on the edge of the road. We came to a stop in front of it. The house was white, vinyl siding, no porch, no shutters, with a picture window so big it seemed from the street you were right inside it. We had a patch of lawn in front, and a little concrete fountain with a cherub perched on the lip of a curved dish that Mommy always turned on in summer.

I opened the car door and called out over my shoulder, "Good night," to Brian and Jimmy, and then ran up the concrete walkway to the front door.

I unlocked the door, and I entered the darkened house. There was a faint, sweet smell in the air, of my mother, Rosemary's perfume always present, everywhere. Everything in our house was so feminine and clean. This was a woman's house. No man could ever stand to live here. One particle on the rug and she was there right away with the Dust Buster. Always had a sponge in her hand and the spray cleaner, as if dirt were a horror and abomination. So were odors, she was always spraying the air with room deodorizer.

It was a soft house, with thick wall-to-wall carpeting everywhere, in the kitchen, in the bathroom. The toilet seat had a flower print cover over it with a ruffle. No man had ever peed in our toilet. No man had ever lifted the seat for that purpose.

Now in the semi-darkness, I could make out her macramé hanging on the walls, the couches and chairs were draped with her afghans, knitted in bright orange and green zigzag patterns.

I knew she was lying awake upstairs in her bed, waiting for me.

Sometimes people took Mommy and me for sisters. Rosemary kept herself up well. She looked so young. We had the same cat's eyes, only her hair was shiny black, cut short like a gleaming helmet on her head. Her skin was tanned and oiled even in the middle of winter. She wore little diamond studs in her ears.

Mommy watched the world for me, her brown eyes filled with intelligence. She missed nothing.

My dad had been night manager at the Stewart's on new 27. I was only five years old when it happened. Some guys drove up in a van, entered the store, pulled out guns, and made everyone lie down on the floor. They emptied the cash register. And even though my dad had obeyed them and just lain down and kept quiet, they shot him anyway. The police said that my dad had offered no resistance. It took the cops only ten hours to find them, way up north near the Canadian border. Ralph Kurt Dewar, age twenty-four, Kevin Valder Leach Jr., age nineteen, their names were always present in my head. I knew their names like a mantra.

At the wake in the funeral parlor, they hoisted me up over the coffin so I could see down at him. My legs were chapped from being lifted up so many times and rubbing the rough cloth of people's clothes.

I looked into the coffin and there was his pale, thin face, his straight brown hair combed flat over his forehead, he was so composed. And on one of his cheeks, I could see a wad of something, like flesh, sticking in a hole. Only it wasn't flesh, I could tell that even then, it was plastic or rubber. There was a hole in his face, and they had plugged it up with something, and then covered it with a thick layer of makeup. I knew even then that hole was where the bullet went in.

Otherwise, I remember almost nothing, except I've put together a memory from her snapshots of him. And in them he seems so young, almost frail somehow, sitting next to her, holding me, smiling at the camera joyously. And then, I remember a vague young smell of sweat, and skin and tobacco, of his body.

Who was my father? Only twenty-six when they killed him.

Never even been a person really. Six years older than I was now, and pretty soon he would be younger than me.

On Sundays, in good weather we visited his grave at the Intercession Parish Cemetery. We had buried him there because we were Catholics before Mommy joined the People's Mission Chapel. In good weather we still weeded the grave plot and sprinkled plant food on the flowers. . . . Ralph Kurt Dewar, age twenty-four, and Kevin Valder Leach Jr., age nineteen, were up north in prison now, in Clinton, Mommy said, in a prison that was like a dark fortress, a place where it snows most of the year and it's impossible to escape from, and she said they would never be released as long as she lived so not to be afraid, they would never get me.

She had never been with a man again after my dad was murdered, but she was still sexy, and yet like a nun too, a beautiful nun, who seemed to have no interest in men. Once, she went out on a date with Mr. Tedesco, who managed Cambria Buick. But when she came home that night, she sat down on the couch in the living room, brushed her knees off decisively with both her hands. "Well, that's that," she said. As if it had been a chore she had to do.

She supported us by working as a secretary at Palatine Travel. I had been trying to get a job of my own now for months, but I wasn't having any luck. Maybe I was lazy, but a lot of the jobs that were available I didn't want. I knew I was spoiled, and I felt so guilty. I didn't want to work at City Shop because I would always get my hands dirty, I would have to wash them all the time, and my skin was so dry, especially in winter. And I tired easier than most people. Mommy said it was because I had low blood pressure, but that was a good thing because it meant I would live a very long time. And in some way I was afraid, I guess, afraid to be out in the world, that I would fail, and that I would be hurt without her.

She had given me everything, ballet lessons, piano lessons. She had paid for a photographer in Albany to make up a portfolio of me so I could be a model, which was something I would like to do. But in Sparta there were no opportunities for models, and I sent away some of my pictures and I heard nothing back. So I was looking for another job, something in Sparta, and I wasn't having much luck.

But she let me be. Maybe she didn't want me to get a job either, so I would stay with her forever, never leave her like my father had done when she was so young. Still, I did look for work, sometimes for days at a time, and then I'd give up and I would stop for a while. I was like a prisoner in her house, a prisoner of love, and it bound me to her in all its softness and its darkness.

In our house now, I climbed the narrow, padded stairs to her room, and entered. Here the aura of her perfume, the deep sweet scent she wore always, hung heavier in the air. That scent was everywhere, in her closet, it was in her towels, in all the linens.

Her voice floated out to me from the shadows of the bed. "Hi, honey. I was worried." She'd say that even if it was five o'clock in the afternoon when I got home.

I said, "I was at a party at Chrissie Peck's house. Brian drove me home."

"I don't like you driving with Brian." I couldn't see her in the darkness, but I knew she would say that, it was predictable.

"He wasn't drinking," I said.

"Still . . ." She sighed.

I walked over, leaned down, and kissed her cheek. "Good night Mommy." Now, so close to her, I could smell even more vividly the sweetness of her cheek and her hair.

When I was little, after my father died, I'd sleep the night with her sometimes. Sometimes still, I'd watch TV in the bed with her, and I'd fall asleep, and I'd end up sleeping the night in her warmth. Her bed was bigger, softer than mine. But tonight, I padded down the hall to my own room.

In my bedroom, in the dark, I could detect the shapes of all my stuffed animals lined up on my bed against the wall. There was the rabbit, the monkey, the bear from my childhood. I still kept them, couldn't stand to throw them out. Now they were waiting for me.

I undressed, and I climbed into bed. The sheets were cold. I was grateful to be under the covers, because I could think of him uninterrupted. And soon I was back in the noise of Chrissie's rap tapes and the smoke and smell of beer, and I could see the boy doing his magic tricks, I could re-create him in my mind, could see his fingers moving so fast, like water.

And I could see the light shining through the lens of his large eyes, and the soft skin of his cheekbone. "You *are* beautiful," he said, and it was as if he were right there with me.

Sometimes still, I let my old rabbit sleep under the covers with me. Now I groped in the darkness with my fingertips searching for his bald, worn coat. I could recognize him by touch.

I found him, drew him into my bed, and wrapped my body around him.

Next day, Saturday, was her day off, and on those days I belonged to her totally. In the morning, we went shopping for groceries. As she pushed the cart down the aisles, I lagged behind. I felt a heaviness in my body, as if *his* presence in my mind were dragging me down, down. I wanted to go back to sleep, though it was morning now, wanted to sleep so I could think about him uninterrupted, without her voice penetrating me. . . . "Look, they got a sale on paper towels. . . . I got to get Ajax, remind me."

On Saturday afternoons sometimes, we would make each other up, or fix each other's hair. Like animals grooming one another, mother and daughter monkeys. It was almost her only hobby, shopping for makeup. She liked to try every single product, usually on me. Like she was a painter or something and I was her blank canvas. And as she studied my face, brushed blush on my cheeks, or shadow on my eyes, I felt as if I couldn't breathe under her hands, and I wanted to escape. But I loved her, loved her more than I wanted to leave her.

Now, when we got home from the store, she sat me down in front of the bureau in her bedroom, and examined me in her mirror. She touched my hair with her fingertips. "Looks dull," she said. "Your highlights have grown out. You need to have it done again." I sat quietly, let her mold me, let her touch me as if I were her doll.

"I don't want to do it myself," she said. "They do it better. They charge a fortune, but they know what they're doing. Just around the face—get a 'framing.' Maybe you can get an appointment this week. I'll give you a blank check to take."

I was her hobby, her project, clay in her hands. She could mold me, make me perfect. Not from my image in the mirror, but from the way people reacted to me. Like Brian. I knew it objectively like you know a fact. And it meant nothing to me. I didn't care, didn't care at all. Somehow, the fact that I was beautiful was outside me. I knew I should be grateful to God for my looks, that they were a gift from God. But all the beauty in the world couldn't bring back my dad who had been taken from me.

And now, even as she brushed my hair, I heard her say softly, " 'Beauty is vain; but a woman that feareth the Lord, she shall be praised.' "

The phone rang. I slid out from under her hands and I ran to the phone by her bed and clutched the receiver.

"It's Dean." His voice on the other end was flat. He hadn't even told me his name the night before, when he had said that I was beautiful. But I knew his name, and he knew I knew it.

"I remember," I said. I closed my eyes. Listening to the sound of his voice.

He said, "I want to go out with you." His voice was clear and direct, as if he had been up all night thinking about calling me, preparing his words.

That evening, snow fell. I watched from the window through the thick flakes as Dean's battered red truck pulled up down below. I saw him walk up the concrete path in his cowboy hat and leather jacket. I saw him press the doorbell, stomping the snow off his boots while he waited.

Mommy, lying on the couch watching the TV, asked, "Who's that?"

I said, "Dean. We're going out."

"Who's Dean? Where're you going?"

"Nowhere." She couldn't tell me what to do every step of the way. Though I still lived at home, lived off her.

I unlocked the front door. It opened directly into the living room.

He stood on the threshold, cowboy hat pushed back from his face, carrying flowers wrapped in paper. He held them toward me, and I let out a little laugh. I couldn't help it. It was so old-fashioned to bring flowers. No one ever brought flowers for people here, except on prom night.

"I got 'em at the Rosary," he said. The Rosary had been on Route 7 for years, next to Flaherty's Funeral Parlor. Somehow, when every other establishment had gone out of business, the Rosary was still there. There was always a need for flowers for funerals, for the dead.

"They looked like you," he said. He held his chin down in his chest as he spoke.

She was watching. I could feel her dark eyes boring into us from across the room.

I took the flowers from him. "Mommy, this is Dean. Dean, my mom, Mrs. Saluggio."

He bobbed his head at her, extended his hand. "Pleased to meet you, ma'am," he said, in his low voice.

She measured him. People around here usually didn't have good manners. It was probably the first time any friend of mine had brought flowers to me, or even shaken her hand. And the gesture was funny coming from him, since he was such a punk.

I left the two of them facing each other, and I went into the kitchen to search for a vase. I tore open the paper wrapping around the flowers. They were roses, dark red buds, almost black. I jammed them into a glass vase without arranging them or cutting off the ends. I was in a hurry. I wanted to get him away from the scrutiny of her eyes.

She asked, "When will you be home?"

"Early," I said.

It was snowing hard now. We drove in Dean's truck along Route 7, onto Route 27, and then the Parkway. The air around us was a wild flurry of white, and as we rode, snowflakes hit the windshield in little bursts. The snow was like a blanket, made it so private inside the truck, him and me, alone together, sealed off from all the world, and as we drove the heavy atmosphere lulled me, made me want to sleep.

Kozlow's stood on a hill over the Parkway at the end of an access road, a plain, red brick flat-roofed building. We always went to Kozlow's on special occasions, on prom night for instance. Tonight there were plenty of parking spaces in the lot because so few people were driving in this weather.

As we stepped inside the restaurant, we were hit by a blast of warm, moist air, and underneath the smell of cooking, you could detect the lingering odor of older meals.

We sat down in a booth by the window. Drops of moisture ran down the glass beside us. Lamps with stained glass shades hung from the ceiling, threw darts of red and yellow about the room. The walls were lined with black mirrors, and planters with long vines in them hung from the ceiling.

The window looked out over the highway, and down below you could see the headlights of cars pushing up through the furls of snow.

Dean said, "I'm paying. Order what you want."

I looked down at the menu. I didn't care what I ate—*if* I ate. I didn't want to bother with eating. I picked the first thing my eye fell on—lasagna. Usually I didn't eat much. My mom was always telling me I was too thin, and then she'd say, "You're so lucky, you never put on weight."

"Two glasses of red wine," he said to the waitress.

"I don't drink," I said.

"Have a little with dinner."

He wore a little gold hoop in his ear. He wore two faded flannel shirts, one bluish plaid, the other green, one on top of the other.

His backpack lay on the floor and he reached down and removed two packages from it. I could tell he had wrapped them himself, the corners of the package were all crinkled and uneven, the bows awkwardly tied without curls. He handed them to me, and I laughed. "You don't have to do this. You brought flowers." I was trying to keep from really laughing now because nobody ever did this around here. It wasn't cool. It was like he was doing something he had been told was right.

He said, "I wanted to give you a present." So I tore open the bigger package. It was a teddy bear, a *real* teddy bear, one of the old-fashioned kind with matted-looking, grayish-brown fur that looked like a real animal's, not all shiny and synthetic looking. "He's so cute!" I cried. How did he know, I wondered, that I still loved stuffed animals? I hugged the bear to my chest as if it were my baby. "I'll always love him."

He nodded at the other, smaller package. I opened that and inside was a bottle of perfume, Passion Flower. I squirted some on my neck and wrist. "Ummm . . ." I held my wrist out for him to smell and he sniffed it. "Nice," he said.

"You didn't have to," I said. "That costs money."

"Money's no problem."

"But I thought Chrissie said you lost your job."

"Yeah, but I got money saved."

He took a cigarette from the pack in his shirt pocket and his Bic lighter and he cupped the two together in one hand, lit the cigarette. Cool little gesture. I watched his fingers, he had smooth, oval nails, and his wristbone was curved like a bird's bone, I noticed.

"So," he said to me, "You with Brian?"

"No. Not in that way. Brian's like my—like my kid. Like a brother. I feel sorry for him."

"You're too good for him."

"I'm not good," I said. "I'm not *good.*" I paused. "Are you with Terry?"

He seemed to think about that for a moment. "We're together," he said, finally, blowing smoke through his nostrils. "But we got problems."

"Problems?" I was always listening to people's problems. He didn't answer for a moment. I remembered Terry Kluge from high school. She was a couple of years ahead of me. I didn't know her that well. She was tall, a little stoop-shouldered like she was afraid of her height. Plain looking, but not ugly. Always with Eddie Lasko. She had his baby.

He was staring out the window of the restaurant, at the coronas of light from the cars on the Parkway below shining through the snow. He frowned. "Terry's good," he said. "I love Terry. But," he shook his head. "I don't know . . ." He left the thought unfinished.

I asked, "She know you're having doubts?"

He shook his head. "Hasn't said anything. Though maybe she feels it." He looked at me. "One thing's Bobby, her kid. I feel responsible for him. I'm like his dad. It's complicated. Terry's so good. . . ." he said, and his voice trailed off. Then he shook his head. It was like he was suffering and couldn't finish the sentence. Now he looked directly at me, his oval eyes wide, as if the expression on his face should say the rest.

The glass of red wine sat in front of me on the table. He nodded at it. "Go ahead. It's a special occasion."

I took a sip, grimaced. The taste was strong, unfamiliar.

"That's cute the way you do that," he said.

When my lasagna arrived, I didn't touch it. Couldn't concentrate on eating. He hardly ate anything either. Kept asking me questions and it was as if he was feeding me, making the words grow inside me, making me want to talk. Most kids around Sparta didn't talk—maybe because we'd all known each other so long.

And as I spoke, he sat still opposite me, his eyes fixed on my lips, as if—if he stared hard enough he could make the language flow out from my tongue, as if, to him, my voice was like music and he wasn't hearing the words but only the sound.

I told him I was lucky, had grown up with everything. I was spoiled, I knew. That was why I was a Christian now, why I had accepted Christ because He had given me so much. It had changed my life, I told him, accepting Christ—hoping to arouse his interest. I told him the most important event of my life, about my dad, and about Ralph Kurt Dewar, age twenty-four, and Kevin Valder Leach Jr., age nineteen, and I told him I knew now I would see my dad again because I knew he would be waiting for me in the Kingdom of Heaven.

He just listened, to the sound beyond my meaning. I told him I was looking for a job. I thought maybe I'd like to be a nurse or do something to help people, but I'd heard you had to have math to do nursing, and I had barely gotten through math in high school and I'd failed chemistry junior year.

"I can tell by your hands," he said, "the way you move your hands." He took my hand, rubbed his fingertip on the back, then turned it over and rubbed the palm. "You'd make a good nurse," he said, with confidence.

I had never had sex with anyone. Never let anyone do it to me. Mommy said, "I want you to pay attention! *Look* at me—don't look away! Look at all those fifteen-year-olds with their babies and their lives ruined. And AIDS. Girls get it easier than boys. No matter what they say, condoms aren't enough to protect you against AIDS."

Now, sitting opposite me, Dean asked, "So, how long have you known Brian?"

"Why do we have to talk about Brian? Let's talk about *you.*"

But he wasn't going to be deterred. "I want to know—tell me about him. If you're not his girlfriend, who is?"

"*I* don't know," I said distractedly. "I feel sorry for Brian. I've always kind of taken care of him. He has a bad family. But girls like him, I guess—he's cute. Let's not talk about Brian," I said again, trying to get him off the subject. "That magic stuff you do," I asked. "Is it real?"

He shrugged, as if the topic didn't really interest him. "Started when I was a kid. Sent away for all these catalogs. I did it to make other kids like me."

I smiled, embarrassed by my next question. "So, is it really magic?" I asked. "I mean, do you really use magic? Or, is it just like—tricks?"

He smiled, a mysterious, teasing smile. "Is there any difference?" he said.

We drove home. The air was choked with whirling flakes. He drove slowly, carefully, keeping his eyes on the snow-packed road ahead, the windshield wipers made a lullaby sound . . . whoosh . . . whoosh . . .

I had always loved the sight of a man next to me in a car driving, maybe it was that he looked as if he had power, and he was in control. One hand on the wheel with his cigarette, the other resting on his thin thigh. Eyes steady on the road. He didn't talk, wore that half-smile, conscious, I knew, that I was watching him.

When we pulled up in front of my house, I could see the lights blazing in the picture window. Ours was the only house on the street still lit up and I knew Mommy was keeping herself awake just for me.

He stopped the truck, but he kept the engine running. He didn't move to get out. There was silence.

We sat still, and I could feel my body inclining toward him like a plant growing toward the light. But he didn't kiss me.

Abruptly, he reached across me, opened the door on my side,

then got out of the truck and went around to help me down, leaving the engine running.

The walkway to our house was slippery, and he held my arm. At the front door, I paused. Hoping he would kiss me. But he took my hand, leaned over, touched me quickly on the cheek with his soft lips. " 'Night," he said, and hurried back down the path to the truck. I watched to see if he would turn back, look at me. But he didn't. Did he think I was ugly or something? Didn't he like me? What had I done wrong?

He climbed into his truck, shifted gear, and moved away, and I watched the truck moving slowly away through the snow. He didn't look back.

CHAPTER 16

MELANIE

When I woke up the Sunday after I'd been with Dean, I had a headache from too much sleep. Mommy and I went to church, and I stood there and I sang the words to the hymn, and listened to Reverend Bill, but I didn't hear what he was saying so passionately up there in his pulpit. I just saw him waving his arms, and his soft, round face, smooth as if he didn't even have a beard yet.

All day Sunday, Dean did not call. He loves *her,* I thought. My thoughts were sluggish, as if my skull were filled with fog. I'd walk into the kitchen for a glass of juice and then wander around, forgetting what I'd come for. I imagined dying. What would be the easiest way?

Mommy would be better off without me. She wouldn't have to support me. Pills. How do you get pills? Jesus would understand I couldn't go on living like this.

Then, Tuesday, 6 P.M., he phoned, and when I heard his voice all my dark thoughts were stilled, like I was a drug addict or something given momentary relief with a fix.

"Can you go out?" he asked.

But I wasn't giving in so easily. I was going to stall. "You still with Terry?" I asked.

A hesitation. Silence, then, "I guess so."

"That's not right," I said. "I shouldn't be seeing you if you're still with her."

"I'm looking for a job," he said. "Soon as I find something I'm outta there. She doesn't know it yet."

I asked, "Do you love her?" Had to know.

"Yeah. I love her. But since you, everything's changed."

That night, he came to get me, and we drove around in his truck. The drive was just an excuse to talk. We drove through the empty streets, turned onto Courthouse Square, where the rich people of Sparta had once lived, the old coal and gas families, in houses hidden behind vines and hedges. We drove past the white courthouse with its wide steps and fluted pillars, like a temple. Behind it was the jail, a relatively new building, shiny yellow brick.

We talked. The talk rushed out of me like a river. The talk was like love, like kissing.

We had stopped by the side of the road, left the motor running for the heat. As I talked, he gazed at my face, as if he were listening to something beyond my words, as if he understood everything, all my thoughts. Talking was like making love would be.

"Talk about Brian," he said, watching my lips.

"What about Brian?"

"You ever kiss him?"

"No. Not really."

"You ever have sex with him?"

"No!"

"Does he say he loves you?"

"I don't know! I don't want to talk about Brian."

He was still staring at my lips, as if a spell had been cast over him, and I thought he was going to kiss me. "He can't help it," he said. "You're so beautiful."

"I don't want to be beautiful. I'm not beautiful."

"Your skin's all transparent. Like glass, or a pearl."

We were related, I thought, brother and sister born on some distant planet, not Earth. He would never hurt me. He was soft. It was myself somehow that I wanted in him.

And as the engine of the truck rumbled, he took my hand,

turned it over, smoothed out my fingers, kissed the flat palm. I could feel his warm breath on my skin. His face was moving closer to my face. As if he were going to kiss me. Then, suddenly, he turned away, sat back in the seat.

He said, "It's okay if we don't make love now. We can go for months and months, and I'll still love you. That isn't what counts for me." He had said he loved me—he had uttered the words.

Then he said, "It's cold. We better go."

We drove home, and he asked if he could come inside the house. Mommy was already in bed, and I let him.

"I want to see your yearbook," he said.

We sat together in the darkness under the light of the brass standing lamp. He paged through the yearbook, his eyes eager for pictures of me. There were the group photos, me with the conflict mediation team. Then he came to the picture of me as Schoolgirl Queen. My crown had flattened my hair down. There were these two bright crazed glints in my eye from the camera's flash reflected in them.

He whispered at my image on the page. "Look at you." As if the picture were the real thing, and I wasn't even there beside him, flesh and blood. I glanced at the photo. What I saw on the page was the face of another person. Even in two years my face had changed, whatever baby fat was there had dissolved, my bones were more defined now. "One of those people nobody can have. . . ." he murmured.

"That's not true," I said.

"Everybody wanted you—right?" he said. "You were perfect?"

"I'm not perfect. Nobody's perfect. And not everybody wanted me."

He raised his eyebrow, grinned, that bad-boy look on his face. "Could *I* have had you?" he asked.

I was gazing at his lips, the pouty lips, creased skin, mole above the mouth. Little gold hairs above the upper lip, and just below his jawline, barely visible unless you were up close. "It's okay," I said. "You can kiss me."

He looked at me hard a moment, then reached forward and kissed me—too quick.

He glanced up at the stairs, looking to see if she was there.

"She's in bed," I said.

"She can hear us. I know she can."

"She can't. I know what she can hear."

He took both my hands in his. "I'll still love you. Even if we don't do it. Let's wait. Till we're ready." And then he turned back to the yearbook, his eyes fixed on my photo again.

I had heard someone say once that desire is one half curiosity. Now I was all curiosity.

Next evening, Mommy was lying on the couch, the TV droning, her eyelids drooping. She was always tired from her job, always fell asleep right after dinner.

It was snowing again. I could hear the grinding of the plow on the road. They said this was the most severe winter in years. It seemed like there was no oxygen in the house and I couldn't breathe, I wanted to get out, wanted the sensation of the cold air on my face.

The doorbell sounded and I got up to answer it. Dean was there standing on the threshold.

"I gotta talk to you!" he said. I felt my heart rise. I stepped aside and let him in and as he brushed past me, the cold from his leather jacket ruffled my skin.

Mommy, on the couch, opened her eyes, and he nodded toward her. "Mrs. Saluggio."

She nodded back, her expression grave, her dark eyes watchful. "Hello, Dean. Close that door, Mellie. It's freezing." She was accepting him in some way. She guessed—with that sixth sense of hers—that we weren't having sex.

Dean glanced toward the kitchen. "Can we talk in there?"

I led the way. We stood there, the humming of the big refrigerator filling the room. Most beautiful thing in the house, the refrigerator. Special-order, powder blue, ice maker and water spout, everything you needed, too big for the two of us really, but she liked the vertical freezer because it held more and you could buy food on sale and keep it.

He glanced toward my mother in the living room, and moved closer to me, lowering his voice. "Listen," he said, "I need a place to stay."

"What happened?"

"Terry knows about us. She's freaked. She threw me out."

My heart raced. "I'll ask her. Wait."

I ran from him to the living room, knelt down on my knees at the couch in front of her. "Can Dean stay here tonight?" I asked. I saw her look doubtful, her lips part to say no. "Please," I begged. "Please—please—please! He's got nowhere to go. He got kicked out of where he was staying." Drowning out any chance for her to say no. "He'll be homeless!" I cried.

She scrutinized me with those dark brown eyes, knowing everything, careful. Knew we weren't sleeping together. Maybe some part of her had chosen him for me because she thought he was safe. I had a fantasy—we would *both* be her kids, we would live here together, the two of us, under her protection.

At last she said, "Well, a few nights, I guess. Get the extra comforter out of the upstairs hall closet, and a pillow."

She switched off the TV and climbed the stairs to bed, and I carried the pillow and comforter down to him. And as I held it out to him, I envied this cloth that would touch his skin. Anything that would touch him, I wanted to be.

We were alone now, the house dark except for the light from the single lamp. I wondered, would he change into his pajamas?

He bent down, unzipped his backpack, removed a black ditty bag from it, placed it on the coffee table. His movements were tentative, careful, as if he were worried he was taking up too much space.

126

Then he stood still in the middle of the room. I realized he wanted me to leave.

"Let me cover you," I said. I wanted to do that, make him like my child. If you loved someone, he was many different things to you. Lover. Father. Child. All those things. I wanted to cradle his head, to surround him completely, cover him with my body.

But he slid under the covers fully dressed. I tucked the comforter around his body. He reached up as if to kiss my forehead, but at the same moment I moved suddenly toward him, and caught him on the lips with a kiss. He seemed surprised.

Upstairs, in my own bed, I lay for hours thinking of him down there on the couch, imagined him breathing. And his whole being seemed to hang in the air of the house.

I couldn't sleep. At 2 A.M., I tiptoed downstairs again. She had kept the light on the stairs burning. As if to sanitize the place, a warning to us to keep away from one another.

In the living room, I could see the mound of his body on the couch under the comforter. He lay still, as if he were sleeping. I stepped closer. He was on his stomach, his arm pushed up under the pillow. I could see his face in the light from the stairs, his eyelashes resting on his full, round cheek. He was still wearing his day clothes, his flannel shirts.

I could hear the hum of the refrigerator in the kitchen, clicking on and off. Had he heard me come down the stairs? Was he just pretending to be asleep? I touched him on the shoulder, he turned over suddenly on his back. I thought for a moment he was irritated at being touched because I had startled him out of some deep sleep of exhaustion.

In the semidarkness, he opened his eyes. He looked panicked, as if he didn't recognize me. "Melanie," he said, and he closed his eyes again.

"I can't sleep," I said. "I came down to get some juice."

"Hi," he murmured, eyes still closed, as if he hadn't understood me. As if he were not fully awake, and was pulled back into sleep.

The house was so cold. She always kept the heat down at night to save on fuel. I clutched my arms around my chest and shivered. Hoping he'd realize I was cold, that he'd sense I was naked under my nightgown, that he'd invite me in under the covers. I sat down on the edge of the couch, perching my hip there, but he didn't move his body aside to make room for me.

"I'm cold," I said. "Can I get inside with you?"

Eyes closed, as if concentrating on sleep, he reached his hand up, touched my hair. "Can't," he said. "She'll throw me out. Then I'm fucked."

I could feel the warmth emanating from the opening between his body and the comforter, could feel myself drawn to the warmth there as if he were a magnet, as if I were an animal who belonged there in his heat. "Please," I said.

He opened his eyes now, and I could see them wide and gleaming. "We can't," he said. "She kicks me out, I got nowhere else to go."

CHAPTER 17

MELANIE

For the next few days, Dean and I rode around in his truck while my mom was at work at the travel agency. We were both supposed to be looking for jobs. Sometimes we'd stop in at a store and ask if they were looking for someone and they'd always say nothing right at this moment, or the manager was out and come back tomorrow, or try again in another week.

We drove around in the yellow winter light, up and down between the rows of cars in the parking lot of the mall. One afternoon we went to the half-price matinee to see *True Lies*. The theater was empty, only a couple of men there, probably off-shift. I couldn't concentrate on the movie because of Dean next to me, I would never remember it. Just noise up on the screen, and shapes moving, and him next to me, watching intently. I took Dean's hand in mine. Wished we were alone, wished he'd take me somewhere so we could be alone.

When the movie was over, we walked out across the parking lot to his truck. A cold, wet wind swept across the asphalt. The traffic on Route 7 was thick, headlights on though it was only 5 P.M. This was what passed for rush hour in Sparta, the pulse of excitement in the air, the day's work done, everyone pointed homeward. Seemed as if only Dean and I had not worked today.

We came to his truck, were standing on either side, about to open the doors, when I looked up and saw Brian's blue Camaro turn in to the mall, Brian and Jimmy in front.

I knew Brian had been cruising around, looking for me. I thought sometimes that Brian spent whole days at a time driving around, hoping to spot me somewhere in town. He'd probably gone to my house and discovered it empty. Somehow, Brian always knew my schedule. I hardly paid any attention to him anymore, except for this awareness I had that he always seemed to be nearby. Sometimes he'd show up at a place just seconds after I arrived, as if he had mysteriously learned in advance where I'd be, before I even knew about it myself.

Brian had spotted us, and he drove diagonally across the lane toward me. He stopped his car abruptly next to Dean's truck, rolled the driver's side window down.

I saw this look of raw pain shoot across his face. He looked from Dean to me, and back again, and his mouth opened, as if he were about to say something. For a moment, his expression was like the face on that gargoyle above the door of the old Opera House on Washington Street, the corners of the mouth turned down in tragedy. It was as if someone had struck him. And for a second, I felt guilty and I wanted to touch his shoulder and comfort him.

"Melanie," he said. His voice seemed to choke up. He hadn't known for sure, but now he knew.

Then that cold smile came on his face again, like he cared about nothing.

Dean stared at Brian, a little smile on his face. "Hey Brian," he said, taunting him.

"Dean," Brian murmured.

We waited, very still. I was uncomfortable, I turned toward the truck. "Well," I said, "see you, Brian."

And then Dean and I climbed in and drove off, and Dean waved over his shoulder at Brian smiling, smiling in his little triumph, but Brian and Jimmy just sat there, looking after us and they didn't wave back.

A few nights later, when Dean and I came into the Wooden Nickel, Brian and Jimmy were there already sitting at a table in the big room. Chrissie Peck was at the bar reading her book and writing in a notebook. As we walked into the bar, I sensed that Brian was aware of us, though he didn't look up.

Dean and I sat in silence for a half hour or so, just listening to the music on the jukebox. Sometimes I was afraid to speak for fear I would sound like a fool. I loved Dean, and I was afraid of him.

Then suddenly Dean stood up. "I'll be right back."

"Where you going?"

He didn't answer and left the bar.

After fifteen minutes, he returned and sat down again beside me, and we stayed sitting there, side by side, saying nothing.

At 2 A.M., Carl said he was closing up, and we went outside. Across the lot, Brian and Jimmy were getting into Brian's car, when suddenly there was a commotion inside. I saw Brian ducking up and down in the front seat, his arms up, shielding his face like he was being divebombed by something.

Next to me, Dean started laughing. Pretty soon, he was bent over and hysterical. "What is it?" I cried.

I could see Brian panicked in the front of the car. Jimmy opened the front of the Camaro and started swiping at something, trying to bat whatever it was away.

From where I stood I could just make out this little yellow thing whirring around inside Brian's car. "What happened?" I asked.

"It's a canary!" Dean said. "A baby canary! I got it at Petland. I got his car door open and I put it there." And then he started laughing again, laughing so hard at the spectacle of Brian and Jimmy frantically trying to get the little bird out of their car that he had to hold on to the side of the truck for support.

"I don't see what's so funny," I said.

"Scared of a little bird!" Dean spluttered. Indeed, you could see Brian was terrified of this tiny alien thing flitting about inside his car, beating its little body frantically against the windshield.

131

People had paused in the parking lot on their way out of the bar to watch the crazy scene. "Oh Dean, why'd you do that?" I said. "You'll just make him crazy!"

But Dean wasn't listening to me. He was transfixed. "Look at him! Freaked out of his mind over a little bird!"

I could see it flapping crazily around the interior, bumping into the glass blindly, completely disoriented in its terror. "Oh God!" I cried. "It's gonna die!" I ran toward Brian's car as if to rescue it.

Brian was backing out of the car, arms raised in front of his eyes, and the little speck of yellow came whirring out after him, then flew up into a pine tree.

"How could you, Dean!" I cried. "It's gonna freeze to death."

Dean ran over, stood at the foot of the tree. "Here, little little little bird. Here . . ."

Brian was brushing himself off and glaring at Dean. "Fuck," Brian said. "Fuck . . ."

"Here bird . . . Here bird . . ." Dean cooed.

Brian had recovered himself a little now and he walked over to Dean. "Fuckin' asshole," Brian said, so Dean could hear. But Dean just smirked. Then Brian climbed back into his car and just sat there darkly, panting and humiliated.

People had begun to drift away. After a few more minutes, Dean gave up trying to get the bird down from the tree and we drove home, leaving Brian sitting in his car with the door open, his legs out, and Jimmy standing over him protectively.

At home, Dean ingratiated himself with my mom. We'd cook dinner together for her when she came home from work, to show her how much easier it was to have Dean staying with us, how I was being good because she was letting him stay. Dean would make himself useful, he would clear the table, shovel the newly fallen snow from the walkway in the morning. When her car wouldn't start one day, he tried to get it going, as if he knew how to fix cars. He looked inside the hood and fiddled around, but no luck. He couldn't find the problem, and Mr. Lyon had to come over from next door and help us. Mr. Lyon said the battery was cold, and he jump-started the engine and had it going in a moment.

After dinner, Dean played hearts with her at the dining table, popping Skittles, his can of Mountain Dew at his elbow, while I lay on the couch watching TV, listening to the hum of their conversation and the sound of their cards slapping on the tabletop.

He showed her how to do magic tricks, though she didn't really want to learn but was just humoring him, like she would a child. "See, what you do, when you're talking to the other person, you touch the card just like this and you say, 'You could have taken a card from here, looked at it, and replaced it here. . . .' But really, when you're handling the card, you let the card hang over the pile, like that. And you press your thumbnail on the edge, see—just enough to make a tiny cut. . . ." And she would try it and laugh. He was just making her love him too, pulling her in, I thought.

On Sunday, Dean went to church with us. The People's Mission Chapel was in a small red brick building that didn't even look like a church from the outside, and today Reverend Bill, with his round body, his hair flat on his forehead, was giving a sermon on the subject of "Until." "We must learn to live *until*. . . ." Reverend Bill said.

Dean looked so beautiful standing there between us, his soft, wispy hair damp from his shower, his almond eyes, his full, red lips, his face soft from his night's rest and glowing with health.

"*Until* we lose that ten pounds!" Reverend Bill was saying. "*Until* we pay off that mortgage. *Until* five o'clock comes and we can walk away from that job we hate. . . ." I wondered how many more "untils" Reverend Bill would say. "*Until* the Lord Jesus comes!" he cried at last.

In the pew behind us, someone's stomach rumbled loudly and Dean stole a glance at me and smiled, and suddenly in the middle of the service we were both giggling out of control like third graders.

That night, as I lay in bed, I heard Mommy enter the room. I felt her standing over me in the darkness. As if she were waiting for me to say something. "I like Dean," she said, finally. "I feel like he's part of the family . . . as if he were my other child."

I could just make out her form above me. I saw her shake her head, as if she had surprised herself, and now she was mocking her own love.

He had us both in his power now, I thought. The power of not doing. The power of holding himself back, of being mysterious, always keeping you wanting to know more, to hold him until you learned it all.

In the mornings, Dean and I would sleep late. She would leave early for work, and Dean would be asleep on the couch downstairs, and I'd be upstairs in my own bed. There was a world of work out there, people going to their jobs in the daylight, while he and I slept in the close, still air of the house, sleeping, sleeping, because there was nothing else to do. Sometimes I wouldn't get up for hours, until I had a headache from oversleeping and I was almost sick with it and forced to get up.

He had been with us about a week, it was nine o'clock in the morning, I was still in bed, when I heard the doorbell ringing downstairs. It was a harsh, rude sound, penetrating the silence of the house.

I climbed out of bed, pulled on my bathrobe, and stumbled down the stairs. Through the glass pane in the front door, I saw two policemen, a man and a woman, standing on the front steps. I unlocked the door. A blast of cold air hit me in the face.

"I'm Officer Jubey," the man said. He was skinny, with buck teeth and a big Adam's apple and hardly any chin.

He nodded over his shoulder at the woman cop standing behind him. "Officer Payette. Sparta Police." The woman cop was short and squat, with bright orange hair, and a little pug nose all red in the cold and her policeman's pants tight on her wide hips.

"We're looking for a Dean Lily," the man said. "He around here anywhere?"

Instinctively, I blocked the door, protecting Dean. I saw the cop swallow hard, his Adam's apple traveling all the way down his throat, his eyelids fluttering in the cold. I saw the woman cop raise her hand to her hip and rest it on the holster of her gun.

"We got a complaint here about him stealing from a Terry Kluge," Officer Jubey said.

Dean had come up behind me. He stood on the threshold in his socks, his face sleepy. "Whassup?"

The cop stared at him. Hesitated. "You Dean Lily?"

"Yeah?"

For a moment, he just stared, as if trying to figure out what Dean was. Then, momentarily, he seemed to recover himself. "There's Terry Kluge says you been writing checks on her account?"

The cop said, "She got her checks back from the bank and she says you stole her checkbook and her ID?"

He waited for an answer. "You steal Terry's checks, Dean?" He was calling Dean and Terry by their first names, as if he knew them both.

Dean was still groggy from sleep. "Whah?" Dean said.

The cop took a piece of paper from inside his notebook, unfolded it, and held it out toward Dean. I saw it was a copy of a check, for 123 dollars. There was a signature at the bottom in squiggly black writing, deliberately indecipherable.

"This your writing, Dean?"

Dean fixed his eyes on the paper, he seemed to scrutinize it, slowly, thoroughly. "No," he said, finally, looking up at the cop, square in the face. "No. That's not mine."

Officer Jubey said, "Mind if I check your wallet?"

It was cold. I wore only my bathrobe and Dean had no shoes. He stepped back into the house and let the cops pass in front of him into the living room. As they moved by me, I sucked in my breath, I knew it smelled from the night. I rubbed my fingers under my eyes. I probably had raccoon eyes, the mascara smudged there. Always did in the morning.

Dean reached behind his back, slipped his wallet out of the back pocket of his jeans, and extended the wallet slowly to the cop.

"Would you empty out the contents on the coffee table there, please?" the cop asked, his voice all nervous. I noticed bits of moisture in the corners of the cop's mouth as if he couldn't swallow properly because of his buck teeth.

Dean removed the bills and cards from his wallet, placed them on the coffee table.

Officer Jubey bent over, riffled through the contents of Dean's wallet. He picked two of his cards up and examined them. "You got Terry's Social Security card here," he said. "And her Food Mart card. That's criminal impersonation, Dean."

Dean stared at the cards as if he'd never seen them before. "I do?" he said. Officer Jubey held out the two cards for Dean to see, but Dean didn't touch them.

"Terry's reporting five hundred dollars' worth of checks written on her account," Officer Jubey said. "The checks all bounced. She says this isn't her signature."

"She gave me her cards!" Dean cried indignantly. "So I could go shopping for her and pay by check. I didn't steal them."

"She says you did."

"That's a lie!" he cried. "She's just mad because—" He stopped himself, not wanting to tell them more.

But they took him away anyway. They clamped the handcuffs over his wrists, dragged him out to the police car. I ran after them in my bathrobe with bare feet crying, "Please! He didn't do anything. I swear he didn't! I swear I've been with him the whole time. . . ."

"You'll have to move aside, miss," the woman cop said, "Or we'll have to arrest you for obstruction."

"She's just jealous!" I said. "He didn't do anything!"

But Officer Jubey opened the door to the patrol car, pushed Dean's head down, and backed him inside.

"Don't!" I begged, standing there shivering in my bare feet and bathrobe. "Oh please." I could feel the tears biting into my cheeks.

But now they were disappearing up the street, the red light on top of the police car flashing and staining the pale air, exhaust throbbing, the stink floating back toward our door.

CHAPTER 18

MELANIE

As soon as the cops took Dean away, I pulled my jeans on under my nightie, then my sweatshirt, and my sneakers without socks, my leather coat—and I ran. I ran along Route 7, the icy rain falling like tiny glass splinters on my skin, washing away the snow, the cars passing by me spraying slush on my body. There were no sidewalks on Route 7, no one ever walked here. I could feel the cars slowing down beside me, keeping pace with me, the drivers leaning across their seats to peer out at me. They were not used to seeing a girl running like this on the highway in the middle of winter with her coat flying out, her nightie on over her jeans. But I ignored them, and I kept on running, oblivious.

Along Route 7. My chest began to hurt, the pain filled my lungs, my throat grew raw from the cold. I could feel the pain in my chest expand. But something carried me along, beyond hurt. O my sweetheart . . . ice water was seeping through the seams in my sneakers, the air slicing my lungs, but I didn't care.

At the park I made a left, then a right down Washington, past the red brick buildings with their false fronts. A few solitary souls out in the morning cold passed me on the sidewalk, their heads down, their bodies sunk into their coats, they didn't even see me. They wanted to get where they were going as fast as they could.

O my sweetheart . . . Down Washington, past the antique stores, left onto Court.

Before me, Courthouse Square, and the courthouse itself, the huge, gray building with columns, the park with the gazebo, the big houses lining the square, their windows dark. Across from the courthouse, the red brick police station with the American flag hanging down over the entrance.

I stormed in through the double doors of the police station. The air was thick, stale. Behind the desk a cop stood, a black man with shiny, blue-black skin like silk. Next to him, a police radio squawked.

"I'm looking for Dean Lily." I was panting for breath. "Have you seen him? Is he here?"

A second's hesitation. No expression on the cop's face. "Has he been arrested?"

"An hour ago! At my house."

"Well, if he's been arrested, miss, you can't see him till he's been arraigned." Slow as he could be, with finality.

"But is he here? Where is he?"

"Can't help you, miss. Have to wait till the arraignment."

Like a teacher. He was playing by the rules, he had all the power, he wouldn't tell me, just because I was young.

I turned away, paced the room. There were rows of plastic chairs linked by metal bars, all vacant, and wanted posters on the walls, hollow-cheeked youths with stringy hair, beefy men with stubble on their cheeks and circles under their eyes. They looked like they hadn't slept for days.

Then, I sprang loose again. I ran back out into the square, across the park, and behind the courthouse, to the jail. The jail was built of yellow brick, fronting on the parking lot. It was shiny and slick with rain now. The building was four stories high, each window two stories high and covered with thick bars so you couldn't see in.

Sometimes, in the lot, you would see young women standing there yelling up at the windows. "T-y-r-o-ne!" they would yell. "I lo-o-ove y-o-o!" they would scream. Sometimes they had their babies with them and they'd hold them up in the air like little round balls so the men inside, the fathers, could see their offspring. But there was never any answer from those dark windows. The women, ever faithful, stood there yelling up anyway, they didn't care about the noise they were making, shattering the calm of the square, and the people staring out at them from behind the curtains and the blinds of the grand houses.

Now *I* was standing there just like them and above me there was no sign of life, not a shadow moving behind the windows of the jail. But he was there, I knew it. And just seeing me standing down there would comfort him. O my sweetheart . . . And I yelled, "Dean! Dean—honey. Oh Dean, I love you, honey." And I realized I didn't dare call him "honey" in person, that I was afraid to tell him I loved him, but I could do it here, screaming at the top of my lungs, my voice echoing in the empty square. And there was nothing he could do because he was trapped up there, and now the truth was out. "I love you, Dean!" I cried.

I stood there, the rain falling harder now, slicking down my hair, running down my face, my sneakers soaked through, my feet numb, standing there eyes pinned on the windows where somewhere, he had to be. "Dean! . . . Deeeeean!"

After a while, my voice was gone and my throat was sore. Nothing could come out of it any more, and I turned and began to walk home, slower now because of the driving rain, because I was exhausted. I walked back up Washington through the town, then along Route 7, soaked to the skin.

All day long, I waited by the phone for him to call. At 4 P.M., I heard the sound of the key turning in the front door. The door opened, and she entered. Right away I saw her eagle eyes scan the place. Mommy missed nothing, everything in her was attuned to me, to all dangers, real or imagined, and right away she sensed something was wrong. "Where's Dean?" she asked.

"He had to go see his mom. She's having an operation or

something. . . ." She looked at me, doubt in her dark eyes. She knew I was lying, like she knew everything about me. She could see right through me. But she said nothing.

"His truck's still here," she said.

"His brother came and got him."

"Is the mom okay?"

"Yeah. It's like appendicitis or something." She said nothing. But I knew she doubted me.

That evening, after we had dinner, we watched TV. She was lying on the couch when the phone rang. The sound pierced the air like a scream and I ran to get it before she could. On the other end of the line, there was a clanking sound, of coins dropping in the box, then a series of clicks. "Mellie?" It was *his* voice, it sounded hoarse, weary.

"O God!" I whispered into the phone. "You okay?" I glanced over at her. She didn't seem to be listening.

"Listen. You gotta get me out of here," he said. She was lying there on the couch, eyes fixed on the TV, like she wasn't paying attention. "They put two hundred dollars bail on me," he said. "They put me in with the women. You got to get me out of here, Mellie!"

"O Jesus . . . I don't know how to get you out . . . What should I do?"

"Get some money," he said.

"Where can I get two hundred dollars?"

"I'm gonna die here, Mellie. Please. . . ."

"I'll try," I said. "Oh Dean . . ."

"There's a line here," he said. "People behind me. I have to go. Please, hurry up. Do it now," he said.

I waited until morning. At sunrise I got up and dressed. "Why're you up?" she asked, when she saw me in the hall. I always slept late. She always got up early because she was so fastidious about getting ready for work.

"I wanted to get an early start," I said.

While she was in the shower, I ran outside to the mailbox. I opened it, snatched the *Ledger-Republican* out before she could see it, and stuffed it under my sweatshirt.

Back in the house, she kissed me good-bye. I could smell her sweet perfume, her morning scents of soap and shampoo. She was so pretty going to work, like she was going to meet important people, not just work at the travel agency.

When she had gone, I took the paper out. The front page had a story about a big fire on River Street, two volunteer firemen killed. I didn't stop to read it. I dug through the pages looking for the police blotter. I came to it and there was a headline, three columns wide. "Police Arrest West Taponac Woman Dressed as Man in Check-Cashing Scheme." I read the story underneath it. "Eleven previous arrests," it said. They had listed all his charges, "Criminal impersonation . . . bad checks . . . traffic violations." They said he had been living two months in Sparta, impersonating a man.

It was a mistake. A terrible mistake. They were saying that just because Dean was so beautiful, because they couldn't believe any boy could be that beautiful.

By 8:30 A.M., I was standing outside the check-cashing place on Washington Street, waiting. At 9 A.M., the man arrived and pulled up the metal gate. I was the first customer. I filled in the lines on the blank check Mommy had given me for the highlights, above her signature with the pretty feminine handwriting, handwriting that looked like it was drawing. In the space for the amount, I wrote $200.

There it was, those big figures above her signature. I slid the check under the plexiglass window, and the man counted the bills out, one by one onto the counter. She wouldn't know about this, I thought, till she got her statement at the end of the month, or if she was overdrawn.

I tucked the money into my jeans pocket, and I ran with it to the police station. The black cop was on duty again, cold, silky-skinned. He must have seen so much that I was nothing to him. Every day there were hysterical women standing in front of him begging to see their men. I handed him the money.

"When will they let him out?" I asked.

"Takes time for the paperwork," he said.

"That's okay. I'll wait. I don't care."

And so I waited. In the stale warmth of the police station, I fell asleep. All afternoon, I drifted in and out of consciousness, in the background the radio squawking, and then another radio somewhere, playing tinny music, and voices around me.

I woke up with a start. He was standing above me, his face pale, like a ghost. He was still as a statue, as if he'd been standing there for hours, watching me.

"Mellie."

"Oh my God . . ." I jumped up and threw my arms around him. But he just stood stiffly, arms at his side. He didn't like it when I touched him, I realized, when I got too close to him and my breasts were touching his chest. But now I had permission to hold him. It was okay now because of what happened I could welcome him. And he stood there, arms down at his side, defeated and exhausted. The cop behind the counter was staring at us. I didn't care.

"Oh Jesus, you okay?" I took his arm, and I lead him like he was sick or something outside and away from the police station.

"I'm hungry," he said. Uncle Dom's was on Washington, a block away. "We'll go to Uncle Dom's," I said.

We walked up the silent street, me holding on tight to his arm. "O sweetheart, what did they do to you?" And again, I realized I was calling him sweetheart and that I'd never dared to do that before, that somehow I had been scared of him, scared because though I knew he loved me, he didn't want me to get too close.

143

"I can't talk about it now," he said. So noble, I thought. "It was real bad." He shook his head. Then looked at me. "Thank you, baby. Where did you get the money?"

"From the blank check Mommy gave me for the hairdresser."

He stopped. "She's gonna go batshit!" he said.

"She won't know about it for weeks. Then, we'll deal with it. I'll get a job. I'll pay her back."

"Is my truck okay?" he asked. His truck was his only real possession, it was everything to him.

"It's fine. Still parked right in the driveway."

"Oh Mellie," he sighed. He looked relieved. "I love you. I love you so much."

We walked home together through the town, and then along Route 7, holding hands, him carrying his backpack. When we got to the house, she was there, home from work and waiting. As we entered, she was sitting at the dining table, the newspaper spread out in front of her. When she saw us come in, her eyes widened, but for a moment, she said nothing. Then, "Dean," she said, carefully.

"Mrs. Saluggio, I'm sorry. I really am. I didn't do anything. This woman—she was just jealous, jealous 'cause of Mellie. She wants me to get in trouble."

She watched him with her eyes like shining coals. Planning her reply, I knew.

"What about what's in the paper?" she asked. "What they said about you. . . . They said—this stuff about you pretending to be a boy."

He sat down on the couch, buried his head in his hands. We watched him. There was silence in the house.

Finally, he raised his head, digging his fingers into the side of his cheeks. "It's a mistake," he said. "It's all a crazy mistake."

"It *was,* Mommy," I cried. "They hate him!"

"I'm sorry, Dean," she said. "I can't let you stay here anymore.

I'm sorry," she said. Their eyes were fixed on each other. "But I've got to think about Mellie."

"But I love him, Mommy!" I said.

She kept her eyes on him, ignoring me. "I have to think about AIDS," she said.

He looked up, as if he didn't understand. "AIDS?"

"Yes," she said.

"But I don't have AIDS! What do you mean, AIDS?"

She stood up, removed the dirty glasses and cups from the dining table where they'd been sitting all day because I hadn't cleaned up that morning. "I'm sorry, Dean, but gay people carry AIDS." She stood up, began carrying the dirty breakfast dishes into the kitchen.

I saw Dean's shoulders slump, like she had punched him in the gut.

Then, he took a deep breath. He stood up. He moved slowly around the couch, reached down, and hoisted his backpack on his shoulder. For a moment, he stood there without moving, as if hoping she would change her mind.

"He's got nowhere to go!" I cried.

"I'm sorry, Mellie," she said. "I have to think of you."

He stood on the threshold of the front door, his shoulder slumped and defeated. Then he opened the door, stood there a moment, the cold air rushing in. He turned, and he looked across the room with hurt eyes. "I don't have AIDS," he said. "And I'm *not* gay."

CHAPTER 19

CHRISSIE

The day after Dean got arrested at Melanie Saluggio's house, anyone who didn't already know the truth about Dean learned it from the newspaper. Even when they strip-searched him in the jail, and the cops discovered the truth, Dean still insisted he was a man.

They locked him in the woman's section, which he protested violently, and they had to place him in restraints.

The news about Dean spread, it was bigger news than the fire on River Street, two firemen killed, or the scandal about Police Chief Trevor and the shakedowns of drug dealers. The news of Dean spread through parents to their children, it was out loud what people had already known since the moment they laid eyes upon him. Or *her.* Or—the truth they had realized seconds thereafter, but didn't want to admit to themselves—for their own reasons. Now they were forced to face it.

The news made people smile. Gays were no big deal in Sparta, but the disguise was unusual, the girl committing the crime. Unusual kind of headline in the paper too. Grown-ups had seen it all, but the kids hadn't, and they had to learn. The news was like the movies, something to do, better than *Montel* or *Ricki Lake.* And it was, for a few days at least, a mark of distinction if you could say you had known Dean, even a little. If you had gone to the Laundercenter while he was still there, if he had made change

146

for you, sold you detergent, folded your clothes. If you had spoken to him at the Wooden Nickel.

The night after it was published in the paper, I was at the Wooden Nickel at my usual spot under the Genny sign. It was a neon sign, with a mermaid outlined in bright pink and mauve, her hair long and flowing, her tail curled. At the other end of the bar, Carl was making a list of something on a piece of paper, sipping coffee from the cup at his side.

A few feet away from me at the bar were two men, dressed in camouflage jackets like they'd been out hunting. "She pees standing up," one of them was saying. "I saw it myself in the men's room at City Shop. . . . I walked in and there she was standing at the urinal, I swear to God."

"A girl can't do that," the other one said. "It would get all over."

"I saw it."

"Well, she must have something I don't."

"Yeah—a long tongue!" And they chuckled into their glasses.

Then suddenly Carl, at the other end of the bar, fixed them with his icy blue eyes. "Let her be," said Carl. "Have pity on her. She's just a poor creature." Carl almost never spoke up, mostly he was just a silent presence watching over us, and now the two men were embarrassed and grew quiet.

Carl walked along the bar to where I was sitting. He leaned over toward me and lowered his voice. "Did you hear? Melanie bailed him out?"

"With what!"

"Brian Perez said her mom gave her a blank check to go to the hairdresser's. She told him that."

"Is he still at Melanie's now?"

"Brian said Melanie's mother won't let him stay there anymore. She's afraid of AIDS."

"Where's he going to go then?" I asked.

He shook his head. "Crazy kid," he said. "I don't know. . . ."

His voice trailed off. And he moved off down the bar, wiping the old wood with his cloth, shaking his head as he went.

It seemed like Dean had disappeared. Then a couple of nights later at the bar, Carl said, "I saw him last night. I came outside around two when I closed up, and his truck was parked right there in the lot. He'd taped clothes up over the windows so you couldn't see in. I banged on the window but he didn't answer. But I knew he was inside. So I figured if he didn't want to talk, I'd leave him alone. And when I came in again this morning to open up, his truck was gone." Like some crazy homeless person, I thought, sleeping out in the open where anybody could get at him. And yet still trying to make privacy for himself, doesn't want to be disturbed, the way homeless people sometimes act.

Christmas Eve came a week later. I had Christmas Eve dinner over at my dad and Liz's. As Liz served the food, she was all flustered and resentful, though she put on a cheery face, because she'd had to work all day and then rush home to fix dinner so there could be a Christmas celebration for me because next day I was going to be with my mom and Mason.

The brats Fletcher and Timmy were whining to get their presents early, but Liz said they had to save them till Christmas morning—though I wouldn't be there, of course. And soon as I could, I left. And I knew Liz was glad because she wanted to clean up and get to bed.

Afterward, I drove out to the Wooden Nickel as if for solace, to find my true family. And when I walked into the bar, there he was, Dean, in the middle of a circle of people, doing magic tricks again, cocky as ever. His fingers rippled through the air, behind people's ears, into their pockets. And then, with a flick of the wrist, he'd produce something out of nothing. When Dean saw me enter, he stopped a moment, and he smiled right at me, his face all flushed. He was defying us all.

The place was packed. Carl had decorated it like a mad person. Carl always made a big deal over holidays. He carved pumpkins for Halloween, put up paper turkeys for Thanksgiving, hid little chocolate eggs at Easter.

There was a low, red incandescence in the room from the Christmas lights, and tinsel sparkling everywhere, a Christmas tree up on the bar, cutouts of Santa Claus and red streamers on the walls. Christmas music blared from the jukebox, competing with the noise from the TV.

And there he was! As if risen from the dead, living at the peak of danger, the people around him laughing and egging him on like he was a performing dog or something.

I sat down at the bar with my book. For a while, I read, half watching Dean as he did his tricks. He had a new one. He was making someone tie his wrists together with a piece of rope. "Tight!" he ordered. They covered his wrists with his jacket, and he started to struggle and thrash about underneath it. His face got all red, his body twisted from side to side while his fans stood around watching this oddity. Then suddenly he grunted, threw up the jacket, and his hands were free. He held them up in the air, and people in the group clapped.

Around midnight, I looked up from my book and saw Brian, Melanie, and Jimmy Vladeck enter.

You could feel a stir in the air. Everyone saw it. Brian with this empty smirk on his face, Melanie small and thin next to him, and she wasn't smiling. She looked different suddenly, deprived of her lover. Like a frail little girl, smaller, lost in the big coat, her hair seemed finer, the shadows around her eyes deeper.

Standing in the doorway, she spotted Dean and she stopped in her tracks.

He was shuffling his cards, dealing them, then turning them over and making them magically come out in order from aces to kings. "Okay—let's alternate red and black cards," he was saying as he dealt the deck again. "Okay—display them—"

149

Then I saw him stop. His body grew rigid. He had sensed Melanie's presence. There was this telepathic connection between them, as if his spirit was directly attached to hers. His hands stopped dealing the cards and he turned his head.

Their eyes locked and you could feel the love between them; as if the air was electrified.

Brian was watching Melanie watching Dean, looking from one to the other, helpless beside them.

Dean stood up. He pushed through the crowd of bodies toward her. I slid down from my barstool and hurried over to him.

He kept walking, his eyes fixed on her and pleading and it was as if there were a soundless vacuum between the two of them, sucking them toward one another.

In front of her, he halted. "Mellie," he said, his voice soft, and personal to her. Standing next to Melanie, Brian glared at him, as if to fend him off with pure hate. But Dean and Melanie just kept looking at one another as if Brian wasn't even there.

"Dean," she said, her voice soft, a whisper.

He stood close to her. "Missed you . . . " I heard him say.

Then Brian smiled. "So, *Lily.* How's it goin'?"

Dean didn't look at him, kept his eyes on Melanie. "I'm not Lily," he said, talking to Brian but not looking at him.

"That's what the cops said when they stripped you," Brian said. "Lily."

Dean kept his eyes focused on Melanie. "Please," he said to Brian, his voice soft and even, "don't call me that."

Brian jerked his head back, then thrust it forward in a gesture of fake astonishment. "But isn't that what you are?"

Melanie turned. "Leave him alone, Brian!"

"You think that's a 'him,' Melanie?" Brian said. "That's not a 'him.' "

"He's what he wants to be, Brian," she said. "Shuddup."

Brian smiled. "So, what do you *want* to be, Lily?"

Melanie's eyes, looking at Dean, had become suddenly soft,

distracted. "Be quiet, Brian," she said over her shoulder, still keeping her gaze on Dean.

Brian said, "Admit it, Melanie. He's a fucking girl."

"Leave me alone," Dean said. Couldn't take his eyes off her. Resented the sound of anyone's voice intruding on his concentration.

Then Dean began to back away from her. Slowly, as if he were ripping his skin away from her skin, as if he were detaching himself from her bodily.

I followed Dean to one of the tables, and we both sat down.

I felt breathless. They had been on the brink of danger. Only Dean's backing away had forestalled a nasty fight, a fight that Dean would surely lose. Melanie sat down at a table across the room, as if the encounter had exhausted her too.

For the next few moments, they held on to each other across the room with their eyes, tragic lovers that they were.

Then Brian grabbed Melanie's arm and dragged her up from her chair. It toppled backward onto the floor. Brian pulled at the sleeve of Melanie's leather jacket, and it slipped off her arm. Then he grabbed her wrist and he hauled her to the door, and she stumbled out of the bar after him, all the time looking back at Dean. Jimmy, Brian's sentinel, followed.

I stayed with Dean another half hour, until Carl began cleaning up for the night. "Closing early tonight," Carl said. "Going to midnight Mass."

Outside in the parking lot, the cold air hit us. There hadn't been snow for a few days and the temperature had risen. A brief thaw had followed but now there was a freeze again and more snow to come.

A row of pines sheltered the parking lot from the river wind. Across the lot, in the shadow of the trees, Brian's Camaro was parked with the motor running, and Brian and Jimmy stood against the side of it. I could just make out Melanie hunched down in the front seat. Even though it was cold, Brian had on only a parka, no gloves. And tonight he had a white T-shirt under his parka, though he was dancing up and down on his skinny legs because of the cold.

Dean's truck was parked next to my car. And as we walked across the lot to the two vehicles, I could feel Brian watching us.

Suddenly the spotlight that illuminated the parking lot was extinguished. There was darkness now, and behind us the door to the bar slammed shut, and I saw that Carl had come outside, all bundled up in his wool coat and gloves. Carl paused on the threshold, studied us a second, then turned and locked the door behind him, climbed inside his own car and drove off.

Silence now. Brian and Jimmy leaned motionless against their car. No other cars in the lot now, everyone had gone home but us.

You could hear the wind soughing, an implacable, icy wind, moving through the trees. Down below, the great river was white, beginning to freeze over. Soon it would be solid ice except for the black waters of the channel that the Coast Guard icebreaker cut in the middle of winter to make a path for the big boats going upriver.

Brian reached around and banged on the window of his car. "You think that's a 'him,' Melanie?" he yelled.

She hunched down further in her seat. He kept on banging. "Open up," he ordered. "That ain't no 'him,' Melanie!" He pulled at the door handle, trying to open it, but at the same moment, she slammed her fist down on the lock. He rattled the door, then took out his key and unlocked it, reached inside, and pulled her out of the car.

"Look!" he commanded, pointing to Dean outside in the parking lot.

She turned her face away, refused to look. "He's a fucking girl, Melanie . . . a fucking *girl!*" Brian cried, baring his teeth. But Melanie kept her head down, bent sideways away from Brian, her face hidden behind her hair.

"You're so fuckin' miserable, Melanie!" He spat the words out. "Face the fuckin' truth. Stop wimping around." He grabbed her chin and yanked her jaw around so she was forced to look at Dean. She strained to look away but he held on to her face.

I stepped forward. "Leave her alone, Brian," I said.

Brian spun round. "Shut the fuck up, Chrissie! You're in love with it too." He turned back to Melanie. "I said *look!*" he yelled.

Then Melanie let out a cry, a dry, ratcheting sound coming from deep down in her throat. "No!"

"Jimmy!" Brian said. Jimmy sprang to attention. "Hold her," Brian commanded, and Jimmy grabbed Melanie's arm.

Brian lunged at Dean. He was taller than Dean, and he moved quickly. He gripped Dean's arm, twisted it up behind his back and pushed him toward Melanie.

I grabbed Brian's arm and tried to stop him. But with one sudden quick motion, Jimmy kicked me, and the big, blunt square toe of his boot cracked me hard on my shin.

"Ouch!" I cried, grasping my injured shin with both hands.

Jimmy was holding Melanie's wrists behind her back and she kicked at him, but he dodged her with clever steps. Melanie was nothing to Jimmy in all his hulking hugeness.

"Hold her so she sees," Brian told Jimmy. "Push her face up."

With one hand Brian held Dean's arm up behind his back, and with the other he reached around Dean's body and jabbed his fingers down into Dean's jeans. He yanked at them, trying to pull them down. He scrambled to unbuckle Dean's belt. There was a flash of brass, and he tore the zipper down.

"No," Dean said. "No . . . "

"Pull her jeans down, Jimmy," Brian said.

Brian shoved Melanie backward, her body bounced against the car. Then he turned to Dean again and held on to him. Melanie jammed her fists into her eyesockets.

Dean kept struggling under Brian's grip. "Fuck you!" he spluttered. "Leave me alone, asshole." Brian grabbed both his arms now from behind, held his wrists together in his one wiry hand, as if to show how strong he was, and that Dean was but a flea to him.

"Do it, Jimmy!" he ordered. Jimmy stepped forward, and pulled Dean's jeans all the way down to his feet.

I saw a flash of white, his Jockey shorts, too big for him, gathered between the thighs because there was no bulge there, and his flat stomach, tender flesh trembling in the cold.

Dean tried to jab Brian with his elbows, but Brian just danced backward. "Let me go!" Dean cried. "Let me go. Now!"

But Jimmy ripped down Dean's jockeys. And there it was. Dean's mysterious black blush, a healthy, springy mound of hair. There was no dick. But maybe there was something hidden in the thick, curly mass. Maybe it was extra small or something, because of his deformity. His hips were gently rounded, the frame of his pelvis curved. He shot Melanie a look, his face clouded with rage and shame. I saw tears on his cheeks.

I couldn't help it, but I stared—then I realized what I was doing and quickly looked away. "You shits!" I cried. "You shit, Brian!"

"Shut the fuck up, Chrissie, or I'll fuckin' kill you," Brian said. Dean was quiet now, his chest heaving. Brian turned his attention back to Melanie. "Look at her, Melanie! You see a fuckin' dick there, Melanie? It's a girl! She's a fuckin' lesbian. Make her look!" he told Jimmy.

Melanie raised her chin but kept her eyes squeezed shut. Her mouth trembled.

Dean's face was turned away now as if in shame, his knees pressed together tight.

"Please!" he said. "Leave me alone."

"You're sick, Brian!" I screamed.

Brian's eyes were glued on Melanie. "I'm counting, Melanie," he said. "One—two—"

She opened her eyes, and for a second they darted to Dean's dark bush and rested there, a glance so rapid I couldn't tell if she'd even seen anything, and then she swept her hands up to her eyes again.

"Say it, Melanie!" Brian shrieked. "Say what he is. Say he's a girl!"

"G-girl—..." Melanie faltered.

"She lied to you!" Brian cried and he lurched toward Dean. "I'm gonna beat the shit out of you!"

"N-o-o—" Melanie cried, eyes still squeezed tight.

Brian stood there a moment, fist clenched in the air, ready to strike.

"No," she begged.

He dropped his arm, turned away, his face still tight.

"Let her go," Brian told Jimmy. Jimmy let Dean's arm drop, and Dean reached down, shoulders heaving, and pulled up his Jockeys and his jeans.

Melanie took a step toward Dean, put her hand on his shoulder as if to comfort him. "Oh God," she whispered, and this time Brian didn't stop her. She reached into her coat pocket and took out a Kleenex and began wiping the tears from Dean's cheeks.

Then she put both her hands on Dean's shoulders and rested her face in the crook of his neck. Dean's arms hung limply at his side, but he bent his face down into hers, and they stood there motionless together, their necks entwined, like two swans.

Brian was lighting a cigarette, as if a cigarette were a reward for a task completed, a job well done.

"You satisfied?" I hissed at Brian.

"Shuddup, Chrissie."

"Dean, let's go," I said. "We can go in my car. Leave the truck here till tomorrow. Let's go to my place. You can stay there."

Dean and Melanie were whispering softly together now, as if there were no one else around. "Don't tell anyone I cried, Mellie." His voice was urgent. "Please. I don't want people to know I cried. Only girls cry." Melanie nodded, sniffed.

Dean focused on me now. His face was smudged from his tears. "I can't leave my truck here," he said.

"You're in no shape to drive," I told him. "It'll be okay here overnight."

"It won't fuckin' be okay," and his voice seemed like it was breaking again. "I'm taking it," he said, glaring at Brian. "I'm not leaving it here."

Then Melanie turned to Brian. "I'm riding home with Chrissie," she said. "I hate you, Brian. I hate you."

CHAPTER 20

CHRISSIE

Driving Melanie back into Sparta, I could feel the wind sweeping up from the river and funneling through the valley, pushing against the car. Terrible wind. Big storm coming, power lines would go down, houses would be buried in drifts, old people would be found frozen to death. All commerce would cease.

Next to me in the front seat, Melanie was huddled down inside her black leather jacket. Her mouth was trembling, her teeth chattering.

We were the only ones on the highway, and as we drove the road seemed to be parting in front of us like water. Hard to see because there was only darkness on the road, and even with my brights on, I could only discern a few feet ahead.

"F-r-eezing," Melanie said. "Can you put the heat on?"

I tried the heat, but only a blast of icy air came through the vents. "Gotta wait a minute till the engine's warm. You okay?"

She rested her head against the back of the seat, closed her eyes. She shook her head.

"You had to know, Mellie. You had to."

"No," she said, eyes squeezed shut.

"I don't believe you didn't."

"Doesn't matter. He's a guy."

"Uh-huh. But a lotta guys want to go out with you, Mellie. I don't mean just asshole Brian. Why *him?*"

The heat was starting to come in through the vents, and the car was filling with warmth. "He doesn't hit on me," she said. "He treats me like I'm a—person. Not some—doll."

"That's why he wanted you. Cause you're Miss Unattainable. That's why he went after you."

"Please don't talk about him like he's in the past," she said. Her eyes were open now, they were blazing, fixed on the road in front.

Suddenly I said out of nowhere, "I love Dean too."

At this, her lips parted, as if somehow she hadn't realized this. A car was coming toward us on the road. I saw her face caught for a moment in a ghastly light and I could see her skin was mottled from crying.

I laughed. "Don't worry. He doesn't love me. It's not that kind of love."

She settled back in the seat as if she were relieved. "I guess that's two of us care about him then."

Now Old 27 merged into new 27, and we were coming into Sparta. At the intersection I stopped for the blinking red light. Nobody on the streets, no house lights on. Secret night, I thought, all yours, universal sleep. Night means all things are possible, gives you the feeling you own everything. It's yours, and you are free.

On Route 7, I dropped Melanie off at her house. "It's late," I said, as she got out of the car. "Won't your mom be pissed?"

"What can she do to me?" She went a few steps, then she turned, her face swollen and stained with tears. "When you see Dean, tell him I love him, will you?" she asked. "Tell him I'll always love him, no matter what." And then she stumbled up the walkway to the front door.

I drove off. A fuel truck came barreling toward me, the roar of it filling the hollow air. Then another car, the city was stirring awake.

When I got to Washington Street, I expected to see Dean's truck parked in front of my building, he was to have gone ahead of me. But Dean's truck wasn't there.

PART IV

THE FANGS
OF MALICE

CHAPTER 21

DEAN

Melanie and Chrissie gone. Silence in the parking lot of the Wooden Nickel. Only the sound of the wind whistling through the pines. I'm freezing, shivering in my boots, my teeth clacking. Me and Jimmy and Brian stand there as if we're not even aware of each other, watching Chrissie's car leave, her brake lights blinking red at the exit. And then she disappears.

And now there's no one here but us three—Brian, Jimmy, me. And suddenly Brian turns, glares at me, his mouth set in a thin little line. "Get her, Jimmy. Put her in back of the truck."

Jimmy grabs my arm, opens the back of the cap, and shoves me down inside. And as I slide across the old rug I've put down to make the truck more like a home my shirt rides up and my skin scrapes hard against the grain. The two of them crawl in after me and I lift my head up and I kick at them, but it's no good. "Get her down!" Brian yells.

Brian and Jimmy kneel on either side of me and pin me by the shoulders. I try to sit up, but they shove me back down and my head smashes against the floor of the truck. There isn't enough room in the back for all three of us. We're all squeezed together and I can hear them panting and grunting in the darkness, can smell their stink of beer and mildew and sweat. And I can just make out Brian's eyes, flashing with pure hatred and Jimmy's big fat face, flesh all swollen on the cheeks and forehead, and suddenly in the middle of it all I notice that Jimmy's ears are too small like they're cut off at the top or something.

161

"Get her pants down," Brian tells him, and I'm thinking, they can kill me and nobody will know because no one can see me here in the truck, there won't be any cars going by till morning. I realize I haven't heard a single car pass by on the road since this all started. And it flashes on me, this is what dying is, someone takes you by surprise in some place when you least expect it, and then it happens—in just a second or two, just like that you're gone.

So I go limp. I let my arms lie by my side while Jimmy thrashes open my belt buckle and pulls my jeans down again. Brian unzips his own jeans and I see his hands with their spiky knuckles grasping at the top of his pants and with one quick jerk, he jams down his zipper, fumbles inside, and he pulls out his thing.

He kneels over me holding it down at me like it's a pen or something, it's long and thin and silvery and veiny, curved at the end like a fishhook that will tear into flesh. Stupid stupid looking thing.

Brian flings his long hair off his face, as if getting ready to aim. There are no words in the truck now, only the sounds of the three of us struggling and as I lie there I realize that Brian's thing is going to cut through me like a knife—because I'm sealed there with like this sheet of flesh. It's going to cut me right in half, going to bore this gaping hole through to my backside, and freezing air will rush in it'll be like electricity, and there will be no inside or outside any longer and I'm going to bleed to death right there in the truck.

"Lie still or I'll kill you," he tells me.

I can hear myself begging, "Don't . . ."

"Hold her down."

Jimmy leans down over me, all thick folds of flesh. He clamps his hand down over my mouth, and now I can't breathe and I'm jerking my head from side to side, struggling to free my mouth. I've got to survive, and I'm so strong wanting to breathe, refusing to have my breath cut off, like a kid being smothered who will fight as hard as he can, it's just instinct, like an old person trying to kill himself will pull the plastic bag over his head, but still struggle and fight to breathe.

At last, I free my mouth from Jimmy's hand and I lie back, gasping.

I lift up my head a second, but Jimmy smashes it down again. Then suddenly, Jimmy rears up and brings the heel of his hunting boot right down on my cheek. I can feel my flesh split open and my cheekbone crushed under the sharp edge of his sole and for a moment everything goes black. "Please . . ." I gasp, my voice all tiny like a child's, a little girl's. If I just go along with them, make my body go limp, it won't hurt as much and they might not kill me.

And I feel myself lifting my hips to cooperate, and it's hard to keep my pelvis off the ground to comply with them, and my thighs are trembling like jelly flesh. "Please," I beg them. "Please don't hurt me."

Now Brian's on top of me. He pushes my thighs apart. He aims his thing at me, then rams it up against me, keeps ramming it against me, trying to push it in. And I feel it ripping my flesh apart. And then it's in, and there's this burning pain there like it's this terrible foreign object inside me and he's stretching me, and moving up and down, grunting and each movement's like he's tearing me apart and I think I can't endure this. And I try to pretend it isn't really me, that it's far away somewhere else this pain which is like torture so bad it isn't real.

Then I hear his gasp above me in the air. He shudders. Then, with a violent gesture, he yanks it out.

It's over. His voice comes to me from somewhere above me, "Tell anybody about this and we'll kill you. Go to the cops and I'll fuckin' kill you."

And now they're scrambling out the truck and I feel a sudden rush of cold air where a second before they've been and I hear their car door slam, the engine revving up. I hear them pulling away, the sound of the motor growing fainter and fainter. And now it's quiet again and I'm lying there in the truck alone. But maybe they're still out there, only just pretending to be gone and if they see me try to escape, they'll kill me. So I lie still and I force myself to count to ten. One—two—three . . . I can still smell them in the air of the truck, the odor of hair and sweat and sex. Did Jimmy really leave with him? Have to be sure Jimmy is gone too, not lurking out there in the shadows. But I hear only silence, the wind rising from the river, and I dare to lift my head, to glance out the window of the truck. Nothing.

The real pain takes a moment to take hold. But then I feel it—this raw, burning sensation between my thighs, the flesh throbbing, it's on fire and I'm so torn, Jesus, I won't be able to pee anymore even and my thighs are all wet and Brian's come is running down my flesh. I'm afraid to sit up for fear I'll faint. I touch the place with my fingertips, afraid to touch it for fear of what I'll find and when I bring my hand back up, I see something dark and glittering and I know it's blood and that freaks me out even more 'cause I've got to stop the blood or I'll die.

Then the cold air hits it there and makes it sting worse and I can feel my whole body hurting like I'm bruised all over. I grope around till I find my jeans down around my feet and drag them toward me, then I try and sit up, but my ribs and back hurt like I've been kicked and so I fall back down again. Got to get out of here, is all I'm thinking. They're coming back to kill me.

At last, I succeed in sitting up. I lean over the back of the driver's seat, then push myself headfirst down into the front. I'm afraid to get out of the truck and go around because who knows who's out there. Blood's oozing down my cheek. My jeans are wet between the thighs, blood there. How much am I losing? And suddenly I feel lightheaded, my head's spinning and there's a prickling behind my eyes. Don't faint, I think. Have to get out of here before they come back.

I dig around in my pockets for my keys. Miracle—still there. And somehow I insert the key in the ignition. The engine scrapes, doesn't catch. Please. I turn the key again, and this time the engine starts up.

Jerking the shift down into reverse, I back out of the parking lot. Can hardly see, it's like it's all swollen now around my left eye. The virus gets in through torn flesh, I think. Her mom wouldn't let me back in the house after the arrest. Said I carried AIDS.

I turn onto the road. I accelerate, and then I drive on Old 27 in the dark, driving the truck though I'm practically blind and it's a good thing I know the way along the road by heart.

*   *   *

When I get to the hospital, the hemlock trees in front are hung with tiny Christmas lights winking up and down like water running through the branches. I pull up under the canopy and there's a sign says, Do Not Block Emergency Entrance Private Cars Towed at Owner's Expense, but I leave my truck there anyway, and I struggle in through the doors.

There's a waiting room, but no one there. A nurse's desk, but the chair is empty. From a speaker near the ceiling comes the sound of "Jingle Bells." There's a TV set in the waiting room, and on the screen I notice a figure in a diving mask coming up from under the ocean. It's as if all the inhabitants of the place have been swept away by aliens or something. Yet all the objects of daily life remain, all the machinery's still running.

The bright light makes the cut under my eye burn. In front of me is a pair of double doors with wire-glass panes leading to a long hallway and I push against them but they're locked. I see a man in a white coat walking down the hallway carrying a plastic glass and I bang on the window to get his attention and he hurries toward me. "Can I help you?" he asks.

"Yeah—I been attacked!" I tell him.

He looks blank a moment. "I been sexually attacked," I tell him. "They fuckin' ripped me open!"

He opens the doors right away, guides me in, then down the hall to an examining room with a gurney. "Up here, please. I'm Rob, the physician's assistant," he says. Big, round man in his fifties, little white beard. He holds my wrist to time my pulse, and I can smell wine and garlic on his breath, must be having their Christmas party.

Rob releases my arm and lifts the phone on the wall: "Dr. Chu, room nine. Dr. Chu," and I can hear his voice echo on the loudspeaker outside in the hallway. I'm starting to shiver and shake again, and Rob reaches for a paper gown from the shelf and a thin cotton blanket. "Please change into this. You can put this over you when you're changed."

*   *   *

I lie there on the gurney in the paper gown under the thin white blanket, my teeth chattering and my body shaking so hard now I can hear my bones rattling inside my skin and I'm afraid my bones are going to break. A woman pokes her head between the curtains. "Lily?"

Got to straighten this out. "Dean."

"I'm Debbie. From the Rape Crisis Center." She is maybe forty. Got a wide face and dark curly hair down to her shoulders. Wears jeans and a pink sweatshirt, and you can tell immediately she's a lesbian. You can always tell. There's this seriousness in the eyes. Anyway all those Rape Crisis types are lesbians. She carries a clipboard in her hand. I can tell she's new at this.

"I want to get out of here," I tell her. "I want to take a shower."

"You got to hold on till the police come, honey. A shower'll wash away all the evidence."

At this, I sit up on the gurney. "I don't want the cops!"

She takes hold of my hand. "It'll be okay, Lil—" She corrects herself. "Dean. I'm here to help you."

Once probably she'd been pretty. Probably had grown children, then found herself as a dyke and now she is doing this work, in which all men are brutes, to prove her point.

Just then, a Chinese guy dressed in a white coat comes into the cubicle. "I am Doctor Chu." Sounds like he's not even sure who he is, says it almost like a question. "I will have to examine you." He's afraid too, I think. Looks too young to be a real doctor.

"No!"

"If there is a rape, you must be examined," he says. Like he's reciting something he's learned in a textbook.

"No. Go away."

"We must look for injuries," he says.

Debbie says, "Dr. Chu has to examine you, honey. He's gotta take slides for venereal disease and get a sperm sample for the DNA." A little catch in the back of Debbie's throat, her voice is deep, womanly.

"It hurts. It's bleeding."

But the doctor's pulling on his rubber gloves, like an executioner getting ready to do his work, I think. Drapes the blue cloth over my legs and slides his stool up to the gurney. She's holding my hand firmly, and I realize I'm a prisoner here. "Please," he says. "Please bend your knees."

And now he's looking there, peering in at me where no one's ever seen before except my mom. "Laceration of the hymen." he says. "Bruising of labia majora consistent with forced penetration . . ." Like he's talking to himself or something.

Meanwhile, she's standing at the head of the gurney, gripping my hand while my nails dig into her flesh and my toes are curling in terror and she's acting like she isn't interested in what he's looking at.

The doc stands up. "Please move down to the end of the table toward me."

Then his hand reaches way inside me, and I'm pulling away up to the top of the gurney, almost falling off it. I've never had this before. "Shit oh shit oh shit!"

"Please, you must push down toward me. I cannot do this . . ." He holds his hand up in midair, looking to Debbie for help.

"He can't do it, honey," she says, "unless you cooperate. You gotta move down." I'm a prisoner here, this is legal imprisonment, I got to do what they say.

So I slide down toward the doctor, giving in giving in, but squeezing the muscles between my legs tight as I can. I feel him force his fingers into there and I try to cut them off with my muscles but it's no good. His hand deep into me. He presses the other hand down on my stomach. "Try and relax please . . . the stomach muscles . . . I cannot do it unless you relax the muscles . . ."

"You gotta be kidding!" I yell.

He's looking at the wall as he works. I can feel this little hard thing inside me like a bony tail attached to the end of my spine that I've never known about before and he's flipping the nubby thing back and forth with his fingertips. And now it isn't just pain, it's beyond pain— just unnatural. As if they haven't done enough to me and now they're

doing this. "Shit oh shit oh shit. Why do you have to do this to me?"
And I burst into tears and my face is all wet and I feel like this baby
helpless collapsing inside like I'm just nothing and they're just trying
to hurt me.

"No internal lacerations . . ." Still reciting, at the wall.

"Just hold on to my hand," Debbie says. "We all hate this. Coupla
seconds."

And now he's got this steel instrument like pincers that he's holding
in the air. "What's that?" I cry.

"Speculum," he says.

"So he can really see inside," Debbie says. "Doesn't hurt. Looks
worse than it is."

But I'm sobbing like a baby now. Debbie smooths my hair back
from my forehead with her fingertips. "I know, I know," she says. "You
never had one of these before?" she asks.

I can't talk just shake my head from side to side.

Then at last, he slides the thing out of me. "Now we take care of
your face," he says.

After he's sewn up the wound under my eye, Debbie brings me hot tea
in a paper cup. "I got to get out of here," I tell her.

"You have to wait for the police. They'll be here in just a minute.
They're short-handed because of Christmas."

"I don't want the cops," I say.

She stands looking down at me, trying to figure out her next move.
Somewhere she's rehearsed all this, they taught her how to do this in
Rape Crisis School or whatever—the frightened patient not wanting
to go to the police, terrified to testify. They probably have training ses-
sions on how to deal with hysterical victims.

"If you don't report this," she says, "they're gonna do it to someone
else. Sure as I'm standing here."

"I don't care. He's gonna fuckin' kill me."

Just then, there's a knock on the outside wall and the curtains part.
Why, it's fuckin' Officers Jubey and Payette! Hideous Jubey, round-

168

shouldered, buck-toothed. Squatty little Payette with her bright orange hair.

"Get them out of here!" I cry. "I'm not saying a word. Now I'm really not talkin'."

I see Payette look at Debbie. "She's reporting a rape?" Payette asks. That gets my goat. "I'm not 'she'!"

"You know her?" Debbie asks.

"We just arrested her on a stolen check charge, and for criminal impersonation," Jubey tells Debbie. Jubey pulls his notebook from his breast pocket, moistens his lips 'cause his mouth is always open 'cause of his big teeth. "When did this happen?" he asks.

"I'm not saying nothing. They'll kill me."

"But they always say that," says Debbie. "You got to think about the next victim. The police will protect you, won't you, Officer?" She looks at Jubey.

Jubey says, "If there are any threats, we can arrest—"

"Aren't they better off in jail than out there where they can do it again?" Debbie says.

"I want them fuckin' dead," I say. And then, in spite of myself, I feel the tears welling up again, and they spill down my cheek, burning the torn skin, the place where he's stitched the cut. And I know I don't count for nothing and I just have to do what they say.

Jubey flips open the cover of his notebook. "Ma'am, what is the name of the person you are accusing?"

"I'm not 'ma'am'! It's fuckin' Brian Perez and that asshole Jimmy Vladeck."

"Can you give us an address?" Jubey asks.

"How should I know their address!"

"Were there witnesses?"

"Only fuckin' Jimmy."

"Where did this alleged event take place?"

"It isn't 'alleged.' It's real. In the back of my truck in the parking lot at the Wooden Nickel. Out on Old Twenty-Seven."

"Anybody drive by while you were there?"

"Nope."

"About what time was this?"

"I don't know. I don't have a watch! I didn't keep track of the time for God's sake. Carl, the bartender, he saw us when he was closing up. Then, after the other two had gone, they—did it." And suddenly I can't even say the word, what "it" is.

"We'll talk to them," Jubey says. *"We'll attempt to locate them."*

"You got to arrest them," says Debbie.

Jubey looks at Debbie, hesitates. *"Well, this—..."* he begins. *"We already arrested this person. She claimed she was a man. ..."* His voice dwindles like he's afraid of the whole subject.

"But she can still be raped," Debbie says.

I lift my head from the gurney. *"I'm not gay! I'm not fuckin' gay."*

I see Jubey swallow, his big Adam's apple rippling down his long neck, which is curved like a turkey's. He nods in my direction. *"This a man or a girl, Doc?"* he asks.

Dr. Chu clears his throat. *"Well, we have no sign of a phallus or testes. The examination is consistent with a normally developed female, late adolescent, approximately twenty years old."* Pompous ass.

Payette is still standing there like a fool, gaping at me. *"We'll attempt to locate the parties,"* Jubey says, finally.

They're gone. Debbie leans over close to me, and I can feel her big, soft breasts under the dark pink sweatshirt, breasts like my mother's, against my shoulder.

"I'm gettin' out of here," I tell her.

"Doctor has to sign you out."

She puts her hand on my shoulder to keep me down, but I push her aside and slide down off the gurney and as I touch my bare feet to the cold linoleum floor, I hear ringing in my ears, and I have to steady myself. My clothes are draped across the chair. I start pulling my jeans on under the hospital gown.

"Just a minute!" Debbie says, and she starts for the curtain. "Just let me get the doctor."

I let her go. But as soon as she's gone, I'm out the door. And I am vanished!

CHAPTER 22

TERRY

Dec. 16. I hope he burns dear god, I hope he burns. Burn burn burn suffer suffer suffer. I know that he must still love me somewhere.... How do I know? Because when I lay underneath him with my legs spread apart, wide as wide as angel wings I open my eyes a moment and he's smiling pleasure I never knew anyone who liked it this much, he says, because he's found his purpose in life.... And I took care of him. You're so good, so fine, he tells me. He really loves Bobby—I wish he were mine, he says. I wish I were his dad. I supported him. She cannot support him.... When my head is roaring with pleasure, when it's like I'm riding the waves of a great ...
                                        —From the diary of Terry Kluge

At Christmas, I shopped in a daze. Had to make a Christmas for the sake of Bobby and my dad. Because otherwise I'd kill myself. Bought presents for my dad to give to me and to Bobby, and for Bobby to give to him. Everything an effort, as if I had two-hundred-pound weights on my legs dragging me down.

Christmas Day at my dad's house, I made roast chicken, because there weren't enough of us for a turkey. Easy, the stuffing ready-made, you just add water, chop the apples.

After we'd eaten, we watched reruns on TV, twenty-five years of Christmas specials—the Smothers Brothers, Bing Crosby, and Ed Sullivan. Then I cleaned up the dishes.

I wondered how many more Christmases there would be with my dad. Doctor Vakil wanted him to go down to Albany for pulmonary tests. Dr. Vakil didn't have the right equipment in his own office, he said, but Dad kept delaying calling for the appointment. He insisted he felt fine, though his flesh hung in bluish folds from his skull, his eyes were watery, and I could hear him wheezing as he moved. That was his generation—they always felt fine. Wouldn't go to the doctor unless they were actually dying. After New Year's, I'd make the appointment for him myself, take a weekday off, drive him down to Albany myself. You become like a parent to your parent.

Around five, Bobby and I left. Now, on Christmas night as we rode home, it was already dark out. So brief the day. I was going straight to bed when I got home, all that food had made me real tired. Maybe Bobby would go down early for once. I glanced at him behind me in the car, strapped in his seat belt in the back—I always sat him in the back for safety.

He was wide awake. Sitting absolutely still, gazing out the window at the darkness of the landscape. In that temporarily lulled state that the car always put him in. Practically the only time I could hear myself think was when he was riding in the back of the car and distracted like this.

I drove out toward West Taponac. We passed the white frame church with the wrought iron fence around it, the graveyard, the gravestones sticking out of the snow, their lettering all washed away by wind and water. The little settlement was even more melancholy in the late winter afternoon.

And as I drove, staring out ahead through the windshield, *his* image seemed to be there on the glass, his boy's figure, short-haired, pale and cold in front of me—appearing without warning as it did every day now.

After someone dies, it's the voice that lives forever—not even the image of the face. Eventually, *that* fades. But the voice you can summon in your head, it echoes throughout the skull. I could make my mother's voice come to me by concentrating and re-creating it in my head, the soft round tones of her voice. I should try, as an exercise, to eradicate him. The only way to stop the suffering—but right now I just couldn't. Wasn't ready to destroy the memory of him. Still needed to see his image, to picture him with me, I was still in a fresh stage of grief.

We were in the open countryside now, the land rising and falling all around me, snow-covered fields glowing in the darkness. Pine trees lined the roadside, skeletons of deciduous trees. Now and then there was a house, windows dark. People away for the holidays. Scary it was so cold out there, what if the car broke down? There was no one on the road to help. I imagined the scene, mother and son found frozen to death in a snowbank, their car broken down, mother lying as if trying to protect her baby from the cold with her own body, two lost creatures alone and abandoned by the world.

It would be cold in the house when we got home, though the embers in the woodstove sometimes stayed alight. Even before modern insulation, these houses had to stay warm somehow.

I rounded the curve of Church Road and I glanced up automatically toward my house. I could see the faint shape of it, a blur in the dark. A light was on in the window. I didn't remember leaving a light on. I was always careful because electric was the most expensive utility in the county.

At Schermerhorn I made the left, past my mailbox. Here the road dipped and I drove cautiously because of the icy patches. The county didn't plough because this was a private road and Mr. Jukowski did it for us whenever he cleared his barnyard for the milk truck.

We climbed the hill and I could feel the engine straining. C'mon, baby, you can do it! . . . Hope this thing lasts.

All around me, the immense, navy blue sky, the hills dipping and rising, luminous in the moonlight. Belonging to us alone.

We came to the yard, and then I saw it. The red Dodge truck, parked in solitude. And in the window of the house, there was the yellow light.

They always come back, I thought. They always come back. At least once.

CHAPTER 23

TERRY

The front door was unlocked. Inside, the lamp by the couch was burning. But the house was silent, empty seeming, no sign of him. Bobby trailed in behind me. "Shut the door for Mommy, please." It was cold in here, the woodstove must've died out.

I walked into the bedroom. On the bed, under the comforter, was the outline of a body. In the faint light from the other room, I could see part of a face. At first, I didn't recognize it. I could just discern one eye nearly swollen shut, the skin on the cheek blackened. Then the soft, tufty hair, the oval shape of the head, the high cheekbones, the jaw drawing to a point at the chin. "Dean."

He turned. I saw more clearly now in the light from the main room, the whole face swollen, a vertical black line under one of his eyes, little threads sticking out where they had stitched it up.

"What happened?"

He closed his eyes. "Jesus. Oh God."

He lifted his head, caught sight of Bobby behind me. "Hi, Bobby," he said. Then he sank back down on the pillow and closed his eyes.

"What happened?" I asked again.

"I can't talk. I'm so cold. . . ."

"You need a doctor."

His voice was faint. "I saw a doctor."

I turned. "Bobby, honey, you go get ready for bed now."

"Dean?" Bobby said.

"I know, honey. Dean. Go get undressed and put your jammies on for me, okay? Please, honey."

But he lingered. "I need to help Dean," I told him. "You go get undressed for Mommy."

Bobby drifted back into the main room. I knelt down on my knees by the bed, afraid to sit on it for fear of jarring him and hurting him. I pushed the comforter in around the edges of his body. "You're all cut. Please—tell me—what happened?"

He opened his eyes. I could see them, vaguely, in the dark. "Can I stay here?" he said. "I got nowhere to go."

"I guess," I said. Said it after trying to get him arrested and jailed, after wanting to kill him, wanting him dead. All it took was one small request. "Yes. You can."

"I'm hurtin'," he said.

"Oh God . . ."

"You sure I can stay here?"

"Yes, I told you."

From the other room, Bobby called out to me. "Mommy, I can't get the snowsuit off. Mommeeeee!"

"Let me just get him." I hurried out of the bedroom into the main room, unzipped Bobby's snowsuit, pulled it roughly down off his arms and legs, then removed his jeans and sweatshirt till he had on only his little Jockeys and his undershirt.

"Go pee, honey. Quick. Go pee for Mommy."

I heard him tinkling in the bathroom and then he came back in. "Put these on." I helped him into his blue feet pajamas, took him by the hand, and nearly pulled him into his little room. He lay down on his bed obediently—he always knew when I was pushed to the limit.

"What's wrong with Dean?" he asked.

"Dean got hurt, honey. He's gonna be okay."

"Is Dean gonna stay here?"

"For a while. I gotta take care of him now, honey. You go to sleep, okay?"

I turned out the light by the side of his bed.

"I want the night light!" he cried.

I switched on the little Mickey Mouse light in the outlet. There was a soft glow in the room. "No song tonight because Mommy's too tired. Please be a good boy and go to sleep."

"What's wrong with Dean's face?"

"He got hurt."

"Who hurt him?"

"I don't know. Please go to sleep for Mommy. Merry Christmas, honey. You warm enough?"

"Yeah."

"You got Barney?"

"Uh-huh." He was holding the purple Barney in the crook of his arm. Right thumb went to the mouth, left hand twirling a lock of dark hair. A sign he was preparing for sleep.

As I stood there, I felt the walls of the house quiver in the wind, only a thin membrane between us and the great outdoors, the wind and the cold. On the way across the main room, I opened the door to the woodstove and threw in some logs.

Back in the bedroom, he still lay under the comforter.

I could just see the outline of his features, his dear face. I sat down on the edge of the bed. All in one place, beneath my fingertips. I owned him now. I could hear his teeth chattering, felt his body shaking, the mattress vibrating with it.

"I'm so c-cold," he said. "Can you get in beside me?"

I undressed quickly, put on the sweatpants and sweatshirt I usually slept in. "Stand up a minute," I told him, "so I can get the covers down." With difficulty, he sat up and swung his legs over the side of the bed. He stood up and I gripped his arm and pulled the top sheet and comforter away for him. He lay back down again, and I covered him.

I climbed inside next to him, reached out my arms, tried to

push one of them underneath his body so I could hold him, but he jumped. "Ouch!"

"What hurts?"

"Oh God. I want to take a bath. I gotta take a bath. I stink. I feel so dirty. I can't sleep in these sheets like this."

"You don't stink."

"I can smell them. . . . Can you make a bath for me?"

"A bath?" He never took a bath, usually only a shower.

"A shower will hurt too much," he said.

I climbed out of bed again; went into the bathroom and pulled aside the mildewy shower curtain. Turned on the water, rinsed the grit out of the old clawfoot tub with the palm of my hand, then filled it with hot water.

Back in the bedroom, he had propped himself up on his elbows. He pushed his legs across the mattress painfully.

In the full light of the main room, with a shock, I saw his face. One side green and bruised, streaked with yellow where it looked like it had been washed with Betadine. A line cut right through the flesh from his eye to his cheek. The wound was crisscrossed with black thread, the ends sticking out in a stubble.

"Oh babeee," I whispered. "Your face . . . Your jeans got mud on them—and blood. You can't wear those jeans. I can give you sweatpants and a sweatshirt."

He hobbled into the bathroom—and shut the door behind him. Still wouldn't let me see him.

I listened, heard mostly silence, the water sloshing in the tub.

He was in there fifteen minutes or so. When he came out again, he was carrying his clothes rolled tightly in his hand. "I need a plastic bag." I handed him a grocery bag, and he packed the dirty clothes inside and tied the ends together.

In the places where his face was not greenish brown and streaked with yellow, he was pale, there was a deep groove of exhaustion carved under the left eye, the one that wasn't swollen shut.

The woodstove was humming vigorously now, heating up the house.

"What happened to you!"

"They attacked me. Sexually."

"Who's 'they'?"

"Brian and Jimmy."

"Jesus . . ." Trying to understand. Then, I couldn't help it, I asked. "But—what did they do? I mean—" Did they rape him? It was hard to say that word—the word was too terrible to speak out loud. "I mean—? Did they—?"

"Tore me," he replied.

"Oh God." Made me hurt down there just to think of it. I imagined his flesh flat and taut, like silk. "You gotta go to a doctor."

"I went to the hospital. They called in this rape crisis lady. She keeps on me till I tell the cops. They said they'd kill me if I went to the cops! Brian hates me because of Melanie."

I moved away from him, sat down on the couch, rubbing my face with my palms. "You nearly killed me," I told him. "I wanted to die. You lied to me. Then you stole from me."

"The thing is, I had the money to give back to you. I had it in my pocket. I knew I should give it to you. But Terry, I was fuckin' desperate."

"So, where's the money?" I wanted the money returned—as a symbol. I didn't care about the money itself.

"They fuckin' took it," he said. "The cops confiscated it for evidence. They fuckin' took all my money. They took my wallet. I was gonna give it to you, I swear.

"I saw the paper," he said. "That was lies. All lies. All the sex stuff."

But that part didn't matter to me. Whatever he was, I accepted him. All parts of him, all his "deformities." I didn't care anymore *what* he was. Other people didn't understand it. But I did. Anyway, it was like I was in this daze, my sole focus to be with him, as if there was no time at all, no reality—except for Bobby and Dean—

and no time but those long stretched-between moments we were together.

"But what about all those arrests they said you had?"

I was asking him this to give him a chance to wipe it all away, to exonerate himself so we could finally be together.

"That was just little stuff," he said. "From when I was a kid. It was nothing. I was riding around in a car with my buddies, and we were chasing this other car with our friends in it."

"And the check-cashing stuff?"

"That was one time," he said. "Once. I cashed this check belonging to this woman, the mother of a friend of mine. It was twenty-five bucks. Can you believe they would still hold that against me?" And he looked away, stared morosely at the floor.

"But if this hadn't happened, you'd still be with Melanie?" I asked him.

He walked over to the couch, sat down next to me, touched my hand. I saw the skin on his cheek blackening, the bruise spreading out like a dark stain across his face in front of my eyes. He looked at me straight in the eyes, full of honor, deeply serious. "Terry, I never had sex with Melanie Saluggio. I swear. Ask her! I never saw her with her clothes off. That was only—between you and me. I never fucked Melanie."

"No?"

"It wasn't that kind of thing. It was different. We never even saw each other with our clothes off. I swear—"

"Did you kiss her?"

"I kissed her—yeah. But I never fucked her. We never had sex."

"So—but—I thought you loved Bobby. I mean like he was your own? I thought you loved *me*. I was dying."

"I love Melanie. But not the same way. It can never be the same way as with you. Melanie was like my sister."

"Then why did you leave and steal my money?"

"I shouldn't have done it! But I had nothing—nada. I was

totally freaked. I did that before I ever went to stay with Melanie." He cupped my chin in his hand, looked into my eyes. "Now I want to stay with you. I want to stay here forever, Terry. I'm going to make it up to you, all the pain I've caused you."

"Forever?"

He gazed into my face, one dear eye a slit. "Forever," he said, his voice husky. Then he dropped his hand and looked away. "I need to sleep." He looked at me. "I need you to hold me."

"You nearly killed me. I thought I was going to die," I said again.

"I know. It's over now." He was talking like someone in pain, every part of him concentrated just on the hurting in his body. His voice seemed to fade, as if he couldn't talk anymore.

"You still love her?"

"Yeah. I do love her. But like I told you—it's different." He drew his arms around his body, hugging himself. "It's so cold in here. Will you hold me?"

All that Sunday he slept. Slept like a baby, like a sick person, all his energy consumed in the knitting up of his wounds, duplicating cells to bridge the cut, sending out white blood cells to fight the infection, his flesh reabsorbing the old blood from his bruises.

In the morning, Bobby went to the bedroom door and stood looking in and watching. He turned to me. "Dean sick," he said.

"Yeah. He's sick, honey. Let's whisper. Let Dean sleep."

Around three in the afternoon, Dean finally got up. He stumbled around the house in a stupor. His cheek was getting blacker, though the swelling around the eye had diminished.

I gave him dinner, and he sat, dazed-looking, at the table, picking at the chicken nuggets.

"Your name's not on the mailbox?" he asked.

"No. Just the box number. Like before."

"Nobody'll know I'm here," he said, as if reassuring himself. "They think we broke up." As if that were a good thing.

I said nothing to this. He had humiliated me. Now my pain was convenient to his excuse.

The next morning, Monday, I rose, prepared for work, leaving him and Bobby both sleeping. On my way into Sparta, I stopped at my dad's, left the car motor running, and ran upstairs to his apartment to tell him I wouldn't be bringing Bobby today because of Dean's return. "Sure, honey," he said. He didn't question me, ask me about Dean, where he had been. Anything I wanted was okay.

Now as I drove to work, the sun sparkled off the crusty snow and the road ahead of me and behind me was deserted, everyone away between Christmas and New Year.

At 7:50 A.M. sharp, I arrived at the Home. I was always early. Mr. Ford was there sitting by the front door in his wheelchair, paper bib under his chin, waiting for me. I knew what he wanted. It was always the same.

I pushed through the door. "Hi, Mr. Ford. You have a good Christmas?"

Mr. Ford mumbled something into his chest, his cataracty eyes staring into nothing, his white hair shaved close to his head, his legs hanging atrophied and lifeless over the wheelchair. I gripped the back of the chair and pushed him away from the door. "It's cold here, Mr. Ford. You'll catch the death." He mumbled again, and I leaned down to hear him. "What's that?"

"My wife," Mr. Ford said. "I gotta speak to my wife."

"Mr. Ford, sweetheart, your wife is dead. You know she's gone, sweetheart. I told you that."

He looked puzzled. "Yeah yeah . . ."

Inside the Home, the sunlight hit the waxy linoleum floor. A salmony pink line was painted all along the cream walls so the people with Alzheimer's could follow it and find their way back to their rooms. There were posters of exotic places, Hawaiian waterfalls, the Eiffel Tower . . . places we would never go.

Chrissie Peck was walking toward me down the hall and I

smiled brightly at her. Chrissie was always slow in the morning, like she was in a daze and wanted you to feel sorry for her or something because she had to get up early to go to work. Sometimes she was late, or didn't even show up, and it annoyed the hell out of me, but Chrissie was one of my few good people otherwise. Had a real feeling for the clients, could listen to their stories over and over again. I didn't have the patience. It was hard to find people with compassion, hard to find people who wanted to work hard. You would have thought they would want to work, would want the money. But you can't get people to work these days.

I thought, don't tell Chrissie Dean is back. Don't say anything.

"Chrissie, can you take Mr. Ford to the day room? Mr. Ford, they're having aerobics this morning. Why don't you let Chrissie take you?" I said.

Mr. Ford's chin jutted forward, it was covered in a white stubble. "Chrissie, better give Mr. Ford a shave."

"Mrs. Oakley threw her food tray down again," Chrissie said. "She's mad. She's demanding to be 'released.' "

"Maybe we're going to have to put her in restraints," I said.

I caught sight of B.J. with his mop. "B.J., there's a spill in twelve. Mrs. Oakley got mad and threw her tray down. Can you get that before someone slips on it?"

"No problem," B.J. said. Someone told me B.J. was in radar in the army. Now this is the only job he could get around here. Sometimes I wondered if B.J. was a user. The way his blue eyes— though he was black—were all rheumy and floaty. One of those users who keeps it to himself, could still function. Well, as long as he does his job, doesn't steal . . .

Mr. Hanley was in his office on the phone. His ugly kids' school pictures lined up on his desk, orangey-color skin, deep shadows on their faces. Mr. Hanley was having a fight with someone. "They didn't deliver Friday," he was saying into the phone. Linen delivery. The same contractor serviced all the hospitals and nursing homes in the area. "You said it would be Friday. . . ."

He looked up. "Terry."

"Hi, Mr. Hanley." He was only a couple of years older than me, yet he was my boss and he called me by my first name, while I called him by instinct Mr. Hanley.

"Terry, can you work Saturday night—four to twelve overtime? Time and a half. I was counting on Chrissie, but now she says she can't."

"I gotta check it out with my dad and Bobby." I wanted to be with Dean.

"I have to know by tomorrow. My wife's on me. She's planned this party."

"I'll ask my dad. What happened with the linen?"

"They say the driver didn't come in Friday. Now they're trying to get someone to bring it over today."

I wanted to be with *him* New Year's, alone with him.

All day long, working in the community of the Nightingale Home, not telling anyone. Without this job, I'd die. Why is it that for some people, things can only be right in one area of their lives, either in work or in love? But never both. God doesn't let you have both. *My* area was work; things were right for me in work, but not love.

Right from the start I had done well at the Home. I just worked harder than anyone else. Maybe I just knew somewhere that one day I'd have to take care of Bobby on my own. After only a few months our supervisor left and Mr. Hanley asked me if I could do the job, which would mean $3.40 an hour extra. "You're as well equipped as anyone," he said. "You know the place." And so I got the job, and over other people who'd been there longer.

All day long, my mind back there in the house, on Dean. One thing I can trust is Dean with Bobby. He loves Bobby like his own. Bobby would be in heaven today with Dean back. Bobby brings out the kid in Dean, lets Dean be the little boy he always wanted to be, gives Dean permission. For Bobby's Christmas present, I'd found some beginners' Legos at the Salvation Army. No diagrams or instructions, but the kind with the big holes to make it easier for younger children. They would spend the day building something with it.

Now, at the Home, checking my charts. Mrs. Alderfer on sulfa for her bladder infection, three times a day at meals. . . . Mrs. Cross, probable eczema recurrence in her ear. Picking at it, bleeding. Need doctor's app't. . . . Mrs. O'Connor wandering again. Speak to Dr. Vakil. . . .

Four P.M. on the dot I leave. Outside I hurry across the parking lot to my car. The sky is already darkening. On the other side of the river, to the west, the sun is like a burning coin, and it hurts the eyes to look at it, leaves an afterimage. And the rumble of the cement plant fills the valley like familiar music.

I stop at Food Mart. No one here I know, only that woman from behind the counter at CVS pushing her cart. No one knows my secret. I glide up and down the brightly lit aisles, filling my cart. It's so cold in here I have to keep my gloves on. In my head, I organize the week's needs. Frozen pizza one night, hamburger the next, fish sticks, tartar sauce, cans of pork and beans for Dean and Bobby. I buy candles—pink and silvery aqua—for the evening, after Bobby has gone to bed, when we are going to make love. New dish towels. Nesting. Is it possible we've got something in our hormones that makes us, when we are in love, want to nest, to rearrange twigs and bits of things like a female bird does? Once the father of the baby bird is in place, once the family is complete, you are forever arranging twigs with your beak. . . . You want to bring in supplies, make everything warm and soft.

Now in the supermarket, there's a chill on my skin . . . cans of Mountain Dew, Skittles, all the things he likes . . .

At the checkout counter, while I wait for the clerk to punch in the prices, I pull the *Ledger-Republican* out of the rack. When I get to the police blotter, I see the story. "Police Question Two Sparta Men, Then Release Them in Connection With Rape of

West Taponac Woman." "Name of victim not released. . . . Police say rape occurred in the parking lot of the Wooden Nickel at around midnight Christmas Eve. . . . Victim has a criminal record, check cashing, fraud, criminal impersonation. . . . Two Sparta men, James Vladeck and Brian Perez, have been questioned and released. . . . Investigation continuing."

So, they're out. Free. Roaming around. Now they know that Dean went to the cops.

I glance around the huge room, people bent over the bins of produce, poking at the fruits and vegetables, squeezing them, turning cans of food around and around to inspect them. No one here I recognize—except that woman from CVS. I write out the check, push the shopping cart filled with my brown paper bags out through the automatic doors into the parking lot.

The parking lot is crowded with vehicles. I load up my car, start it up, then I have to wait in a line at the exit. Eventually, the tangle of vehicles breaks and I'm heading out toward West Taponac.

Driving away from Sparta, into the open countryside, my car is the only one on the road.

I approach West Taponac. As I reach Schermerhorn Road, as my car rounds the curve, I glance up at the hill, at my house. Behind it, the ridge of trees, the skeletal shapes of oak and chestnut.

And there is my house, the square shape visible against the lit sky. Don't see Dean's truck. But there's a yellow glow in the windows. He is waiting for me.

Inside, there was a scene of quiet, tense, domestic life. "Hi, guys!"

Dean and Bobby hardly looked up when I entered, they were building a giant Lego assembly, a community with houses and walls, and driving Bobby's trucks along the road. Dean really was a guy, the way he liked Lego and building things. A girl would never do this.

"You parked the truck behind the house?" I said.

"So it couldn't be seen from the road."

"Your eye's going down," I told him, though the skin on his cheek was an even more lurid green than before. Maybe it has to get blacker before it heals, I thought.

He stood up from the floor, came toward me, kissed me on the lips for the first time since his return. I remembered again the feeling of those big, soft lips, lips like cushions, the dry, chapped skin. His tongue prodded my lips and I kissed him back, my tongue poking through to find his, all the pores of my skin like flowers opening up to him. Bobby, sitting on the floor with the Lego, gazed up at us. "I got the paper," I said.

He broke away from the kiss and snatched it from my hand. "They questioned Brian and Jimmy," I told him.

He raked through the pages till he came to the police blotter, then read avidly. "I knew it!" he cried. "They let 'em go." He paused, staring across the room at something, thinking. Then he sat down on the couch, the newspaper flat across his lap, still looking out into the room. "Now they know I went to the police. They said they'd kill me if I told anyone."

"They're full of bullshit," I said. "They won't do anything. Anyway, they don't know where you are. Nobody knows."

But he was looking right through me.

"You'll be okay here," I said. "They don't know where you are. They don't know about me."

Bobby walked up to him on the couch, tugged at his arm. "Dean. Play with me. Play with me, Dean, play with me." Little high-pitched voice. But Dean was still staring into space, didn't look at him, as of he was in some kind of trance.

"Honey," I said to Bobby. "Dean played with you all day. He's talking to Mommy now. Leave Dean be."

As soon as Bobby is asleep, I go to Dean in my bed. I lie down beside him, and almost immediately, his fresh, wet tongue is inside my mouth. Welcome home! Picking right up where we left off.

Yanking up my sweatshirt, he's at my nipples with his tongue.

Driving me nuts . . . can't take it . . . where to go from here. It is torment, and I think he's going to give me relief, but then he finds someplace new with his tongue. At last, pulling down my sweat-pants, finding the place so easily, his lovely wet tongue between my legs, then pushing inside and out, then filling the space. Getting hot . . . hotter. . . . Bedsprings squeaking. I giggle. Can Bobby hear us? No lock on the door and in the middle of it all, I climb out of the bed, brace the back of the chair under the doorknob, and I return. He is healed, all better now.

CHAPTER 24

CHRISSIE

We all knew what had happened. Even though the paper didn't name the rape victim. Everybody knew Brian was crazy jealous of Dean, and they'd all been seen together that night at the Wooden Nickel. The victim had a record, for criminal impersonation. The paper said Brian and Jimmy had been questioned in the case, and then released and were not suspects at this moment.

We had left him there alone in the parking lot with Brian and Jimmy. I'd wanted to take him home with me, but he wouldn't go. Was afraid of leaving his truck there. His truck was all he had in the world. I wanted to get out of there. The violence of what they were doing to him frightened me, and Melanie's anger. I was afraid she'd attack Brian physically and then get herself killed.

A few days after the item in the paper, Brian and Jimmy appeared again at the Wooden Nickel, Brian edgy and over-friendly suddenly, as if he knew he had almost been caught, eyes darting nervously about the room all the time, as if he was looking for someone, as if he was waiting for Dean to arrive. But he was defiant too, he knew he'd gotten away with it.

He disgusted me. I knew what he had done. He was the same as a killer almost. And I kept away from him. Brian was sickness and evil walking among us.

But most people seemed to tolerate Brian. They figured Dean had asked for it, taunting people with his disguise. Dean had challenged everyone, held himself up as a target. He had fucked with Brian. They figured Dean must have wanted it somehow. He was a weirdo, a freak, not subject to ordinary protections.

Meanwhile, Dean had completely disappeared this time. No one had seen him in days. And I knew, watching Brian and Jimmy, that they were uneasy about his absence, and perpetually on the lookout for him.

CHAPTER 25

TERRY

Tuesday, drove to work again. Had my secret life now. My own world—Dean, the husband, our child, the daily routine. Work. Return. Get food on the table, my body alert, tense under his gaze, his little smile, waiting only for Bobby to go to bed, knowing he knew that I was just waiting. Then, when Bobby was in bed, making love. Making love over and over again, our own world of the night.

And each time we made love, it was like entering a new room, a different place. A door would open and then close behind us; and beyond that, there was another passageway and then another door opening and another.

Money was a problem. Car insurance plus the car needed new tires. Mr. Schmidt, who sold it to me, had been totally honest about that. You gotta get new tires before the snow, he said. And now, I was buying food for Dean too. "I don't want you to support me," Dean said. "I feel bad I don't have anything. But I can't look for a job now." When this blew over, he'd get a job. I knew he really meant it. He had only stolen my money because he was desperate.

But then, why hadn't he *asked* me for money? I would've given it to him. I would've given him the world.

Fact is, I had to let him have his head. It was inevitable he'd come back, because he couldn't have what he had with me with anyone else in the world. No way. I believed him truly when he said he never fucked Melanie Saluggio. With me it was different. With me he dared to show part of himself he'd never shown anyone before. I thought, just wait, he will be mine for good.

That night, after Bobby is in bed, we smoke some dope. Then, he gets me ready, torturing me with his tongue and his hard little fingertips pinching my nipples, and working the little knob between my legs, so hard it almost hurts and we are just on this side of his really hurting and I almost can't stand it anymore. "Please," I say, "please," my voice caught in the back of my throat, and I'm ashamed, but need overcomes my shame. "Please," I say, wanting him to stop, to continue, to go on, and I hear a little chuckle come from the back of his throat. Suddenly he stops. The air grows cool and still around us. He's propped above me, leans over me on his fists. I can sense his smile in the dark.

"Y'know," he says, "I didn't know you had it in you!" And then, "Hah!" he throws his head back, gives a laugh, and he plunges down again between my legs, where it is wet like the ocean, and water is flowing from me and it's like he's swimming underwater and he could drown there, both our bodies wet.

Afterward, I lie there with my cheek against his back. "When I first saw you," he says. "You reminded me of like—a teacher or something. You seemed . . . older than you are. I didn't know you had it in you!" And he laughs. "You know, when I saw you, I liked the way you looked, but I didn't know you were beautiful."

His words hurt me. "What do you mean?" I say. "You didn't think I was beautiful?"

"You had those thick glasses. Didn't do anything to your hair . . . It was all straight and everything."

Same old thing. I am not beautiful. And I know it. My nose is too big. Always red in the cold. Even in summer, it's red.

"But now I know," he says. "Now I know. And it's my secret." He turns, smiles his cocky smile. "You are beautiful. But it's private, for me only. . . ."

Then suddenly he lunges at me—"*Look* at those tits!" He cups both my breasts in his hands, pushing them up so they are almost under my chin. "Look at those big titties!" He's practically hissing. "*Mine!* All mine! Everyone thinks you're a prude. But *I* know. I know, don't I?"

And down he goes again, my deep-sea diver, swimming, swimming, swimming. . . . "Didn't know you were beautiful till you met me," he says from down between my legs, "did you?"

"Nuunh . . ." I can hardly talk.

His face buried in my bush. "I think of you, Miss Prim and Proper, they're all scared of you, Chrissie and B.J. You tell them what to do. . . . If they only knew what you're *really* like!" And he's at me like he's starving or something, a starving person, and I'm laughing because I've never known anyone so outrageous, so *ba-a-ad!*

"Let me do it to you," I whisper, with my last breath. "You deserve it. I don't want to be the only one. . . ."

"No," he says. And then he stops suddenly, and pulls his legs together.

Getting up in the middle of the night, I walk to the bathroom, switch on the light. I look at myself in the mirror on the medicine chest, and I realize, I *am* beautiful, even in this sleepworn state. My skin is creamy and smooth like a girl's. I never wear makeup because it makes my skin feel all stiff, like soap is left on it, and lipstick makes my lips chapped. But now Dean makes me feel that I don't need makeup anyhow.

Standing in front of the bathroom mirror, I remove my glasses—hate those fishy-eyed things, always make those deep red ridges on the sides of my nose. It's the glasses that end it once and for all, I think, end any chance of my ever being pretty. But my eyes were too bad for contacts, I'd be blind without my glasses.

I lean in closer to the bathroom mirror, I can see that my eyes are luminous from fucking, and my hair, my no-color brown, sort-of-slate-gray hair—though not gray in the sense that the color has gone from it with age—is clean and shiny and polished-looking now. My breasts high and full, my waist curved—when he touches it, it's like an electric shock. There is another kind of beauty, I think. Men like my kind of looks too. He is the only one who has ever made me feel beautiful and now I can look at myself in any light, and it is true I am beautiful.

Later, on my way back to the room, I glance in at Bobby asleep in his room. In the faint glow from the night light I can see the outline of his form. He sleeps on his back, arms thrown wide, legs apart, head to the side, mouth open. I step into the room, bend down over him. He's sweating, his cheeks are red, strands of dark hair stuck to the sweet white skin of his forehead. It's too hot in here, even in winter sometimes with the woodstove. Those sleepers are really hot and I unzip the top a few inches, pull the comforter down to give him some air.

In my bedroom, Dean sleeps on his side, his back to me. He always sleeps that way, in his own private world. So warm in here, I can smell the night smells, the odor of warm hair, of sweat from lovemaking, the fishy, salty smell of sex.

Dean mutters something, then flips over suddenly on his back. I lean down, my ear close to his mouth, trying to catch his words. His lips are moving. . . . I hear a grinding sound coming from the back of his throat, a sound like a whimpering, a sound meant to be words, but not words.

I whisper, "Wake up, honey. You're dreaming. Wake up."

And his eyes suddenly open wide. He jerks up in bed, stares straight ahead, unseeing. He's still in his dream. He turns his face in my direction, seems to focus on me a second, then lies back down again. "Jesus," he mutters. "Jesus . . ."

Next morning at the Nightingale Home, I'm counting out meds at the nurse's station when I see Chrissie coming toward me, pushing her chart wagon.

"You're lookin' good these days, Terry." Chrissie speaks fearfully, respectfully. I'm her boss. "Like you're gettin' rest."

"Thank you, Chrissie." Have to keep aloof from her.

I can tell she wants to say something more, but is afraid. I hear her take a breath. "You seen Dean around, Terry?" she asks. Fake nonchalance, like she's scared to bring up the subject.

"Haven't seen him. Anyone else seen him? How *is* he?"

She hesitates. Like she knows the truth. "You heard about what happened?"

"No, what happened?"

"You didn't read the paper?"

"Nope," I lie. I keep my eyes on my rows of tiny paper cups. "Two ampicillin, Mr. Ford . . . septra, Mrs. Alderfer . . ."

"Dean said Brian and Jimmy attacked him. They raped him or something. It was in the paper. They didn't use Dean's name. But it was him. You didn't see?"

I look up from my counting. "That's terrible," I say, as if hearing about the death of a stranger. "I'm really sorry. That's terrible." Pretending shock that I actually do feel.

Chrissie is staring at me. She knows I'm lying about not hearing, but she's afraid to challenge me. My reaction is too calm to be true.

"I wish Dean well," I say. "But he's not really part of my life now."

"They took Brian and Jimmy in for questioning and then they let them go because Dean was a known liar," Chrissie says. "The cops already had him on that check-cashing charge from you, so they figured he was an unreliable witness.

"Now the Rape Crisis people are pressuring the cops. They say just because he's gay doesn't mean he can't get raped . . ."

I don't look at her, but I feel her dark eyes scrutinizing me. "Guess that's right," I tell her.

That evening, arriving home, I find him on the floor, stretched out against the couch, watching Bobby. He's smoking—wish he wouldn't do that, because of Bobby's asthma. But I can't tell him not to.

"How'd it go today?" I ask.

"He's a good boy," he says.

"Did he cough?"

"Not once." Bobby is pushing his yellow plastic truck along the floor, making engine noises, "Thrum . . . thrummm . . ."

"I got a piece of steak to broil for tonight. And wine, Folinari, to wash it down." Every night a celebration.

"Good," he says. "We went out in back."

"You didn't drive anywhere?"

"Didn't want to take the truck out and be seen."

I remove my coat, hang it on the hook, turn on the oven to broil. "Chrissie came up to me at work today. Asked if you was with me."

He looks up. "Does Brian know where you live?"

"How could he? Unless Chrissie says something . . . and I told her I hadn't seen you."

"He said he'd kill me."

"He's not gonna do anything. They'd know it was him right away."

"I shouldn't have told the cops."

Something in him enjoyed this drama, I thought. "You're being melodramatic," I said. "This is real life."

"Real life is they fuckin' attacked me! They ripped me apart."

Bobby had stopped playing, holding the yellow truck in midair. How much did he understand? He shouldn't hear this.

I walked over to Dean and touched his arm. "I know, baby," I said. But inside myself, I still didn't know what he meant, what had actually happened. People sometimes said they were sexually attacked and it wasn't true, just said it because they were mad. The feminists created that. There was something in Dean, I thought, that was drawn to Brian and Jimmy, drawn to trouble like a bee to nectar. He wanted them to notice him.

"Poor baby," I said softly. "I love you. Ain't nothin' gonna happen to you. If they come near you, the cops'll know it's them. Just lay low awhile. They'll get themselves in trouble sooner or later."

I started dinner, unwrapped the meat. I'd bought it on sale. It was grayish, larded with fat, and now I lathered it with steak sauce.

"I don' want Dean to go to jail," Bobby said suddenly, worry on his face. "Is Dean going to jail, Mommy?"

"Dean's not going to jail, honey," I told him.

I studied Dean. What part did I love about him best—that groove on the back of his neck, where the hair was all soft and fuzzy? Tonight I would like to run my tongue down that groove, feel the fur on my tongue. Only with your tongue can you really feel, more than with your fingertips.

Today his hair is shiny again—you can see streaks of sun at the ends, golden strands in the brown, then it gets darker at the roots, almost chestnut in color. His hair is so soft. I see the beautiful white teeth between his lips, the long lashes that curl . . .

His fingertips go to his cheek, to the wound underneath his eyes, and he scratches at it, tentatively. "Fuckin' thing itches like hell."

"You're supposed to go back and get them taken out."

"I'm not going back there! You kidding?"

I scrutinize the ugly black strands. There are puncture marks in the skin from the needle.

"The nurse at work says when it starts to itch, that means it's healing."

"I know how to take them out," I tell him.

So, after supper, I sit him down in a chair underneath the floor lamp. I pour rubbing alcohol on a piece of kleenex, wipe the nail scissors and tweezers, lay them out side by side on another tissue as if I'm going to perform surgery.

I dab at his cheek with the alcohol. He gets up from the chair and starts hopping around the room. "Shit!" he shouts. "That burns! It burns!"

"You gotta disinfect it," I say. "Sit down."

He obeys and sits down again, I peer at the cheek, snip at the black strands, pulling them out one by one with the tweezers. "Owowowow . . ." he cries, jerking his cheek away from my hands. "Fuckin' owwwww!"

"Stay still. Can't you say anything but 'fuck'?"

"Fuck! Fuckin' hurts!"

Bobby stands at my elbow, studying the operation. He keeps getting his head in the way so I can't see. "Honey, can you move? Mommy can't see."

"Where'd you learn this?" Dean asks.

"Watching the nurses at work at the Home." I love being so close to his face in the light. Usually, when we are close together it's dark. He always wants the light out when we make love.

Now, under the light, I can see he has long blond hairs on his cheeks, especially under the cheekbones and above his upper lip and along the jawline. Like a teenage boy's before he shaves, golden hairs, lighter than the hair on his head. His eyes glow, almost feverish with health. I have the power to hurt him, I think, he is under my hands.

His flannel shirt gives off its distinctive clean fragrance of cotton. There's always the smell of fresh air on Dean, his breath is like sweet apples. He trusts me. If I tore at those stitches, I could hurt him.

"You'll have a scar," I say. "They should've called a plastic surgeon in for a face wound."

And suddenly, he smiles. "Good! I *want* a scar! Right under my eye! A scar'll look good."

What did I know about him? What did I know except that he could betray me?

Dean was like water, always changing to fit the form around it, moving faster than you could grasp, forever out of reach. The more you reached for Dean, the further away he slipped from you. Love goes beyond betrayal, I think. Love is a burden, love is a curse.

CHAPTER 26

MELANIE

When Dean got arrested for the check-cashing charge with Terry, and I bailed him out, Mommy went berserk. "You used the hairdresser money—I can't believe it! Two hundred dollars!"

And she wouldn't let Dean come back and live with us—because of AIDS, she said, and I said we aren't even having sex, how could he give me AIDS, but she said, she's gay isn't she, gay people carry AIDS. I said "But Dean isn't gay!" "She's gay," Mommy said.

And then, for the first time after the check-cashing arrest, I saw him at the Wooden Nickel, and I was like a person in the desert dying of thirst coming upon a pool of water.

Later I read in the paper about what happened in the parking lot of the Wooden Nickel after Chrissie and I drove away that night. I knew the victim was Dean, it was him they raped, knew it was my love, and those animals had done it to him.

He had gone, gone from my life. I didn't know where he was, if he had returned to his parents' house up in St. Pierre, or if he was hiding out somewhere in the county. I called Chrissie Peck and she didn't know where he was either.

I could only think of him, of seeing him again. During the day, when my mom went to work, I would watch TV, hoping the phone would ring and it would be him.

I prayed hard as I could, my jaw clenched. "Please Jesus, make him come back to me. I'll do whatever you want. Please Jesus." If I prayed hard enough I could bring him back to me through sheer will and effort.

I didn't care about anything. Eating. Getting dressed in the morning. It was like I was in mourning for him, one of those Indian widows who when their husbands die, burn themselves to death on his funeral pyre.

Sometimes I'd walk into town and just wander through the streets, hoping to catch sight of him. I had no car, but I'd walk along the road through snow and rain, my coat flapping open around me, hoping that we would find one another, I didn't care. I couldn't feel anything, the cold and the rain meant nothing to me. And the cars would slow down next to me, their headlights on because it was so dark out, and the drivers would stare at me, this weird girl walking alone along the highway.

I didn't care about the snow and cold. I was desperate, searching for him, wanting my sweet guy.

I'd started smoking, and I'd make that the point of my walk, going to the CVS in Sparta every day to buy my cigarettes.

One afternoon, the snow was coming down hard, but I went out anyway. I pushed my way along Route 7, through waves of whiteness. It seemed like I was the only person outside in the whole of Sparta. But I didn't feel cold even though it was storming all around me. Somehow it was warmer when the snow fell like this, the snow was like a blanket. I'd be freezing when I went inside and thawed out, but for now I was okay, and so I kept on going.

The whole city had shut down. Ahead of me on the road the snow was piling up, soft and white and clean where there was usually gray slush.

Turning down Washington Street, I saw ahead of me the lights from CVS, which was always open no matter what the weather.

I went inside, a lone clerk stood behind the counter, a young woman. I was the only customer in the place. I bought my Marlboros, and I stepped outside again, back into the snow.

As I began walking up Washington Street through the blur of air I saw this vague, red shape, ahead of me, emerging through the white.

As I drew closer, the shape became more distinct and I saw that it was his truck parked on the curb. I drew nearer and I saw, through the snow melting on the windshield, the outline of his head, the flesh of his face. He had been waiting for me.

I ran to the truck and hammered on the window, and he rolled it down.

"Dean! I've been looking everywhere for you! Are you all right? Tell me you're not hurt!"

"Baby . . ." he said softly.

I clutched at the glass, wanted to tear it away, the barrier between us.

Inside the truck, next to him, strapped to the seat, was the little boy, *her* boy, bundled up in a blue snowsuit, blue wool cap on his head, scarf wound round his neck, staring at me.

"Where've you been! Oh God! Oh I've been so worried. I read in the paper what happened. I knew it was you. Those animals!" I spat out the words. "Those pigs!"

"I've been driving around looking for you," he said.

"Did they hurt you? Did they hurt you bad?"

I couldn't imagine what they had done. I couldn't bear it.

"I'm okay," he said, and there was something noble about the way he said it, and that he didn't want to tell me any more.

I looked at the boy. "Where's its mother?" I couldn't bear to give the kid a name, to refer to him directly. To give *her* that. I was punishing the child too, by not saying his name, though he couldn't understand.

"She's working," he said. "A lot of people didn't come in today because of the snow."

"You're staying with her?"

"I got nowhere else to go," he said.

He saw the pack of cigarettes in my hand. "You smoking?"

"I got no reason to live now," I said. "Are you okay?" I asked again. We had to talk loud over the throb of the truck engine. I could feel my feet burning in the snow now that I was standing still, like I had frostbite.

"I'm fine," he said. "Right, Bobby?" He glanced at the boy. He was being brave. But the little boy just kept staring up at me silently, like I was an alien or something.

"How's your mom?" Dean asked. "I'm sorry she's pissed at me."

"She's not pissed. Just ignorant."

"I can't give you AIDS," he said. "We never did anything."

"I know." He said it as if it were all right with him, that we never "did anything," when with me it was not all right. Which was something I couldn't figure out because at the same time I respected him so much for not coming on to me, for not just loving me for sex.

"He's getting cold in there," I said of the boy. "You shouldn't keep the window open."

"You look bad, Mellie," he said.

"I don't care." He had said it almost as a criticism, that I wasn't beautiful anymore, though I knew he meant I looked sick.

"You eating right?"

"I can't eat. I don't care. I don't care if I die."

"Don't say that," he said.

"Do you love her?" I asked, through the snow. That was all I could care about now, since I couldn't give him shelter, just the words, just let him say the right words.

"I love her," he said. "But not the way I love you. You're soaked," he said. "I could take you home in the truck. . . ." He looked guilty, uneasy. "But I'm scared. Brian said he'd kill me. I can't let him see me with you."

"Please," I begged. "Say you love me again."

"I love you," he said.

The snow was falling down around us harder now, completely enveloping us. "You having sex with her?" I asked.

"No," he said. He looked me straight in the eye. "No. It's not like that."

And I believed him. Once words are spoken, they hang there in the air, hard as diamonds.

He rose up from the seat toward me, touched his lips to mine. For a moment, I could feel his warm breath fanning my face. He touched his lips to mine. Then, "I better go," he said. "I don't want them to see me." The boy's lips were trembling. "He's getting cold."

"I love you," he said. And he reached up again and touched my lips. He looked at me intently. "Nothing else matters. No matter what happens, Mellie, you'll always feel it inside you, the love. Once it's there, it stays forever. Even if I die, it stays there."

"Don't say that!" I cried. "Don't say 'die'!"

But he rolled the window up now, and then I heard the grinding sound of the gears and he was pulling away from the curb. I still touched the window with both hands, walking alongside the moving truck as if to keep him there.

I let my hands drop. He was moving up the street. I could just make out, in the rear window, his face turned back toward me, looking at me.

I watched the truck move up Washington, and within seconds, the red shape disappeared, blending into the whirling snow.

CHAPTER 27

TERRY

Four P.M. at the Nightingale Home, when work ended, I said good-bye to Chrissie and I went outside. I could hear the sound of the cement plant filling the valley, echoing against the cliffs as usual. Down below, the river was the color of liquid steel, the sky above it pale, yellowish in the cold, the mountains beyond like gray shadows in the air. A strong wind swept in off the water, and I wrapped my wool scarf tight and pulled on my mittens.

Across the parking lot, a figure leaned against a car, watching the entrance to the Home. At first I couldn't make out who it was. The person was forlorn-looking. I could see the fuzzy, long, pale blond hair. His parka was unbuttoned, his shoulders were hunched over, he was smoking a cigarette. There was something broken about him. He didn't have a hat on in the cold, or gloves. Brian Perez. I wondered how long he'd been there waiting.

He caught sight of me, threw his cigarette to the ground, walked across the lot toward me. "Terry." His voice echoed in the cold. No one but us here.

I stopped. "Yeah?"

"I'm looking for Lily Dean."

His eyes had big black pupils, looked almost as big as the iris itself. I wondered if the holes in his eyes went all the way back into his brain.

"I don't know who you're talking about," I said.

"I mean Lily Dean."

"I don't know Lily Dean." I was carrying my car keys in my hand in readiness and now I brushed past him and leaned down to unlock the door.

"You know who I mean."

I stood up straight and faced him. I was his height, maybe an inch taller. I was pulling my schoolmarm bit.

"No. I don't know Lily Dean." Best loyalty I could give Dean—call him what he wanted to be called, respect that. Define him as he wanted to be defined. That was the most profound loyalty you could give someone.

I unlocked the car door, and I slid down into the front seat. But he put his hand on the door and I slammed it shut quick so he had to pull his hand away or it would've chopped his fingers off.

I backed the car back out of the parking space, wheels spinning in the slush, and made a U-turn. And then I slid down the driveway of the Home, leaving him there, looking after me, his parka unbuttoned in the cold.

When I got home that night to West Taponac, I told Dean, "Brian Perez was in the parking lot at work."

"Now he knows I'm with you. He knows how to find me. He's gonna follow you here. You can't go to work anymore."

Bobby was sitting up at the round oak table, crayoning something, a project that Dean had started. He seemed absorbed but I wondered how much he understood. "I got to work," I said. "How're we going to eat?"

Dean paced about the room, punching his fist into the palm of his hand, peering into the corners as if searching for something. "He's gonna kill me. He'll kill you too—and Bobby. He's capable of that. He set fire to his landlord's apartment building."

It's the mention of Bobby that does it to me. I look at Bobby, sitting up at the table, his feet not even touching the floor yet, the tendrils of dark hair against his pale skin. Bobby's been quieter lately, watchful, as if he knows something is up, as if he's afraid and trying to understand. He doesn't look at us, but I know he hears everything.

I say to Dean, "I've got sick days coming. I'll take a few days off. Till it dies down."

Later that night something wakes me. I climb out of bed, walk into the bathroom. Through the little rectangular window, I can see only wave after wave of white fields, and silence. I see the ridge in the distance, and a faint light behind the trees, beginning to blend through the sky. No sign of animal tracks on the icy surface of the snow. I study the contours of the fields, so smooth and white, as if they are bathed in all the reflected light of the universe. This inhospitable land.

Mr. Jukowski's barn is down the road, out of sight. That big brown bear they talked about in the *Ledger-Republican,* it must still be somewhere out there. If bears get hungry enough in winter, if the snow is deep enough, they'll approach your house, they'll forage. Hunger makes them unafraid.

It's so still here. I can hear a faint crackling from inside the woodstove, the embers still lit even after all night. In the kitchen beyond, the dishes are stacked clean on the drainer, Bobby's toys picked up, put away for the night in his basket. There is the faint tick tick tick of the clock on the wall.

I walk over to Bobby's room and peer in. The little night light sends out a faint, warm glow into the room. I see Bobby is sleeping with his back to the door. The two of them, I think, the two I love most in the world, so still here under my protection.

Back in the main room, I sit down on the saggy couch. I'm wide awake, as if it's morning.

Then I hear a sound. I look up and Bobby's standing in the doorway to his room, rubbing his eyes.

"Why're you up, honey?"

But he only rubs his little fists into his eyes more fiercely, and I realize he's sleepwalking.

"Wanna go pee-pee?"

He nods, rubbing at his eyes now as if he's trying to gouge them out. I take his hand and lead him into the bathroom, unzip his sleeper pajamas, and stand over him while he aims in the bowl.

He does all this automatically, and then I pick him up and carry him back to bed, his head resting in the crook of my neck, fast asleep.

That night, the real snow came. A blinding blizzard, the air outside went solid white, so that you couldn't see in front of your eyes. A heavy wind was pushing behind the storm and it was impossible to leave, but we had enough wood stacked on the porch to last for months. We were trapped, warm and cosy.

In the early morning of the next day Mr. Jukowski drove up the hill and plowed us out. I could see him from the window up on his plow, red wool hat, face red too from the weather.

Midmorning I drove cautiously out to the Taponac convenience store on the Parkway to buy some food. The store had mostly canned goods, frozen pizza, supplies for campers. Everything was more expensive here, but I didn't want to go into town.

That night for dinner we had frozen pizza and leftover wine, which was sour, but went right through my body anyway. I wanted Bobby in bed, wanted him asleep so I could be alone with Dean. "It's late," I said to Bobby.

"I don't wanna. . . ." Bobby said, knowing I meant it was time for bed.

"Look!" I cried. "Look at the snow!" I pointed to the window, trying to distract him. The flakes were falling again, harder. "You gotta go to sleep so you can get enough rest and play in the morning."

"Not sleepy," he said irritably, showing me he was sleepy.

"Let's have a bath. That'll help you sleep. . . . He doesn't get out enough," I said to Dean. "He didn't get out today so he's not tired."

After his bath, Bobby made me read to him, *Green Eggs and*

Ham. I recited the words of the book mechanically, knew them almost by heart. Felt guilty because reading to him should be a pleasure, but he was delaying me and I just wanted to finish it so I could be alone with Dean.

So I raced through the book, and when I finished, I slapped it shut, and led Bobby into his room. "You go to sleep now," I said, firmly, almost cruelly, I realized. Usually I was not firm enough with Bobby, let him do almost whatever he wanted to do. But he knew I meant business now, and he went down without any more fuss.

When I went back into the main room, Dean was standing at his usual spot by the kitchen window, looking out. It was as if he was drawn to that window irresistibly, as if it was a magnet. But there was nothing there but the steady beat of snowflakes, all lit up near the house by the light from the window.

"Nobody can drive up on that road now," Dean said. "He won't even be able to plow in the morning."

"They always plow, not matter what."

"Not if it keeps up like this."

The TV was on. It was *Roseanne.* The voices were chattering, and every couple of minutes there was a splutter of laughter. I hated Roseanne, there was something crazy about her eyes.

A weather bulletin moved across the base of the screen. "Winter storm warning . . . accumulations up to twenty inches . . ."

Abruptly, he turned the TV off. "Can't take it anymore! I need a blunt," he said.

"Make one for me," I said. "I want one too."

This was our language, the language we both understood. It was about sex, fuck me, let's have some dope and then we'll fuck.

He rolled the blunt, lit up, took a drag on it, then handed it to me. I moved close to him, bent down over him, and I ran the tip of my tongue along his lips, then down the side of his neck, tasting the salt of him, smelling the faint animal smell where his body's breath came up through the opening in his shirt.

As I licked him, "Oh God," he said. "This is what gets me about you. Nobody else would know you're hot like this."

I giggled, slurring it at the end. I was standing over him now, he was kissing my breasts through my T-shirt, sucking on my nipples. "Ummmm," I said. "Nurse me, nurse me."

He pulled on my nipples with his teeth, making a vacuum with his lips, hurting me. "I'm gonna draw milk," he said, through his teeth. He buried his face between my breasts, and I was burning now.

I came to consciousness a moment, glanced at Bobby's door. He saw my look. "He's asleep," he said.

Then, in the little bedroom, can't get my pants off quick enough. He arches over me, wants to watch my face while he's got his hand inside me, wants to see me go out of control, that's his thrill. Likes to watch me, reaching his hand, his whole fist practically, deep, deep inside me.

Then, we're finished. Resting, I turn my face to him. "Now you," I say.

His hands fly to his chest. But I pin his arms back at the elbows, and when I release him, he folds them back again over his chest. I force them open again, and down flat along the side of his body.

I lift his T-shirt. His flat breasts are exposed, I can see the silky skin shining and I wet the nipples with my tongue.

At first, he's reluctant. Then his chin starts to move, side to side.

"Oh baby," I say, "trust me . . . trust me . . . I love you. . . . I love you—whatever you are. . . ." Wetting the smooth skin of his breasts with my tongue, circling his nipples.

His thin thighs are locked tight together. "You've never known anyone you can trust like me, baby," I murmur. "I know everything . . . yes, I do, I do . . . I *am* you. We're the same, you don't need to be afraid. . . ."

And now in the dark, my hand's going slowly down his belly, as light as I can make it so he won't notice, toward the mound of his crotch. His legs are still locked tight. "Let me try," I say. "Trust me," I say. "It's our secret. We got nothing to lose, baby. Have we? We got nowhere to go but up, huh?" And I slip my hand into his jeans, and force my fingers between his legs.

This time he doesn't squeeze his legs together like he usually does, but I can't get my hand in all the way because of his jeans, the space is too tight. Pulling my hand out for a moment, I unzip his fly and he doesn't resist. And then—my fingers find him there—warm and wet and thick.

His legs relax and his thighs spread apart wider and wider and I pull the jeans down at the waist, then his Jockeys. I try to keep my fingers inside him while I do it because I'm afraid if I take them out he'll forget how good it feels and he'll close his legs up tight again. He's not wearing shoes, so it all comes right off. I'm a mother, I know how to do this, I'm used to it. Now in the dark, I can just see his dark mound, but I can't tell what it is—male . . . female. . . .

Slowly, I lower myself down between his parted legs, slowly so he almost won't realize what I'm doing, and I move my face into his warm center. He lets me find him. And he lets me taste him. He's all fresh there, like cucumbers, a little salt. He lets me find the little knob with the tip of my tongue. "See, it doesn't hurt," I say. My voice is soothing, like he's my baby, don't frighten him. "Nobody'll know. . . . You deserve it. . . . Don't be scared. . . . Don't be afraid, baby. Don't be afraid. . . ." And soon our bodies are all tangled up together, and inseparable, and we can no longer tell where one of us begins and the other ends, we thrash wildly, each of us selfishly wanting it, and wanting to give it to the other at the same time and it is like we are fighting, between love and greed and love again.

Afterward, he lay on his back, not moving, eyes wide open. I could see a beam of light from the other room in his eyes. It was as if he were suddenly grief-stricken.

I nestled down against his side, making myself smaller so I was looking up at his face.

"Never happened before?" I asked. "Happy New Year," I said. He didn't answer.

"Well," I said. "I'm glad it was me."

Next day, we woke up late because Bobby didn't come in to get us till eight. It was still snowing out, and almost dark, as if it were the late afternoon, not the morning. The heavy atmosphere must have made Bobby sleep too.

Dean sat up in bed and knelt on the mattress at the window, springs creaking, peering out the window in his boxers and T-shirt. "Did he plow?" he asked.

I had never seen Dean completely naked, except in total darkness. "Wouldn't do any good if he did," I said. "It just keeps coming. He's probably waiting till it stops. Nobody could get up that road. My dad couldn't get up here."

"We've hardly got any food left. We've got a can of pork and beans. Maybe enough milk for one more day."

"We don't need milk," he said.

"He needs milk," I said. "What should we do?"

He didn't answer, but gazed out as if he were transfixed by the snow.

"Maybe I could walk to the convenience store," I said, thinking of Bobby's milk.

"Four miles! You're gonna walk four miles?"

I was too scared to walk through the snow, he was right.

"We'll be okay. It's good," he said tensely, as if trying to reassure himself.

It was hot inside the house, there was no air in this small space. Bobby was at the front door, tugging on the doorknob. "Out," Bobby said. "Out . . ."

"We can't go out, honey," I told him. "It's too cold outside."

"I wanna go outside" His lower lip trembled, he was going to cry. So I pulled on his snowsuit, and his mittens and scarf, and opened the door for him. "Stay on the porch where I can see you."

I positioned myself at the window so I could watch Bobby tottering around. The snow was so thick it was impossible to see beyond a few feet from the house. I could just discern his little blue snowsuited body through the flakes raining in on the porch, the wind buffeting him and whirling him around. Then I saw him start to cry, and he was at the door again, trying to get back in. "Wind hurt, wind hurt," he cried when I let him in. Usually, Bobby loved to play in the snow, but today it was too rough even for him. But even just five minutes with him outside was a respite for me.

After lunch, at one o'clock, I tried to put him down, but he started crying. "I no wan nap. No!" He threw his Barney on the floor and I walked out of the room, shutting the door behind me, needing to be away from him.

I could hear him screaming. "Maaaaaa . . ." He could outscream me when he wanted to. He was perverse that way. Sometimes he'd just accelerate, push me further and further as if he were going out of control because I was out of control.

I sat down opposite Dean at the round table, trying to ignore Bobby's crying in the other room. I could see a frown of annoyance on Dean's face.

After a few minutes of the crying, Dean said, "I can't take it! Can't you make him shuddup?" The word "shuddup" made me wince, its brutal shortness, the coldness of it, the distance that Dean really felt from Bobby. Made me realize Dean did not love Bobby absolutely, the way I, his mother, did. To Dean, finally, Bobby was just another person.

That was the difference—I was always Bobby's mother, but Dean was the visitor. It was finally necessary that only *my* patience be infinite. "It's hard when he can't go out," I said. "He hasn't had any fresh air or exercise."

He stood up suddenly, paced around the room. "I'm goin' fuckin' crazy here!" But I said nothing, just watched, holding myself still.

I saw him go to his jacket, rummage around in the inside pocket where he kept the dope. He tore the little plastic bag out of the pocket. Only a few grains left.

"Shit. Fuck, I'm all out."

At 5 P.M., I noticed Bobby's nose was running, his cheeks were red. His head was all hot. I found the thermometer and took his temperature. "It's a hundred," I said to Dean.

Dean looked at Bobby and frowned. Now he seemed genuinely worried. "We ought to take him to the doctor," he said.

"We can't drive through this. I don't want to take him out."

"Maybe just give him the mask anyway," Dean said.

"Try and prevent it," I agreed. I plugged the Pulmo-Aide into the wall. "Sit on Mommy's lap," I instructed Bobby.

The machine started up. Bobby lay against me, the mask over his face, holding his *Green Eggs and Ham* while the machine went whoosh-whoosh-whoosh. As he inhaled the medicine, I lay my palm against his chest and I could feel his little heart beat, thump thump thump. The rapidity of it always frightened me, but Dr. Vakil had told me not to worry, a child's heart can beat much faster even than an adult's and it will still be okay.

That night, Dean and I didn't make love. Perhaps it was because we were both so worried, listening for Bobby to cough. It seemed as if I didn't fall asleep for hours, tossing and turning. I found it hard to go to sleep now without making love.

At last I fell into a shallow sleep. Then, somewhere in the middle of the night, I heard it—a barking sound coming from the other room.

"Bobby." I was out of bed like a shot, Dean right behind me.

Bobby hadn't even woken up, but I knew the signs of trouble, as surely as I knew my own breathing. His face was flushed. I unzipped the sleeper pajamas as he lay there and studied his rib cage. There was no retraction in his rib cage. Dr. Vakil said always look and see if there's retraction, like the stomach's sticking to the back of the ribs. That means he's having trouble getting air. I waited a few minutes, watching him. He wasn't waking up. After a while I decided he was okay, and we returned to our bed.

But at dawn, I heard the sound once more, an inhuman cry, like an animal's.

"When did I give him the last mask?" I asked Dean. My head was all fogged up, I couldn't remember.

"About eight," Dean said.

"That's nearly twelve hours. I can give him another."

I took Bobby into our bed, and I held him against me while he dozed and breathed in though the mask and Dean sat at the end of the bed watching us.

"Maybe I can handle it myself," I said. "We got it early. Dr. Vakil said if you catch it before it really starts you can prevent it sometimes."

Bobby finished the medicine and lay back against my breast, fast asleep. He was exhausted from the effort of trying to breathe.

Outside the window, the snow had stopped. The sky was growing lighter, it was a flat gray color, the world out there empty seeming. You could only see white now, miles and miles of white. I lay back against the headboard, holding Bobby, and closed my eyes. "Yesterday was my last sick day," I told Dean. "If I don't go in today, they're gonna fire me."

CHAPTER 28

MELANIE

There's no difference between night and day now in our overheated house. Mommy comes and goes to her job at the travel agency and I can feel her worried eyes on me all the time. And I'm just lying there on the couch with the TV going and a blanket over me. If I can't actually die, this is the closest I can get to it, hardly ever going out except to buy my cigarettes—maybe the cigarettes'll kill me— I don't care—not talking to anyone, seeing anyone, eating only candy, Skittles, and Mountain Dew to survive, sleeping all day.

On Sunday morning, she stands there all beautiful and ready in her camel hair coat, her little boots with the fur trim, fresh lipstick, sweet-scented, holding her keys, ready for church.

"You better get dressed. It's quarter of."

"I'm not going."

"Why!"

She already knows I'm not going. I told her that after what happened to Dean. But she won't believe me.

"Why should I go?" I say. "I prayed and prayed. It didn't do me any good."

"C'mon, it'll make you feel better."

"Oh yeah," I say, turning my eyes back to the TV.

"Come. We still have a few minutes. I'll wait for you. Just come with me."

"If you'd let him stay with us it wouldn't have happened."

"I did it out of love for you, Mellie." She is beseeching me. She knows what she has done. "I'm your mother. My job is to protect you. Besides, he was a criminal, a thief. I couldn't have him here." She waits, watching me. "Why don't you just get dressed? Come with me."

But I refuse to take my eyes off the TV.

"God did this. God let him go away from me."

"Come on, Mellie. God didn't take him from you. God's got better things to do." She hesitates. "You can't stay like this."

I say nothing. Just keep my eyes on the TV, and the documentary about people who are a hundred years old and how they've managed to live so long, and one man is saying he ate lots of fatty foods and he lived a long time anyway.

"It'll help you get over it," she says.

"What does 'get over it' mean? I'll never get over it. I'm not going."

I hear the jangle of her keys, the signal she's given up. I hear her open the front door, feel her hesitate, hoping I'll change my mind. But I don't.

One day during this time the doorbell rings. It's the middle of the day. I get up from the couch, my worn nylon blanket draped around my shoulders, wearing my bathrobe and my big socks for warmth. I look through the glass and I see that it's Brian. He's right there at eye level, just a few inches between us, his face peering in at me. "Go away! Get out of here!" I cry.

I turn away. He sees me walking away, and he starts banging on the front door and I can hear his voice muffled through the wood. "Melanie! I gotta talk to you! Open up!"

I lie back down on the couch and pull my blanket over me, and ostentatiously I turn my eyes to the TV so he can see through the glass that I'm going to ignore him, but he keeps on banging and banging until finally I get up and I unlock the door. But I keep the chain on.

"Go away." I practically spit the words out. "Get out of here or I'm going to call the cops."

"Please, Mellie." He jams his foot in the space between the door and the house, keeping it open. "Please, lemme talk to you."

"You make me sick."

"Just talk to me. Please." Now he's banging his body against the door, pounding it.

"I know what you did and you make sick."

"I didn't, Mellie. I didn't."

"No!" And I try to slam the door closed, but he stops me with the full force of his body.

He rams his shoulder against the door and I can feel the chain straining and I know he's going to snap it. It's a cheapo door, not even solid wood. "Stop it. You're going to break it. Okay," I say. "I hate you."

He steps back, and I unhook the chain, and I let him in.

His face is pale, his skin all rough and dry with the cold, I see, his hair wild and curly, hanging around his face like a white cloud. "I hate what you did," I tell him. "I hope they put you in jail forever," and I walk away back to the couch.

He follows me. Brian towers over me. Everyone else is afraid of Brian. But I am not.

I sit down on the couch, and suddenly he's on bended knees in front of me. "I can explain it! I can. Listen to me," he says.

"You can't explain it."

"I was wrong, Mellie. I was real crazy." And now his wiry hands with their chapped knuckles are actually clasped together, as if he's praying or something. I refuse to answer him.

"You know about Cecil?" he asks.

"Cecil? Who's that?"

"Remember Cecil? My mom's boyfriend?"

I remember now. The one who used to beat him, and then locked him in the room without food.

"That fire down on River Street," he says. "The two firemen

killed. One of them was Cecil." He looks at me for a response. Like I should be sorry for him or something, like that was going to justify what he'd done to Dean.

His mother had still let that bully live in the house, even after what he did to Brian when he was a little boy, never could get rid of him. Let him live with her even after what he did to her own son.

"That doesn't make what you did right," I say.

He backs up onto his haunches, and sits on the recliner in front of me. He hangs his head down between his knees, his long hair falling like a curtain over his face. "I was fucking crazy, man," he says.

"You are sick, you are evil, Brian."

"I know," he says. "I know." He raises his head, looks at me. And now I see that his face is covered with tears, gleaming like a sheet of glass. I see he is actually suffering, and for a moment I remember the kid in the yard blinking blinking like he'd just been struck. The little boy with the blank angel face not showing anything, any pain or awareness.

"Then turn yourself in," I tell him.

"I was—" he begins. "Couldn't look at him." I hear his voice break. He swallows. "I love you, Mellie. Since we were kids. When the others kids—"

"That's a great way to pay me back."

"Just the sight of him. Knowing you liked him . . ." He squinches his eyes shut, like he can just see Dean in his mind, and the thought of it is unbearable. "Couldn't take it, man." He opens his eyes, looks at me again. "Forgive me, Mellie."

"Ask *Dean* to forgive you. Not me."

"Dean's not here," he says. "Jimmy's turning on me, he's talking to them."

"Good. Tell them you did it."

"Jimmy's my buddy. . . . He's the only other one. . . ." He stops. "Except you."

"Jimmy!" I say. "That animal."

"I don't know if I can take it again, Mellie, back in the can. You don't know what it's like in there. I can't do it again."

"I wish I'd never been nice to you, Brian. I should've known. . . ."

At this, I see his eyes widen with surprise and hurt, like I've just hit him. "But I did it because I love you, Mellie," he says. " 'Cause you're the only one who's ever been good to me. I couldn't take his lies anymore. I wanted you to know the truth about him. You won't believe it, Mellie."

"I know the truth. I love him, every little thing about him I love." And suddenly I feel this rage boiling up inside me, consuming me. "Get out of my house! There's no way I'm gonna love you now, Brian. Ever."

And I get up and I start pushing him toward the door, and though he's bigger than me, against the full force of my will, he is pushed back, like he's nothing and I have all the strength. "Just get the hell out," I tell him. "I can never love you now, Brian. Never. Ever!"

CHAPTER 29

TERRY

I had broken Bobby's asthma. Done it myself. His breathing was even, calm, his eyes had lost their glassy look, his face was less red. But I was irresponsible, I hadn't taken him to the doctor, even though I could see the attack coming on. I could've gotten through the snow, though maybe the cold would've been worse for him. If I'd gotten stuck . . . still. It was my child's life, and I didn't take him to the Emergency. Dean didn't want me to because he was fixated on the idea Brian was hunting for him. I had to choose between my child and Dean, and I was choosing Dean. I was willing to lose my job because of him, just to stay with him. To give up the money we needed to eat. That was what love could do to you.

Late afternoon, and there was still a blizzard out. I had Bobby on the floor, sheets of newspaper spread out, doing Play-Doh. I'd found some old stuff, all dried up and crumbly in the bottom of his toy chest. But I was slowly running out of ways to keep him occupied. "Tomorrow," I said to Dean, "one of us is going to have to walk to the store."

Dean said nothing. Just sat at the table smoking his cigarette.

I'd lost track of all time, the days were one long, airless white tunnel now, merging into night into day again.

Through the window I saw the black sky, snowflakes illuminated by the light from the house coming down steadily like a curtain of lace.

222

He stood up, walked over to the kitchen window, and looked out through the snow toward the ridge.

"What do you see?" I asked.

"Nothing."

"It's New Year's," I said. "I gotta write in my diary. I've missed days." My diary was in the top drawer of my bureau in the bedroom. The key was attached to it by the little chain, the brass rusted now because a full year had passed.

I carried the diary back into the living room. Dean was still standing at the window over the sink, his back to me. "You read my diary, don't you?" I said.

"What?" he asked, his eyes still on the horizon beyond the house.

"My diary," I said.

He didn't answer. Seemed transfixed by the falling snow, by the wild ridge beyond, the dark shapes of the trees.

He didn't care what I knew. He wasn't even there with me anymore.

"Love me?" I asked him.

"Yeah." He didn't look around, he was concentrating.

I unlocked my little book. Pale blue leather, with a gilded line around the edge. I flipped through the pages. There was an entry for almost every day, though lately I'd missed a few, I was so distracted because of Dean. But when I did miss an entry, I caught up the next day, recapitulating the events that came before.

I began to write:

> *We're together now for good, I think. I think he'll stay with me because he's got nowhere else to go. I think he loves me. . . . I know he will read this! Are you reading this, baby? When you read this, know that I love you and hope you love me. I have had happiness with you, Dean. . . . Happiness comes in strange forms—*

"Terry—See that?"

"Yeah . . ."

"Up there, on that ridge?"

I got up, went over to the window, stood beside him. I looked out. But I saw nothing.

"I don't see it."

"Thought I saw something. . . ."

"Probably just a deer." I turned back to my diary, continued writing:

> *Who is to say how we will be happy? I don't care what you are. You have made my life better I found part of myself I didn't know about You are like a father to Bobby, the father he never had. And I know you really love him. Maybe you see yourself in him and you can do it right. Dear diary, everything will be okay I know it. Oops . . . gotta go Dean wants me. . . . He's calling to me. . . . I will just finish this please do not leave me again baby I can't help it I can't help it. Please do not—*

CHAPTER 30

CHRISSIE

After the holidays, Terry didn't return to work. Mr. Hanley said she'd called in sick with flu and was taking sick days.

But after a few days when she still hadn't shown up, Mr. Hanley phoned her house and there was no answer.

So, Wednesday, lunchtime, I drove over to West Taponac.

It was twelve-thirty. The sky above was a pearly color, there was no sun out, just a dull, quiet light as if it were going to storm again.

Terry lived up on Schermerhorn Road. A steep incline that led up the hillside through the trees to where her house was. Someone had plowed the road that morning, and I was able to get up it. When I reached the house, I saw Dean's truck parked next to Terry's little black Honda.

I climbed out of the car, and I stood a moment. There was a silence all around me, except for the faint, intermittent brushing of the wind through the trees.

It looked like no one had come outside yet this morning. Maybe they were sleeping late. As I plowed across the yard to the house, I noticed old footprints on the ground softened at the edge by new snow. The prints led from the house, across the yard, up into the fields.

As I approached the front steps, I looked down. On the snow at the foot of the steps, there was a red stain. It was dark at the center, then dissolving into pink at the edges.

The porch was covered by an inch of new snow, I noticed, the firewood stacked there was powdered with it.

I paused. All around me, the only living sound was a bird cawing somewhere in the distance, its cry echoing through the fields.

I rapped on the front door. No answer. I turned the knob. The door was unlocked.

As I entered the house, the air was still and cold. There was no welcoming warmth, not even the heat that human bodies massed together inside give off. The temperature inside the main room was the same as outside.

I stood in the center of the room. Everything was orderly, the dishes stacked in the drainer by the sink, a child's toy trucks parked in a row along the wall. Only one thing seemed out of place—on the floor there was a small blue book facedown, splayed open as if it had been flung there. I bent down and picked it up, and saw the familiar handwriting. It was a diary, Terry's diary. I recognized her writing from all the orders she had written out at work, all the notes I had seen from her, her round, neat script, as if she always wrote everything slowly and carefully. I had watched her write many times. Someone's handwriting, the way they write, is a clue to their soul. How many times had I stood by Terry at the Home and watch her do her orders, noticed how slowly and carefully she wrote. I glanced at the words, *"Who is to say how we will be happy? I don't care what you are."*

In the window, a fly buzzed. There were two doors leading off from the main room. They were open. Through one door, I glimpsed the edge of a wrought iron bed frame.

I stepped across the threshold. It takes a moment for the brain to sort out the outline, the meaning, of the shapes in front of one's eyes, of something like what I saw there in that room. At first I saw only a room, very still. And then, on the floor by the bed, I saw the figure of a child, facedown, in blue sleeper pajamas. The back of the head dark red, hair matted with blood. On the bed, two figures facedown, in blue jeans, their hair also dark with blood.

I stepped forward into the room. They lay like dolls that had just been thrown there. I recognized Terry and Dean. For some reason I noticed the blood on the hair looked dried. On the floor, the child looked he had just been thrown there, like he weighed nothing. If you hadn't seen the dried blood on the hair, a glimpse of the dead white skin of his face, you would have mistaken him for a doll. I saw a fly crawling on Terry's arm, and as I moved, it flew off and I knew the bodies had been there for many hours.

The bedsheets were stiff with blood. Behind the bed there was a spray of red on the wall as if someone had flung a can of paint on it.

The stillness told me all. I was too frightened to go further into the room and I cried out, "Terry!" and then I rammed my fist into my mouth, and I ran back through the main room into the smaller bedroom.

My memory of what happened next is blurred. I ran to the telephone and I dialed 911, screaming that there had been a murder, weeping and sobbing as the operator kept asking me over and over again the exact location of the house.

Then, I threw down the phone, and I cowered in the corner of the room, afraid whoever had done this was still there, although I knew that there could be no other living being with me in the house. But what if he came back? I had never been so close to death before. The silence of it terrified me. But within seconds, I heard the distant sound of sirens in the still, midday air, growing louder and louder across the countryside. And soon the yard was crowded with ambulances and police cars converging all at once. Men were running up the front steps, and I could hear the urgent squawking of police radios.

I sat huddled at the kitchen table. The police stood over me, asking me questions. "Did you know the victims, ma'am?" "Do you know if there are next of kin?" But it didn't take them long to realize I knew nothing.

And by now I was crying so hard that I could hardly get the

words out. And it was so cold in the house because the fire in the woodstove had died out, and I was shivering and my teeth were chattering like china rattling, and this little orange-haired woman cop brought a blanket for me and wrapped it around my shoulders and I was grateful.

I heard grunts as stretchers were lifted across the room and I saw the bodies covered up, the tiny little one in the body bag like a dog or something.

There was a blast of freezing air as they opened the door of the house and carried the bodies out into the snow. And all the time it was so cold in the house, as if the inside were outside because the cold had seeped into the very walls and beams and settled there.

And after a while the woman cop with orange hair drove me to my dad's. We didn't talk the whole way because it was as if she were scared too, scared of the whole huge thing. When I got to my dad's, Liz was kind to me and made a hot bath for me, and put me to bed in the boys' room and made them sleep in the living room. And all through the night, I kept waking up, and I would sense Liz there, coming in to check on me and see if I was okay.

The next day at dawn, the cops found Brian Perez's Camaro abandoned on the edge of the Parkway. There were footprints leading from the car into the fields. The police followed the prints over the ridge and across the fields again to Terry's house. They figured he must have taken Terry and Dean by surprise. Probably killed the child because it had been woken up by the noise and run into the bedroom to see what was happening. Brian must have killed them all in a some crazy, blind rage, spraying bullets all over the place.

He must have wanted them very badly to hike in across the snow like that. And I pictured Brian plowing knee-deep through it with a deadly determination, the wind cutting his face, looking like some wild creature, his body shagged with white, not caring anymore if he lived or died, not capable of feeling cold or heat, not capable even of dying in the cold on his journey, couldn't die because he was completely animated by hate.

They instigated a statewide search for him, calling in reinforcements from other counties. But that night, they discovered him in the old ice house down by the river, cowering and hypothermic. He hadn't gone far. It was almost like he wanted to get caught. He didn't resist, they said, just put up his hands and went along with them. There were signs he had tried to build a fire, but he couldn't get it going. Arsonist that he was, Brian couldn't even start a fire in snow. He had no weapon with him. But they found his gun thrown out onto the ice on the river. It was a 9mm and the bullets matched those in the bodies.

He gave himself up without a struggle, he was nearly dead with cold. And besides, he had destroyed the object of his hatred, Dean, and he had nothing left to fight for—indeed, to live for, anymore. It didn't matter now whether he lived or died because he was never ever going to have Melanie—never, never, once and for all.

Later, as I lay in my own bed in my apartment, huddled under the blankets, still shivering though it was warm, I watched the whole thing over and over again on television, the woman reporter from the Albany station standing in the yard outside Terry's house, dressed in a sheepskin coat and hat, the snowflakes melting on the lens of the camera and making blotches of white on her face, talking into her mike. "This is the first multiple homicide in memory in this quiet, rural county fifty miles northwest of Albany," the woman said. "This place, of quiet farming communities, where neighbors help one another in time of need . . ."

PART V

I Am Not
That I Play

CHAPTER 31

CHRISSIE

There was a week of funerals. The whole county turned up at the little white church in Bergen Falls for the joint funeral of Bobby and Terry. The church was filled, and they had to have speakers hooked up in the trees outside so all who had come could hear the service and people stood in the freezing cold, or sat in their cars with the motors running for the heat, listening. Even the cops who were involved in the case came.

Up by the altar, with its plain brass cross and threadbare vestments, the two coffins stood side by side, the little coffin in the shadow of the bigger one, as if seeking its shelter.

I sat in a pew with B.J. on one side of me, and Carl on the other. B.J. was crying, though he was a man, the tears streaming down his dark face. And whenever a prayer was uttered, Carl crossed himself. Though this was a Lutheran church, he was Roman Catholic. Terry's father was unable to attend, they said, because he had had to be hospitalized with heart fibrillation.

There was a woman minister, fresh-faced, short hair, young. She was itinerant, and made her way across the area from one Lutheran church to another to perform services. She did not know Terry and her boy personally, she said, but she knew from talking to the people of Sparta that Terry was a kind person, and conscientious, a hardworking supervisor at the Nightingale

233

Home, beloved by all the patients, and above all, a good mother to her child.

A couple of days later they had Dean's funeral all the way up in St. Pierre. Melanie insisted on going, and her mother too, and they asked me if I would drive with them, because they didn't want to make the journey all that way alone in winter and I told them we could take my car.

At 6 A.M. on the morning of the funeral I picked them both up at their house. It was still dark out and our breath steamed in the black air as we got into the car.

Mrs. Saluggio sat in the front next to me, beautiful, with her golden skin, her perfect bowed lips. Didn't look much older than Melanie, they could have been sisters. Despite the hour, Mrs. Saluggio was all dressed up, her dark hair perfectly combed, she was wearing a neat camel's hair coat, her slender legs gleaming in their shiny stockings. She had on little boots with a fur trim and her perfume filled my car with a rich, sweet scent.

As we drove out of Sparta, Melanie sat in back, peering out the window at the roadway with glittering eyes. She was hunched over in the folds of her black leather coat, puffing on a cigarette with frantic, jerky gestures, as if this was the only language she knew to express all her anger. She looked thinner, her neck was scrawny, her cheekbones were hollow, there were dark circles under her eyes. Her hair hung limp and dull around her face, and she wore dirty jeans and a soiled aqua-colored sweatshirt under the coat. A gold cross hung on a chain around her neck.

We took the Sparta bridge across the river, then the Thruway north. They kept the Thruway cleared in all weather, and the driving wasn't bad. Mrs. Saluggio did most of the talking, her voice blending with the throb of the motor. "I blame myself," she said. "I should've let him stay with us."

"Then maybe Brian would've gotten *you* too," I told her.

"True . . . but I loved her—or him." That was easy to say now, I thought, now that he was dead and no threat to anyone. "She was like another child to me. But I couldn't have her back after all that stuff in the newspaper, saying she was a girl. . . ."

She glanced behind her at Melanie. "With all this AIDS, I had to protect Mellie."

Melanie, hunched over in the back, said nothing, just puffed away angrily at her cigarette, glaring out the window.

"Mel, honey," Mrs. Saluggio said, "open that window, will you? The smoke is too much."

With a spiteful, violent gesture, Melanie jerked the window down, and cold air swept through the car.

We drove awhile, then Mrs. Saluggio said, "Now it's freezing, honey. Can you throw that thing out and roll the window up?"

Melanie threw her cigarette out and turned in her seat, watching it disappear behind her, and then sullenly rolled up the window again.

Mrs. Saluggio was watching her. "You didn't take a shower this morning. You should've, for the funeral."

In the rearview mirror, I could see Melanie's lips tighten.

"You should've," Mrs. Saluggio said, "out of respect, honey."

And I realized suddenly that the pungent, salty smell of sweat and old hair that was permeating the car was Melanie's smell. Playing the role of the widow, I thought, establishing herself as the widow. That would be her whole identity from now on. Dean's widow.

Mrs. Saluggio leaned back in her seat. "I guess sometimes the only thing to do is trust in the Lord. He's the only one who can make sense of this."

"I hate God!" Melanie said suddenly from the back.

"Don't say that, honey. You don't mean that."

"Yes I do."

"Well, I know you don't," Mrs. Saluggio said, softly. "You're just upset. Sometimes we don't understand. . . ."

"Could you check the map?" I asked. "It's Route Twenty-five, isn't it?"

Mrs. Saluggio peered down at the map spread across her lap. "I'm looking for the exit," she said. I could feel her guilt.

We drove on north up along the Thruway. The traffic was mostly trucks now, the beam of headlights filling my rearview window though it was finally daylight out.

A sixteen-wheeler swept past my car, washing it with snow and ice, the boom of its wind pushing my car out toward the median.

"You okay?" asked Mrs. Saluggio. "You're a good driver," she said, encouragingly, knowing her life was in my hands.

"I'm okay." I'd been driving since I was seventeen.

"You didn't have any breakfast," she said to Melanie.

"No." Melanie's teeth were clenched.

"I'd give anything for a cup of coffee," Mrs. Saluggio said.

"They'll probably have some there, after the funeral," I said.

"They must be just shocked at the Home," Mrs. Saluggio said, "about Terry Kluge and her boy."

North, north, past Manorville. Then Lima, West Lima, Manatock, Florence, Delos, Thrace. All those classical names. What did the people have in mind when they named these towns? The ministers who led the settlers must have had a classical education, knew their Latin and Greek, and in the New World they must have had a longing for it, so they named these towns to remember the past by, their schools, all their learning, the Old World.

Gradually the landscape changed. It was more deserted, the hills steeper, there were fewer stretches of flat land. The houses seemed sparer, with raw siding, gray with age, the light here thinner and blue.

I saw the sign for St. Pierre and I turned off onto the exit. The mountains seemed to loom closer to the road here than in the southern part of the state. We were in a narrow valley now. We came to a scattering of houses, passed a gas station, a diner. And then I saw a sign with gothic lettering, Picavet Funeral Home, and a low white wood building, the lights on inside the windows though it was late morning, the parking lot filled with cars.

*   *   *

Inside, the funeral home was packed. People were sitting on metal chairs. All dressed up and clean, the men in shirts without ties, the women wearing dresses.

As you entered, your eyes went right to the coffin, which seemed almost to fill the room.

Melanie saw it first, screamed, and ran to it, before Mrs. Saluggio or I could stop her.

Inside the open coffin was Dean, lying with his hands clasped over his chest. His cowboy hat rested across the top of his head, as if to hide the wounds there. He had been shot in the back of the head, but the bullets must have gone through and damaged the front of the skull. You could just see the full lips underneath the brim of the hat.

A silk comforter covered his body up to his waist. But then, the weird thing, Dean was wearing a girl's blouse. It was a white, silky material with a V neck and a seam along the breasts, and long sleeves. You could see the little bumps where his breasts were. A little gold cross rested on his chest.

It was if someone had twisted the lens on the camera, and brought him into a new focus and suddenly he was a girl, a thin girl who went to church. It was as if in the end they had won. They had snatched his body, made it theirs only. I closed my eyes for a moment, and imagined his tears and rage if he had known this, that they would dress him like a girl at his funeral. They had taken possession of him, made him what the little town thought he should be. In the end, he had lost the battle. Only she was wearing this weird cowboy hat. A concession, maybe, to what he had loved in life.

"Deeean!" Melanie flung herself on Dean's feet, her sobs tore the air. People were staring, Mrs. Saluggio gripped her arms, trying to pull her away. And all around, the strangers watched stiffly. To them, Melanie was just one more weird thing about Dean.

In the front row right next to the coffin, Dean's parents sat.

The father was slender, youthful looking, with a wide handlebar mustache that looked like it was waxed or something, his hair freshly slicked down. He wore a short-sleeved shirt, though it was winter. Next to him sat a tall, pale, skinny youth, the brother. Raymond. Miserable-looking and embarrassed, a beanpole of a kid. The two of them, father and son, leaned forward in their chairs, hands hanging awkwardly between their legs.

And then, next to the father, the mother, dark curly hair, full, soft body, wide breasts, shiny glasses, biting her lip, staring at the coffin. In her lap she held a photograph in a silver frame, and she kept raising it and looking from the picture to the figure in the coffin, as if comparing the two images.

Melanie had noticed the mother and with a moan, she broke free from Mrs. Saluggio and hurled herself across the room to where she sat. Suddenly Melanie, with her soiled sweatshirt, was on her knees at the woman's feet, her hands on the woman's lap. The mother looked down at her, not moving, bewildered.

"You're Dean's mother!" cried Melanie. "Dean and I were together!"

The woman's eyes gleaming behind her glasses. She dabbed at her cheeks with a Kleenex.

Mrs. Saluggio was standing over both of them now. "We're so sorry," Mrs. Saluggio was saying in her melodious voice. "I can't tell you. As one mother to another . . ."

"I was his girlfriend," Melanie said to the mother. People had stopped talking completely now and were listening.

The mother looked down at the framed photo on her lap as if for confirmation. I moved closer and looked down over her shoulder at the picture. It was a picture of a girl, eight or nine years old, a girl with a wide smile and pigtails sticking out on either side of her face and one front tooth missing. The pigtails were tied with a ribbon and the little girl was wearing a dress with a floral print and an eyelet collar.

You could see in the photograph the beginnings of Dean's face, the shadow of emerging cheekbones, the adult bones forming in the girl's face and starting to harden, you could see the full lips, the almond-shaped eyes. A happy child.

"That's him!" Melanie cried, and she snatched the picture from the mother and stared into it while the woman watched her, as if in a daze.

"Oh my god!" Melanie cried at the picture. "That's him!" She was on her knees, clutching the photo to her breast with both hands as if it were him, then holding it out in front of her and scrutinizing it avidly. Melanie looked up at Dean's mother. "Can I have this, please?" she asked. "Please? Do you have another one?"

The mother's eyebrows creased. "You knew her?" she asked.

"Yes!" cried Melanie. "And he loved me—he loved me more than anyone!"

CHAPTER 32

CHRISSIE

Winter was deep-set now. It was never full daylight anymore, the sun seemed never really to rise. You got up in the morning and it was dark out, and at the end of the workday when you came outside it was dark again. Like that story in the Greek myths of the beautiful girl who is sent underground every year to live with her husband, Hades, and the whole world darkens in mourning for her and all light vanishes until spring. In the sky beyond the river you could sometimes see a glimmer of light along the mountaintops on the horizon, as if behind the mountains there was a warm, light place where the sun whirled at the proper angle to shine upon the earth. But in our county it was mostly darkness and people huddled in coats and scarves looking downward as they passed one another in the street, and the only warmth was the light from people's homes, the golden light from windows that signified there was life continuing within.

After all the funerals, I returned to work at the Nightingale Home. I kept going to my classes at the college. My first-semester grades that year were all A's, and in February, I went to the college advisement office and looked through the brochures for four-year schools. The counselor said I would be eligible for money if my dad filled out an affidavit saying I was "emancipated"; then I could get TAP and PELL grants.

The brochure for Caledonia seemed like the best. Caledonia

was a branch of the State University, up north. The pictures on the brochure showed old red brick buildings with bell towers and columns from when it was Caledonia Normal School. There was a big new library with dark glass windows, and behind that, a hilly, wooded campus.

The college had rolling admissions, which meant you could apply year-round. I filled out the forms, and within only a couple of weeks, I heard back from them, accepting me for next fall. I'd major in English, I decided, and then I'd teach school. In some warm place, I thought, maybe in the South, where it was always warm, a location with a growing population where they needed teachers.

Meanwhile, through Student Services at the college I got a job as a summer replacement in the Caledonia library stacking books, and they said I could start right after Memorial Day, which meant I could quit the Nightingale Home in May and leave town. They also found me a room, which I rented sight unseen, from some old lady who let to students. The woman told me over the phone that the room was on the top floor of her house, which was right opposite the library where I would work.

So all winter long, I saved everything I could from my paycheck. And when Carl found out I was saving for school, he started giving me free beer at the Wooden Nickel.

That April, they had Brian Perez's trial at the courthouse, and people went just to watch the proceedings as if it were a movie or something. Some local writer was even doing a book about the murders. The trial lasted only three weeks. They gave Brian life for the murders, and Jimmy got a reduced sentence in the rape case for testifying against Brian.

At the Rape Crisis Center on Washington Street, as a response to the tragedy, they began holding regular workshops on rape and gay awareness. The antique dealers on Washington Street really supported the workshops, and there were signs all over town advertising them.

*   *   *

Gradually, winter began to recede from the county. At first it was just that the snow stopped, and the rain washed what was left away and you looked up at the trees and you saw that the buds on the branches had suddenly swelled. And while the earth waited, along the roadways you'd glimpse here and there amid the sparse branches a shad tree feathered in tiny white blossoms, life emerging while all the trees around it were still dark and bare.

And then, just as you had hope, had thought spring had finally come, there would be biting rain and cold again, followed suddenly by a day of bright sunlight, and hearty souls, men in their T-shirts as they unloaded their trucks or dug ditches by the roadside, and you'd even felt a little sticky from the heat. And then slowly, the green washed across the county, as if someone was coloring the earth with a paintbrush, and soon the days were bright and filled with promise and the evenings were warm and alive.

In springtime in Sparta, you are reminded of when it was a real city. There is life on the streets, people sitting in the shadows of their front porches watching the cars go by, kids allowed to stay up late playing on the sidewalk. You would almost think Sparta was a viable city then, instead of a place where once there had been a thread mill, and a ball bearing factory, and a cord and tassel factory, and now down by the river there were only the shells of buildings covered in ivy and bindweed. There is a sweetness in the air in Sparta then, the fragrance of new leaf flesh, the soft breath of the river rising from its banks and filling the streets of the city.

On the last Thursday in May, I drove over and said good-bye to my dad and mom. My dad gave me big hug and a check for $250, and then he turned away to play with Fletcher and Timmy, who were fighting on the floor while I was trying to talk to him. He was trying to be a real father to Liz's brats. It was as if my dad had this faint memory of what it was like to be a father to me—Chrissie—and felt guilty because he had gotten it only half right then. Now he wanted to do it really right with those two. He was even coaching the boys' Little League team. He must've always wanted a son, I thought. And his love for Liz was so great that he was able to take on those two, even though they were not his own. If I'd been a boy, I wondered, would he have still left us?

At my mom's house, my mom was now linked tenaciously to Mason. Her eyes never left him; she watched him warily at all times, anxious and tense. And she talked less and less these days in his presence. Mason did the talking for both of them now. No matter what happened, I felt like a guest in both homes.

Friday, my final day of work at the Nightingale Home, they held a good-bye party for me. There was a big square cake with "Good Luck, Chrissie" written across it and Kool Aid and music—music for the patients, like "Good Night, Irene," and "Tennessee Waltz." Some of the residents actually danced, and those who were in wheelchairs joined hands and swung their arms together and clapped and tapped their feet. And even the really senile ones, the ones who were totally into themselves, like Mr. Ford, who probably didn't even understand that I was leaving, were smiling. For some of the clients, those old songs were almost the music of their youth.

Terry's murder had bewildered them, and they had sent in grief counselors to talk to the patients. My going-away party was really the first happy occasion since that bad time. At the party, Mr. Hanley stood up and said, "I'd like to offer a toast to Chrissie on her new life. And let's take a few minutes to remember our dear friend, Terry, who was taken from us far too soon."

The residents and workers bowed their heads, though some of the residents looked a little confused. Then after thirty seconds it was over, and time for more music.

B.J. stood up and sang "My Girl," and "Since I Lost My Baby" a capella and everybody sat there listening without moving because B.J.'s voice was so sweet and unexpected and it almost made you want to cry. Afterward, while people applauded, B.J. mopped his face with his handkerchief and said he used to have a group in the Bronx where he grew up, and they did real street-corner stuff, singing at weddings and birthday parties.

When it was time for me to go, Mr. Hanley shook my hand and said, "Sorry to lose you, Chrissie. You've been a very good worker." I said good-bye to Mrs. Alderfer and Mr. Ford, who were, miraculously, still alive, and I leaned down into their wheelchairs and gave each of them a hug. "Good-bye, darling," Mrs. Alderfer said. "You're a good girl. We'll miss you."

"Bye-bye, Chrissie," they said, like children. "Bye-bye. . . ."

Outside, the parking lot was filled with light from the windows of the Home. I got into my car and pulled out of my spot.

I was about to turn right, toward my apartment, when, on an impulse, I decided to say good-bye to Melanie. I hadn't seen her since the funeral. I'd called a couple of times, and when I asked Mrs. Saluggio how she was, her voice had seemed guarded, but she said that Melanie was "fine," and when I spoke to Melanie herself, her voice was bright, and cheerful, almost unnaturally so.

I drove out of town along Route 7. On either side of me, the land was flat and treeless, with only an occasional house, vulnerable and unprotected in the wide space. I came to Melanie's house, small and spare, right on the edge of the road, a little fountain with a cherub in the midst of its neat plot.

I stopped my car, walked up the concrete path, and rang the doorbell. As I stood there waiting, I could hear the sound of the television coming from inside the house.

The door opened, and there was Mrs. Saluggio, slender and beautiful, her skin tanned and oiled, wearing pedal pushers on her slim legs, and mules on her delicate feet. "Chrissie," she said.

Beyond, in the room, lying on the couch, was Melanie. She was wearing shorts and a T-shirt, and I saw that her arms and legs were pitiably thin, the bones curved, the joints big. Her skin had a yellowish cast, and there were brown circles around her eyes, and all the light had gone from her hair.

"Mellie . . ." I said.

She saw me, sprang from the couch and ran to me. She was smiling, her eyes feverish. "Oh, Chrissie!" she said. "I'm so glad you're here." But it was as if she were speaking not to the person in front of her, but to some other being, in some other realm.

"You look so thin, Melanie."

"I feel fine!"

Her mother stood still, watching her with dark, worried eyes. "She doesn't eat," she said. "But we're working on it, huh, Mellie?"

But Melanie didn't answer.

"I came to say good-bye," I said.

"Where are you going?" Melanie asked, with a brightness that could shatter glass.

"Up to Caledonia, to college."

"Oh that's wonderful, Chrissie!" Then she said, "I gotta show you my room, Chrissie. I haven't seen you for months. Come and see what I got!"

And before I knew it, she was headed up the stairs.

As I followed her, I could feel Rosemary Saluggio standing at the foot of the stairs, watching us from below.

At the top, at the door to her room, Melanie paused, then threw open the door. "Look, Chrissie, look what I've done!"

I peered at the room. It looked unlived in, the pink chenille spread smooth as if no one ever lay upon the bed, Melanie's stuffed animals lined up neatly. The white curtains in the windows had little ruffles, and the wallpaper had a pattern of yellow roses. The air was warm and close, as if no life ever stirred it.

"Look," Mellie said, sweeping her arm across the room.

The bureau was crowded with objects. She had made a little shrine to Dean. There was a newspaper clipping from the *Ledger-Republican*, in a frame, and in another frame, a photo of herself and Dean taken in the Wooden Nickel. They were sitting in the shadows of the bar, he was leaning over the table in a masculine pose, the arms of his T-shirt rolled up, butchy, elbows resting on the table by his beer mug, and she, beside him, was demure.

Mellie was all made-up and beautiful, her shoulder-length hair fine and gleaming, the mysterious smile on her face. She was glancing over her shoulder at something. She looked just like a movie star.

Next to the photo were two books, *Modern Magic,* and *Magic Secrets of the World.* "Those were his," she said. "They help me to understand him better."

In a silver frame on the bureau was the picture of him as a little girl, the one his mother had held at the funeral home, Dean in pigtails, front tooth missing, cheekbones large even then, pointy chin. The look of surprise at the camera, the delight. "His mom sent it to me," she said. "I wrote her and begged her for something of his. We've been writing. I guess I'm her only connection to him."

A teddy bear sat on the bureau. Melanie picked it up and hugged it to her breast. "He gave it to me on our first date. I call him Dean. Isn't he cute? Want to hold him?"

I took the bear, petted it like you would to oblige a child, then tried to give it back to her. "No, you can hold him," she said, watching me, studying me, as if she was trying to remember the image of me holding the bear because I was tied together in her mind with him.

"You're the only other person left who was close to him," she said.

On top of the bureau was a scrapbook with "Dean Lily" in big black letters.

She opened the book. Pasted on its pages were more newspaper clippings from the case. "Area Man Convicted in Multiple Killings." She turned the pages. An empty Skittles bag stuck down, an advertisement for Mountain Dew cut from a magazine. "That's what I'm mostly eating now. Skittles, because of him," she said with a little laugh.

Pasted on a page under a piece of Scotch tape was a lock of golden brown hair. "His mom sent it to me with his picture."

"Oh, Mellie . . ." I said. And I sighed.

I sensed a movement behind me. I turned and I saw that Rosemary Saluggio was standing in the doorway. I hadn't heard her.

"You gotta eat something other than Skittles, Melanie," Mrs. Saluggio said. "You gotta drink milk."

But Melanie was staring at the photo of Dean as a little girl, as if she hadn't heard her mother.

"Didn't you know?" I asked Melanie. "I mean, how could you not have known?"

Still staring at the picture, "No. I never knew."

"But it was obvious. I knew."

"I didn't know. I believed him."

Her head angled toward the picture. As if I was not even there now. "It didn't matter," she said. "Because Dean acted like a man, he did everything a man does. He loved me the way a man loves a woman. I mean, if he does everything that a man does? What does it matter?"

And now she seemed not to know we were there at all, me, and behind me Mrs. Saluggio in the doorway, her hair like a gleaming cap on her head, dark red lipstick, watching with her dark eyes, watching her daughter, who had become a child again, a child with a thin body and no breasts, little and frail, and lost, forever lost to her.

It was still early evening when I entered my apartment on Washington Street. The atmosphere was close and it smelled of warm wood and I pushed up the window to let in some night air.

Everything was ready to go. I didn't have many belongings anyway. The futon was too heavy to load into my car. I would leave it here for the next tenant.

I had borrowed a suitcase from my mom and all my clothes fit into it. My precious things—my yearbook—I would take them with me. My books were packed in a box. I had almost as many books as clothes. The Mariah Carey poster was too torn to salvage so I ripped it off the wall and crumpled it into the garbage.

In the bedroom near my mattress was my green fireproof box. I knelt down, pulled up the lock, opened the lid. Inside was my birth certificate. I kept my Social Security card there too, in case I lost my wallet. I saw the big manila envelope with the writing on it, Bureau of the Public Debt. That was my savings bond. I pulled the envelope out of the box and opened the flap.

Inside it was empty. The savings bond was gone.

I sat up on the mattress. "Son of a bitch! Shit!" I cried, into the empty room. He had taken it. Screwed me too. I had begged him not to steal from me, but he must have stolen it while he was actually staying here with me. I had trusted him, I hadn't bothered to look in my green box for months.

Now, crouched on the mattress, I felt my face heating up in anger and sweat spring from my body. He had dared—he had counted on my trust, counted on the fact that even if I discovered the savings bond gone, I wouldn't throw him out of the house. He knew he had me under his spell.

I felt the tears well up in my eyes. It wasn't just the money, it was the fact that, in the end, I was just an object to him too, like all the rest of them were.

I dropped the envelope back into the box, closed the lid. So, that was the ending, I thought, even our friendship couldn't transcend who he really was, a compulsive betrayer of all people. In the end he trusted no one, except maybe Melanie—the one girl he wouldn't let himself have.

It was ten o'clock now, and my apartment seemed to have a harsher light because everything was packed away. The windows were open, I could hear noise, children playing. Outside in the humid spring air, the fake gaslights on the street were surrounded by a golden aura.

The room looked clean and anonymous, as if I had never even lived here. The wainscoting on the walls was smooth, the brass sconces gleaming. The phone rested upon the bare floor. My suitcase was closed up, the box of books sealed with tape. As if the room were waiting now, for the next stranger.

I hadn't done any damage to the place. I hadn't paid Mr. Chin, the landlord, for May—he could have my security for the rent.

I was taking off at 8 A.M. and I would be in Caledonia by lunchtime, and have the weekend to settle in.

I needed a drink and to say good-bye to Carl. "Don't you leave without saying good-bye," Carl had said. Funny, I had never seen Carl actually in town, as small a place as Sparta was. I knew he lived in the Sparta Apartments off Courthouse Square, yet I'd never seen him on the street. His only life was the Wooden Nickel, I thought. I'd go over to there, have a drink, and just say good-bye.

As I drove up Washington Street, I could smell the spring air. There was the tinkling of bicycle bells, and the sound of a calliope somewhere from an ice cream truck. Kids were riding their bikes on the sidewalk while their mothers, wearing shorts, thighs still pale from winter, sat on the stoops talking.

I passed the Opera House and I saw a line of cars. They had raised enough money to restore just the ground floor of the building. And tonight was the opening of an art show by local artists. While they were mounting the exhibit, I had peeked inside. There were paintings of the river, and of Washington Street itself, with the red brick buildings seeming to glow in the light; there was even a painting of the CITGO station, all squares and triangles, bright oranges and yellows.

Now, driving up Washington Street, I came to the New York, New York store. The old lady who ran the antique shop next door to it had been complaining to the cops about all the drug dealers hanging around New York, New York, claiming they were keeping legitimate customers away from her place. You could see her sometimes, a tiny, white-haired figure dressed in blue jeans, standing there yelling at the kids to get off her stoop. The old lady said she wasn't afraid of the drug dealers killing her. She was too old to worry about dying.

And as I drove through the crazy spring air, the city seemed to glow and there was life echoing in the streets. At the end of Washington Street, I turned onto 7 and coming through the window of the car was the fragrance of cut grass—people had already begun mowing their lawns. In the shadows of covered porches, old women swung back and forth.

On the steep banks rising from Noland Street, people had planted begonias and impatiens, even though it wasn't officially Memorial Day yet and there was always the danger of frost before then. But after the long harsh winter, people were in a hurry.

On the rise above the river, I saw the lights still blazing in the windows of the Nightingale Home. I could hear the soft clanking of the cement plant across the river, the sound filling the humid air.

I curved around to Old Route 27. Down below, the river ran parallel to the road, a milky color in the spring night, and the sweet smell of the water permeated the air.

Occasionally, as I drove, I passed a lone house, the curtains in the window drawn, the blue light of a television set leaking out from around the edges. So that you saw a darkened house, the shape barely visible from the road, and a blue light emanating from it. Little families in their homes. Little families all together, life within.

Cars whooshed past me. People out late because it was spring, a holiday weekend. There was the old trailer lot, giant trailers unsold and abandoned, looming. And a stretch of dark road now.

I saw a white clapboard building ahead of me, The Wooden Nickel. It seemed almost to glow in the thick night. Funny, I'd never been upstairs in the place. Carl said the second floor was just storage, filled with junk. Once, long ago, when this had been a real inn, the proprietors had rented out the rooms on the second floor to weary travelers on the old coach road. Two hundred years ago, before the white man came to Palatine County, Old 27 was probably an Indian trail, and there had probably always been a trading post of some kind here. It was a natural spot on the road for it. And then the white man had built his inn.

There were cars parked in the lot now. The sign with the Indian head was all lit up. Funny old gnarled Indian head. The place was probably named "The Wooden Nickel" because of the Taponacs. The Taponacs were all gone now. Except maybe for their descendants intermarried with the blacks.

I pulled into the lot. It was lit up almost like daylight by the harsh spotlight.

As I entered the Wooden Nickel, people were watching the local news on TV and customers were playing video games in the back. Bruce Springsteen was on the jukebox singing "Glory Days." Carl had the top ten of all different years on his jukebox— strange, random years that made no sense. Must have been some package deal he got from a distributor. There were new releases and oldies. Oldies to cater to the older patrons, and on some nights the older customers would take over the jukebox completely and just play record after record of *their* music, and the younger patrons would jeer and laugh, and there would be actual music wars. It seemed like the older group had won tonight.

I sat down at my usual place at the bar, underneath the Genny mermaid, and Carl caught sight of me. "Hey, Chrissie. Tonight's the last night. What time you taking off?"

"In the morning. Around eight."

"Packed yet?"

"Don't have much to pack."

He wiped the bar down with his white cotton towel. I noticed his muscular forearm, the red tattoo of the heart on it. Carl's eyes were crisp blue, his hair white and springy, his cheeks ruddy. He stopped to ring up a tab for a customer, then poured some drafts out. He walked back to my end of the bar.

"So, looking forward to it?"

"He fuckin' stole my savings bond," I said to Carl. "Took it right out of my box by my bed. While he was living with me."

"Your savings bond?"

"Yeah."

"Well, how much was the thing worth?"

"Hundred dollars. I discovered it just now when I was packing."

"I'm sorry," Carl said.

Carl cleared some glasses from the bar top, stacked them in the sink. "Hundred dollars not worth much these days."

"Yeah! But he stole from me. I asked him not to. I said to him, 'Don't steal from me. Please!' "

He considered my words. "Well, maybe to him it wasn't really stealing."

"What do you mean? It wasn't his savings bond."

"In his world, he probably felt you owed it to him."

I sat a moment. He poured me a beer, didn't even ask me if I wanted one.

I could feel tears welling up in my eyes. "This place is just grief," I said. "All it is is grief." At that moment, I could not wrap my mind around the grief. Whenever I pictured the scene that day at Terry's, the bodies lying there, I made the thought go away. I knew I was doing it. I wondered if there would ever come a time when I could let myself think about it really.

"Everything about this place is sorrow, isn't it, Carl?"

"I don't know, it's home to me."

"I hate it."

"I'm sorry, Chrissie."

"What do you like about it?"

"Oh, I dunno. I grew up here. I like the seasons. The river. Hunting season. It's home. There's a lot that's beautiful here."

"What!"

"The river's beautiful. Sparta's beautiful."

"Hah!" I said.

"One day you'll know. When you're an old lady you'll pine for it."

"I don't know whether to cry, or to be angry at him because they're all gone," I said. "I can't believe I'll never see him again as long as I live." I looked up at Carl. "Carl, do you think he changed things?"

"What do you mean by that?"

"I mean, did what happen make people any better? Because what happened was so awful, will anything change?"

He shook his head. Then he looked at me, his white towel was poised on the countertop. And suddenly it seemed that there was only me and Carl now in the bar, and all the noise—the laughter and the music and the conversation had receded, and for a moment we were enveloped in a silence. Carl's bright blue eyes were sad and kind, the skin on his face was thick, middle-aged, his arms still had the power of his youth. And suddenly he seemed even older than he actually was, like a teacher or a father. "That's the mystery, Chrissie," Carl said. Then he sighed. "That's the mystery, honey."